Lexile 760

Lone Star 2007-2008

The WIZARD, the WITCH & TWO GIRLS FROM Jersey

Razorbill books
by Lisa Papademetriou

M or F?
(with Chris Tebbetts)

THE WIZARD, THE WITCH
& TWO GIRLS
FROM
Jersey

LISA PAPADEMETRIOU

raz**O**r
bill

The Wizard, the Witch & Two Girls from Jersey

RAZORBILL

Published by the Penguin Group
Penguin Young Readers Group
345 Hudson Street, New York, New York 10014, U.S.A.
Penguin Group (USA) Inc., 375 Hudson Street, New York, New York 10014, U.S.A.
Penguin Group (Canada), 90 Eglinton Avenue, Suite 700, Toronto, Ontario, Canada M4P 2Y3
(a division of Pearson Penguin Canada Inc.)
Penguin Books Ltd, 80 Strand, London WC2R 0RL, England
Penguin Ireland, 25 St Stephen's Green, Dublin 2, Ireland (a division of Penguin Books Ltd)
Penguin Group (Australia), 250 Camberwell Road, Camberwell, Victoria 3124, Australia
(a division of Pearson Australia Group Pty Ltd)
Penguin Books India Pvt Ltd, 11 Community Centre, Panchsheel Park, New Delhi – 110 017, India
Penguin Group (NZ), Cnr Airborne and Rosedale Roads, Albany, Auckland 1310, New Zealand
(a division of Pearson New Zealand Ltd)
Penguin Books (South Africa) (Pty) Ltd, 24 Sturdee Avenue, Rosebank, Johannesburg 2196, South Africa

Penguin Books Ltd, Registered Offices: 80 Strand, London WC2R 0RL, England

10 9 8 7 6 5 4 3

Library of Congress Cataloging-in-Publication Data is available

Printed in the United States of America

This book is dedicated to Jersey girl Liesa Abrams.

Special thanks and lots of love go out to Craig Hillman and Christopher Graybill, for the inspiration they provide by being hilarious, and to the Cheer Squad: Ali, Mom, Bob, and Ro Stimo.

THE WIZARD, THE WITCH & TWO GIRLS FROM *Jersey*

ONE

King Xanthor—son of Pericorn, Duke of the Pearlish Sea, and newly made Sorcerer of Tandrahor—thrust forth his gauntlet, and a stream of dragons roiled toward the horizon. Their wings hissed on the air as, one after another, they disappeared into the clouds. Finally, the last one—

"Veronica!"

—paused on the warm air. It was Nenemeh, the Golden One. He—

"Veronica! Mom wants you!"
Veronica didn't even look up. "I'm almost done," she announced, flipping the page.

—looked toward the king—

"You're always almost done." Luz cracked her gum and leaned against Veronica's door frame. "But you're never done. You know why? Because the minute you put one book down, you pick up another one, that's why." She stood with her arms folded across her chest, not leaving in spite of Veronica's blatant attempt to ignore her. When Veronica refused to give in and look up from her book, Luz walked over to Veronica's dresser and sat down, as though she intended to stay for a few hours, maybe give herself a makeover.

Sighing, Veronica peeked up at her younger sister. She and Luz had been born only a year apart and looked almost identical. Still, Veronica knew that most people thought of Luz as "the pretty one." Veronica wasn't really sure what that was all about. She supposed it had something to do with the four hours Luz spent every morning styling her hair and piling on makeup. When Veronica had started high school two years ago, her sister had given her a makeover. But Veronica found makeup, high heels, and short skirts to be too much work. It had taken only two weeks for her to revert to her ponytail-blue-jean-college-sweatshirt look. "Call it my signature style," Veronica had said when Luz complained that Veronica was setting a poor example.

Luz peered at herself in the mirror. She checked her lip liner, then reached for one of Veronica's lipsticks and twisted it out of the tube. "Oh, ugh, Veronica." Luz pursed her lips in disapproval. "This color was out three years ago."

"Maybe that's why you gave it to me for Christmas," Veronica shot back. She held up her book. "Look—I've only got two paragraphs left. Do you mind?"

Luz's plucked eyebrows crept halfway up her forehead as she eyed the novel. "What is that?"

Veronica glued her eyes back on the page, knowing that if she made eye contact for even a moment, her sister would try to drag her into some dumb conversation about celebrity weddings, and she'd never know if Xanthor fulfilled his destiny. "It's a book," she snapped. "Not that I expect you to know what that is . . . "

"I read," Luz huffed, flipping her long black hair over one shoulder.

"*Teen People* and the instructions on the back of your shampoo bottle don't count," Veronica replied.

Just then, a bulky figure appeared in the doorway. It was their brother, Esteban. Esteban used to be fat, but then he'd started working out. A lot. He'd turned from an oval into an inverted triangle. Right now, he was holding a dumbbell, working his left bicep. "What's going on?" he asked. Grunting softly, he muttered, "Ten," then asked, "Why is everybody hanging out in here?"

"Mom needs Vero to set the table, but she won't put down her dumb book," Luz explained.

"It's not dumb," Veronica muttered.

"Fifteen," Esteban said. He switched the dumbbell to the other hand. "One—what's it about?"

"It's about a guy raised by dragons who discovers a lost treasure and is made king." Veronica held up the cover of the book. It had a picture of a man in a hauberk riding the back of a golden dragon.

Esteban paused mid–bicep curl. "Nice tights."

"That was the style!" Veronica insisted.

Esteban looked dubious. "Back when dragons used to raise people?"

"See?" Luz said, curling her lip. "At least the instructions on my shampoo make sense."

"Wash, rinse, repeat," Esteban said, nodding. "Always repeat."

"Always," Luz agreed.

"Will you people get out of my room?" Veronica slapped the book down onto the worn quilt that covered her bed.

"Ay, Díos mio! Porqué están todos aquí?" Veronica's mother, Carmen, poked her head into Veronica's room. A strand of curly black hair had escaped from the barrette at the back of her neck, and she tucked it behind her ear absently, then went back to worrying the dish towel in her hands. "Dinner's almost ready, and none of my children are in the kitchen helping me?"

"I told her, Mama," Luz said, folding her arms across the word *flirty*, which was written in bold, sparkly letters on the front of her tight T-shirt. "She won't stop reading."

Carmen gave her a heavy-lidded look. "And why aren't you making the salad, like I asked you?"

"I was just about to." Luz pulled herself from the chair and ducked out of Veronica's room.

Carmen looked up at her son, whose muscles rippled as he worked the dumbbell.

"Fourteen. I'm just about to wash up. Fifteen," Esteban said. "I'll be right there." He hurried down the hall.

"Veronica?" Carmen pronounced the *V* like a *B*. "Porqué no estás en la cocina?"

"Ma—two paragraphs," Veronica said, holding up her book. "Almost done."

Carmen planted a hand on her hip and flipped the dish towel over her shoulder. She sighed. "Tu y tus libros," she said affectionately.

"Just a minute," Veronica promised.

Chuckling softly, Veronica's mother shook her head. "It's okay," Carmen said. "Finish your book. Then come."

Veronica smiled. "Thanks, Ma."

"It's okay," Carmen repeated, her black eyes dancing. "Read." She turned away and strode toward the kitchen.

Veronica smiled at her mother's broad retreating back. Carmen Ramirez worked all day, cleaning houses. Then she came home and took care of her three kids. She even found time to tidy up Veronica's room when Veronica forgot, which was fairly often. Veronica loved her mother and respected her. And she knew that her mother loved the fact that she read so much. Carmen's dream was for her children to get a good education. It had been both her parents' dream. That was why Veronica's father had started reading to her when she was six years old. The first book he'd chosen was *Queen of Twilight*, by Fabiella Banks. Even though Veronica was really too young to understand the whole thing, she had loved the steady rumble of her father's voice as the words floated from his lips and formed pictures in her mind. She had been hooked on fantasy books ever since.

It was kind of funny, actually, because her English teacher had just assigned *Queen of Twilight*. In fact, the essay was due tomorrow. Not that Veronica was worried. You see, Veronica was the smartest girl in her class. That wasn't an opinion—it was a fact. Whenever Ms. Jackson had a tough question, she called on Veronica. Veronica always got the highest grades in the class on tests. Her papers came back with glowing comments, which Veronica often didn't bother to read. English was Veronica's thing, and nobody else even came close to topping her in it.

But to be perfectly honest, Veronica was a little cocky. Which was why she was reading *Xanthor's Destiny* instead of re-reading *Queen of Twilight.*

I don't need to read Queen of Twilight, Veronica had told herself. *I already have a topic for my paper—how modern fantasy books mimic traditional epic stories, like* The Odyssey. *For example, in* Queen of Twilight, *when Princess Arabelle gets that orb thing . . .*

The Orb of . . .

Oh, wait, Veronica thought, *the Orb had a name. What was it? Hmm . . .*

The Orb of Inflation, her mind supplied unhelpfully. She knew that wasn't it, but suddenly, she couldn't think of anything else. Her brain was rattling with *inflation, inflation, the Orb of Inflation—No! That's not it! Orb of Inflation. Stop thinking that!*

That's going to drive me to the nuthouse, Veronica decided, hauling herself off the bed. *I can't write about the Orb of Inflation in my paper. I guess I will have to peek at the book after all.* Crossing her room, Veronica scanned the bookshelf, which was crammed with fantasy titles. Her finger skimmed along the spines.

No *Queen of Twilight.*

Veronica frowned. *Where did it go?* she wondered, scurrying into the living room to search the shelves there.

"What are you looking for?" Esteban asked as he chopped up a red pepper. The kitchen had an open counter that looked out into the living room.

"My copy of *Queen of Twilight,*" Veronica said absently. "Ma, have you seen it?"

Carmen looked up from the pot she was stirring.

"What?"

"Have you seen my copy of *Queen of Twilight*?" Veronica repeated. "I need it for a paper."

Carmen bit her lip, thinking. "Was it in the box of books that we packed up?" she asked, referring to their recent frantic spring-cleaning effort.

"Yes!" Veronica cried, suddenly remembering. "Yes—where's the box? In the basement?"

Carmen winced. "I gave it to the Bookmobile."

Veronica's eyes went wide. "What?"

"Lo siento, amorcita," Carmen said. "I didn't know you still wanted it."

Veronica felt a pang in her chest. Okay, true, it was just a battered old paperback. Her mother had been right to give it away. Except that it was the very same copy her father had read to her. Suddenly, she wanted that book back. *But I'll never see it again*, she thought, her head spinning dizzily. "I need that book," she whispered.

"What's the big deal?" Luz asked, pulling four glasses out of the cupboard. "Just get another one from Barnes and Noble."

Veronica took a step toward the door, but her mother said, "Excuse me?"

"I have to get the book," Veronica explained.

"After dinner," Carmen corrected. "Now you set the table."

Veronica had to fight the panic rising in her chest. *Okay,* she told herself. *It can wait an hour. The book will still be there when I'm done with dinner.*

It was only when she started toward the table that Veronica

realized she was still holding *Xanthor's Destiny*. She peeked at the last page.

> *It was Nenemeh, the Golden One. He looked toward the king, his emerald eyes gleaming. "Good-bye," called the king. "The land of Silba-a-La'eth-Dal-Nimbrahal thanks you!"*

Veronica put the book down on the table. So it had all turned out fine in the end. As usual.

"How was it?" Luz asked.

"It was okay," Veronica told her. *Better than a shampoo bottle,* she thought.

But not as good as *Queen of Twilight.* Suddenly, she couldn't wait to read that book again.

⚜

"I don't know; something about it just doesn't feel right," Heather Simms said as she shook her head sadly.

Amber Smalley looked up from her latte. "I thought you said you were in love," she said, running her fingers through her blown-out do.

"Love at first sight," Amber Wilkinson added from behind her frappe.

Heather shrugged. "I guess I was wrong." She looked down at her carefully manicured nails. "I've been wrong before."

"If it's not right, you've got to just forget the whole thing and start over," Skylar Delissio put in. She pulled her long blond hair over one shoulder. "Remember how I had to get my pedicure totally redone after I picked that gross purple?"

"It looked really good in the bottle," one of the Ambers

said loyally. Truthfully, Heather found it kind of confusing having two friends named Amber. And it didn't help that they were both brunettes with the same sort of breathy voice. They were kind of interchangeable, in Heather's opinion. She had been thinking of maybe giving one of them a new name. It would clear up a lot of the confusion in her daily life.

"I'm not talking about a pedicure, okay?" Heather snapped. "Nail polish is easy to change." She pressed her lips together and fought back tears. "I'm talking about highlights." Heather dabbed at her eyes with a napkin. *Oh, great,* she thought miserably. *Now my mascara's going to run. Can this day possibly get any worse?*

"They look really good," Skylar told her.

"Oh, absolutely." The Ambers bobbed their brown heads.

Heather sniffed and looked up hopefully. "You don't think they're too blond?"

"It's almost spring," Skylar said. "Blond is in."

"Everyone's going blond," Amber W. agreed.

Amber S. must have seen the look on Heather's face, because she quickly added, "Everyone who's anyone. You know, not just *everyone* everyone."

Heather took a deep, cleansing breath, just like her yoga teacher, Guru Stacey, had taught her. Then she smiled gratefully at her friends. "I just love you guys," she said, tearing up again. "You're the best."

"Stop it," Skylar said. "You're going to make me cry."

"I'm already sniffling," one of the Ambers agreed.

"Well, well," said a honey-sweet voice, "it looks like everybody's crying. What happened? Somebody chip a nail?"

Heather looked up into the green eyes of Walker W. Walker

III, who was smiling down at her, holding a tall paper cup of coffee in one hand and a book in the other. Heather swallowed hard and ran a quick finger under her bottom lashes. Walker was the hottest guy at her school, and she had a major crush on him. True, somewhere in the deep recesses of her mind, Heather knew he was a jerk. But Walker was hot enough to temporarily short-circuit that part of her brain. Heather flashed him a bright smile. "Hi, Walker!"

"Hello, Heather. Hello, Friends of Heather." Walker smiled smugly and took a sip of his coffee. His eyes flicked to the novel lying on the varnished wooden table in front of Skylar. "Working on your paper?" he asked.

"I haven't even finished the book yet," Skylar admitted. "Fantasy is so lame."

Why is she talking right now? Heather thought as she sent Skylar a hands-off! glare. Everyone knew that Walker W. Walker III was positioned dead center in Heather's relationship crosshairs. "What paper?" Heather asked, flipping her thick golden highlights over one shoulder.

Walker cocked an eyebrow. "The one that's due tomorrow." His voice was almost sneering.

"Tomorrow?" Heather repeated, racking her brain. She glanced at Skylar's book. *Queen of Twilight*, the cover read. *By Fabiella Banks.* "Oh my God, you would think that Ms. Jackson would mention something like that," Heather huffed. "I've never even heard of that book!"

"She's been talking about it every day for the past three weeks," Skylar said.

Heather narrowed her eyes at her friend as Walker snorted.

"Sorry," Skylar said quickly, her brown eyes wide.

"Well, it looks like you've got some work to do, then," Walker said smoothly, grinning at Heather. "Catch you later."

"'Bye," Heather called softly after him. *Great,* she thought. *Now Walker thinks I'm an idiot, and I have a paper due tomorrow.* Heather didn't usually sweat stuff like that—she just read the back of the book and the reviews on Amazon.com and faked her way through it. But Ms. Jackson had been riding her tail ever since she'd handed in a paper on 1984 that offered a critique of eighties hairstyles.

A very valid critique, too.

But that didn't seem to matter to Ms. Jackson. She kept pestering Heather about "substance" and "thought," and Heather knew that if she didn't hand in something decent on *Queen of Twilight*, her grade would be flushed.

"Guys, what am I going to do?" Heather whispered. "I haven't even bought the book!"

"I'd loan you my copy," Skylar said, "but I need it."

Thanks for nothing, Heather thought. *Note to self: Skylar = useless.*

"You could ask for an extension," Amber suggested.

"From Jackson?" Heather rolled her eyes. "No way."

"Pretend to be sick," the other Amber said. "Stay home tomorrow."

Heather sighed. Usually, that idea would be perfect. After all, her father was on one of his business trips. He was only going to be home one day this month. And her mother was off on one of her harebrained "save the world" trips to the African jungle—or was it the Amazon jungle? Anyway, she wasn't around. Not that either of Heather's parents would be likely to notice that she hadn't gone to school even if they were home. But . . . Ms. Jackson was one of the most hard-core teachers on planet Earth, and she had a strict no-excuses policy.

"The paper is due when it's due," Ms. Jackson always said. If you weren't at school, you had to e-mail it to her by 11:00 a.m. "If you've been sick for a week or more before the paper, I'll give you an extension," Ms. Jackson would say. "Other than that, the only excuse for a late paper is death. Your own."

Heather sighed. She was going to have to buy the book, read the first and last page of every chapter, and pick a few random quotes to fill the paper.

"I have to find a bookstore right away," Heather said.

Her friends exchanged glances. "Um, Heather," Skylar said finally, "we're in a bookstore."

Blinking, Heather looked around. Wow. She'd never actually glanced beyond the magazine rack at the end of the café before, but it looked like Skylar might actually be right.

"Skylar, you're a genius," Heather said as she pushed back her chair. "I'll see you guys later."

"Call my cellie if you need help," one of the Ambers called.

"Or if you want to procrastinate," the other Amber added.

"I will," Heather promised.

 ✿

Heather paused uncertainly at a circular table stacked with a tower of best sellers as she gazed past the rows and rows of book-lined shelves. Green signs atop the bookcases trumpeted the types of titles in each section. She headed past Travel, Self-Help, Gay and Lesbian, and toward the back of the store. She had almost reached the far wall when she realized that she had no idea where she was going. What kind of book was this *Twilight* thingie? Fiction? Literature? What? Heather's heart started to pound. She didn't like not knowing where she was going.

Heather hovered uncertainly at the edge of a table stacked with sale items. As she took a deep, cleansing yoga breath, her eyes scanned the clothbound journals, skipped over the bookmarks, and came to rest on a snow globe.

Her heart resumed its normal rhythm as she focused on the snow globe. Around her, the rest of the store went dim as she stared at the light that shone through the glass ball. The snow globe was ugly, that was for sure—although someone had gone to great lengths to make it look like a "special collector's item." The round sphere stood in a cheap stand, and at the center of the globe was a small, black plastic Empire State Building. Some of the letters on the stand had rubbed off, so that it now read, *Welcome to New Yo. We aren't even in New York,* Heather mused idly. *Why would anyone come to the Jersey suburbs to buy a tacky tourist snow globe?*

Reaching out, Heather plucked the round ball from the cheap plastic pedestal. White flecks drifted around the black tower, creating a plastic New York City snowstorm that reminded her of the shopping bags that swirled lazily in the air around Herald Square. The price tag at the edge of the plastic stand indicated that the globe had originally cost fifteen dollars but the store was now willing to let it go for seven-fifty. *An overpriced piece of junk,* Heather thought. *Who would want this ugly thing?*

She tucked the globe into the pocket of her pink denim jacket with feather trim and walked away from the table.

I know, I know. You're shocked. You're disappointed in Heather. She's a thief! It's true.

But Heather couldn't really help herself. She didn't understand why she took things. Her brain would scream, *No! No! Don't take that!* But it was as though her fingers had a mind of their own. In fact, at the very same moment that she was putting the snow globe in her pocket, she was commanding herself not to take it. So forgive her. She didn't mean to do it.

Heather's mind felt muddy as she walked toward the information booth. Her thoughts were far away as she said, "Excuse me."

A girl with heavy black eyeliner and a lip ring looked up from her computer screen. "Yeah?"

Heather blinked. It took her a few seconds to remember why she was standing there. "I'm looking for a book," she said finally. "*Twilight* something. *Twilight Princess?*"

Lip Ring Girl rolled her dark eyes. "*Queen of Twilight?*" she guessed.

Heather nodded. "That's it."

Lip Ring Girl scoffed. "It's a classic," she spat.

"So—it's in Classics?" Heather guessed.

Lip Ring Girl sighed and then made a *hhcchh* sound in her throat, as though being forced to deal with someone as uninformed as Heather was the absolute worst kind of torture. "It's in Fantasy."

"Okay," Heather said, turning away. She looked back. "Where's that?"

Lip Ring Girl rolled her eyes, presumably to indicate that she thought Heather was too dumb to live. "Right mezzanine." She jerked her thumb toward the ceiling.

Anger simmered in Heather's chest, but after a moment— and a cleansing yoga breath—she decided not to say anything rude. Instead, she just pictured the girl with a huge glob of spinach caught in her piercing.

Visualization is a key to peace of mind, just as Guru Stacey always said.

"Thanks!" Heather said brightly.

When she reached the top of the stairs, Heather headed to the right and came to a nook with a few oversized chairs. *I should have known I'd find this book in the Dork section,* she thought as she scanned the shoppers. She eyed the skinny guy with stringy hair, the pasty-faced overweight dude, and the girl with the scraggly ponytail wearing a giant sweatshirt and sweatpants. Right mezzanine would be the perfect location for a makeover show. These people needed some serious help.

Actually, Heather thought as she looked at the girl in the sweatpants more carefully, *Little Miss Needs to Brush Her Hair has potential.* Just then, the girl pulled a book off a high shelf. As she did, she turned her face slightly, and Heather realized that she knew her. Well, knew who she was, anyway. It was Veronica Lopez, the smartest girl in her English class. That chick was always reading these weird books with dudes in tights on the cover.

Heather glanced at the book in Veronica's hand. *Queen of Twilight,* the cover read.

Ha! Heather smirked. *So, the smartest girl in the class and I are both scrounging for the book at the last minute, eh? Well, if she can get an A with a last-minute paper, so can I.*

I guess.

As though her thoughts had just been broadcast over Brain Radio, Veronica looked up, blinking.

"Hi," Heather said.

Veronica's eyebrows lifted slightly, almost imperceptibly. For a moment, she looked like she wasn't sure that Heather was talking to her, but finally she seemed to decide to risk it and said, "Hi."

"Paper for Jackson?" Heather asked.

"Mmm." Veronica nodded.

"Me too. Where did you get the book?"

"Under *B*," Veronica said. She started to walk toward the stairs. "For 'Banks.' It's by Fabiella Banks."

You really need to tweeze your eyebrows, Heather thought. How could this girl live in civilized society and not know that the untamed brow is out?

"See you," Veronica said.

"Good luck," Heather told her.

Veronica laughed softly. "Yeah. You too." Then she headed down the stairs.

Heather scanned the shelves. "Banks, Banks, Banks . . ." she muttered as she ran her manicured pink fingernail along the spines. "Balin, Balmer, Bamson, Banner, Bantlinger . . . wait." Heather's eyebrows drew together. She scanned the names again. Banks wasn't there. The book wasn't where it was supposed to be. There was only an empty space. . . .

Crap! Heather realized. *Veronica just took the last copy!*

That little sloppy-haired, sweatpant-wearing book-I-need taker!

The skinny geek looked over at Heather and adjusted his glasses. "Come here often?" he asked.

That was the catalyst that sent Heather bolting down the stairs. Scanning the bank of cash registers, she spotted Veronica's ponytail across the counter at the third register from the left.

The clerk fired his laser scanner at the book. *Bleep!*

"Hmm," the guy behind the register said. He stroked his goatee. "This scanner has been acting up all day."

"I'm in kind of a rush," Veronica told him.

"It's not my fault that the scanner isn't working, miss," the guy snapped, arching his dark brows. "I'm not the King of Technology, okay? I don't have power over electrical objects."

"Okay, okay," Veronica said, holding up her hands.

Heather pushed her way to the front of the line.

"Excuse me," said a heavyset woman with way too much blue eyeliner as Heather tried to squeeze past. The woman was wearing a flowered shirt and holding a stack of self-help books. She stuck a meaty hand in front of Heather to stop her from getting to the register. "I'm next."

"This is an emergency," Heather explained.

"I've been waiting," the woman snapped. Heather tried to scoot past her again, but the woman barred her way with her stack of books. Heather glanced at the titles in her hands. *Learn to Love Yourself*, one read. *Think Yourself Thin*.

"Look," Heather said, "I'm about to save you ten minutes and fifty dollars. You don't need those books—you need a new look. Go with brown eyeliner and finish with black mascara, switch to solid colors and wear a shoe with a slight heel, then get a cool short haircut and dye your hair blond—it'll look a lot fuller. Now,"—Heather slapped the books out of the heavy woman's hands—"excuse me."

With a shriek, the heavy woman lunged after her books, and Heather squeezed past her and tapped Veronica on the shoulder.

Veronica gave Heather an up-and-down glance. "What do you want?"

"You know what I want," Heather replied. "That's my book."

Bleep!

"Ooh, this scanner is giving me a headache," said the guy behind the counter.

"It's not your book," Veronica pointed out. "It's mine. I'm buying it."

"Okay, look," Heather said. "I really, really, really need that book. I'll fail if I don't do this report."

"Is that my problem?" Veronica asked.

"Oh, rowr," said the guy behind the counter. He pursed his lips and leaned forward, resting his chin in his palm.

Heather glared at him. "Do you mind?"

"No, no." The guy waved the book scanner in her direction. "This is the most interesting thing that's happened all day, and I've been here since one."

"Look, I'll give you fifty bucks for the book," Heather told Veronica.

A gasp from the guy behind the counter.

Turning to face Heather, Veronica folded her arms across her chest. "You really think you can buy everything, don't you?"

Heather considered this for a minute. "Of course," she said finally. "I mean, if it's a book."

"Well, you can't buy this book," Veronica said. She wasn't even sure why she was refusing to give Heather the book. But there was something about the girl that really rubbed her the wrong way. Besides, this was *her* book—the book she had shared with her father. And she just didn't want Heather to have it. "It's mine."

"What are you doing?" said the guy behind the counter. "Take the money!"

The scanner beeped indignantly.

"You haven't even bought it yet!" Heather pointed out. "The scanner isn't working."

"I'm the one standing here," Veronica said, holding up the book. "I'm the one with the book in my hand." She planted her other fist on her hip and waved the paperback in Heather's face.

"You know, we could order the book for you," the man behind the counter suggested.

"Shut up!" both girls shouted at him.

"Okay, jeez. I was only trying to help."

Heather looked at the novel, her nostrils flaring. In a flash, she grabbed it from Veronica's hand and darted away. Veronica leaped after her, and both girls sprawled onto the floor in a heap.

"Ow! You're squashing me!" Heather cried.

"Give it back!" Veronica shouted, reaching for the book.

The guy behind the counter leaned forward to get a better look at the action.

Bleep!

The scanner fired—directly at Heather and Veronica. Light flashed. Thunder rolled.

When the smoke cleared, the bookstore clerk looked to where the girls had been fighting on the floor. They had disappeared. All that was left was the copy of *Queen of Twilight* and two smoking coals.

The clerk stared for a minute, then did the only reasonable thing he could think of. He pressed the button on the intercom. "We need a cleanup in the checkout aisle," he said. Then he gestured to the heavyset woman with the self-help books. "Next."

TWO

Veronica's face dug into something soft as Heather shoved her aside.

"Get off!" Heather shouted.

Veronica looked down at what she expected to be the maroon-patterned carpet that lined the bookstore. Instead, she found herself staring into a silvery-green floor covering. It gave off a sweet smell, like a combination of licorice and cinnamon, and it wasn't smooth. Its small curled tendrils were feathery, almost moss-like. Reaching out, she touched one carefully with a finger. It was soft and gave easily, springing back when Veronica pulled her hand away. *Cool carpet,* Veronica thought. *How come I never noticed this before?*

"Who turned out the lights?" Heather wailed.

Blinking, Veronica realized that Heather was right. The light was dim, the way it is when the sun has just disappeared below the horizon. Looking up, she saw slim trees with white bark towering above them. They glowed strangely in the low light. The place was eerily quiet, as though the forest was holding its breath.

Veronica's heart started to pound.

Trees? She looked down at the carpet again. Only this time,

she realized that what she was seeing wasn't carpet at all—it was moss. Which explained the moss-like quality.

Something told her she wasn't in New Jersey anymore.

Pain rocked through Veronica's body as Heather kicked her in the ribs.

"You witch!" Heather shouted. "You hit me and now I'm going blind! Security! Secuuuriiiiteeeeee!"

"Will you shut up?" Veronica demanded. For some reason, Heather's screaming was making her very nervous. Above, leaves rustled uneasily.

"*No!*" Sitting up, Heather cupped her hands around her lips. "Security!"

"Shut up!" Veronica reached over to cover Heather's mouth.

"Get away from me," Heather screeched.

The two girls got into a mini–slapping fight.

"Give. Me. The. Book!" Heather said, slapping at Veronica with each word.

"I. Don't. Have! It!" Veronica slapped back. "Look around! Can't you see we're not in the bookstore anymore?"

Heather froze. Her blue eyes rolled like marbles as she took in the forest for the first time. Her chest rose and fell with her breathing. "Where are we?" she whispered.

"I—I need to think." Veronica shook her head. There was something about that silver moss—the scent. It was so familiar somehow . . . and yet, she was certain she'd never smelled anything like it.

"Oh my God!" Heather sniffed. "Don't you get it? We're dead!" She looked at Veronica through teary eyes. "And I've been sent to hell—with you!"

As Heather unleashed a series of noisy and snuffly boo-hoos, Veronica took a deep breath and counted to ten. She had to admit that being stuck with Heather did seem pretty hellish. Still . . . Veronica didn't feel dead. "We aren't dead," she said.

"Yes, we are!" Heather cried.

"No, we aren't."

Heather glared at her. "Prove it!"

Reaching out, Veronica slapped Heather across the face.

"Ow!" Heather put her hand to her cheek and gaped at Veronica in surprise.

Veronica stood up and brushed off her jeans. "See?" she said, looking down at Heather. "If you were dead, you wouldn't have felt that."

Heather scrambled to her feet. She was just about to lunge at Veronica when something crackled behind them.

A moment later, a woman rode into the clearing on a white horse. She was wearing a dark cloak, and her hair hung past her shoulders in golden waves. Her face was young, but her regal posture made her seem much older. Her eyes were green and almond-shaped, catlike. Behind her were two ponies with two riders—dwarves in chain mail, one with a long black beard, one with a short red one.

"Oh my God," Veronica breathed.

The woman stopped her horse, and the dwarves rode their ponies forward, halting on either side of her. One drew a battle-ax. The other drew a sword.

For a moment, no one spoke.

"How is it that two human strangers walk alone in the Shadow Forest?" The woman fixed Heather with a steely stare. "Did the wizard send you? Speak."

Heather rolled her eyes. "Um, no," she said, and added, "We aren't into your gross Dungeons and Dragons game, okay?"

"Wait," Veronica said quickly. "Wait—did you say, 'Shadow Forest'?"

"Oh my God." Heather groaned. "You *are* into Dungeons and Dragons. I should have known."

The golden-haired woman's catlike eyes narrowed. "I was told to look for the wizard in the forest," she said, slowly pulling a golden sword from the sheath at her side. "So, either Strathorn sent you . . . " Here she pointed the sword's delicate tip at Heather's throat. "Or She did."

Veronica had opened her mouth to say, "Strathorn?" but before the syllables could pass her lips, Heather started screaming. Her scream was high-pitched and piercing, like a teakettle or an opera aria, and it cut through the silent forest like a scythe.

"Quiet, stupid girl!" hissed the black-bearded dwarf. "D'ye want Her to hear?" He swung his battle-ax at Heather, who ducked—still screaming—and scooted under the woman's horse, so that she was facing the rear of the crowd. The black dwarf's ax stuck firmly in a tree trunk. "Skeech knees!" he cursed.

As he yanked at the ax, something cut through the air with a hiss and buried itself in the black dwarf's back. "Streck necks!" he grunted, and fell off his pony. With a final gasp, he lay on the soft silver moss, motionless. A black arrow tipped with bloodred feathers protruded from his back.

"She's found us!" The golden-haired woman's horse

reared, and in the next moment, several muddy greenish figures dropped from the trees.

"Ookies!" Veronica shouted.

The golden-haired woman and the red-bearded dwarf hacked at the hunched creatures, who reached with long webbed fingers for their poison-tipped arrows. The Ookies' large yellow eyes burned as they launched their attack. In a moment, Veronica found herself surrounded by chaos. Without thinking, she reached for Heather's hand and yanked her out of the way as another Ookie dropped behind her.

Luckily, Veronica realized, they were between the horse and two ponies and were thus more or less protected on each side as the dwarf and the lady hacked at the attacking Ookies.

Swish! Swish! Red Beard lopped off the heads of three Ookies at each stroke. The golden-haired woman fought with her sword. She split the cranium of one Ookie, then sliced another in half.

"Oh, gross!" Heather screeched. She turned away, then let out another scream as an Ookie head rolled past her foot. She kicked at it hysterically. The spongy green flesh gave slightly as her kick sent the head flying into the woods. "I'm going to vomit!"

"Hoook! Hoook!" cried an Ookie as his hideous green hand reached for Veronica.

The lady chopped it off and it fell—still grasping at the air—a hand's length from Veronica's leg.

Screaming, Heather kicked that away too.

The Ookie howled in pain and scrambled off into the forest.

After a few moments, all but two of the Ookies had either

fled or been killed. The remaining dwarf lunged at the Ookie captain—but before he could deliver his stroke, there was a flash of light. He and his pony froze in place, glimmering dimly, like an ice sculpture.

Heather's screams reached a new pitch.

Turning, Veronica saw a figure standing at the edge of the clearing. She was wearing a subtle gray cloak that made her hard to spot in the dim light. But Veronica saw her pale face and noticed her red lips as they curved into a smile. The woman raised her wand.

"The Fragile Hag!" shouted the golden-haired woman just as the Hag took aim.

Veronica darted away. *Zap!* The fern that had stood at her feet a moment before turned to glass. The Hag aimed for the golden-haired woman, who kicked her heels to her horse and reached into her cloak for something. *Zap!* The shot went wild, hitting a tree. Overhead, glass leaves tinkled in the wind.

Heather screamed again, and the Hag turned to look at her. She lifted her wand.

Without thinking, Veronica reached down, wrapped her fingers around a heavy white fallen branch, and swung it with all of her force against the Hag's arm.

With a crunch and the sound of breaking glass, the Hag's arm dropped off, the pale fingers still holding the wand. The Hag cried out in pain as light flared from the wand . . .

. . . turning the golden-haired woman to glass.

The Fragile Hag turned to face Veronica. "I'll kill you!" she cried in fury.

Veronica raised her branch, and the Hag cringed.

"This isn't over," she hissed as she reached for her fallen arm. In a moment, she had disappeared.

With a howl, the two remaining Ookies disappeared into the forest.

Heather continued to scream.

"Heather," Veronica said, shaking Heather's shoulders. "Heather! Snap out of it!"

Heather's head lolled back and forth, and her scream started to sound a bit like this:

"Aaarghllaaaaaaaarghlaaaaarghlllcchhh . . . "

. . . until her head flopped forward and stayed there. Finally, she coughed a little, then took a deep breath.

Veronica looked around. They were surrounded by dead Ookies, a dead dwarf, and two glass figures. The dead dwarf's pony wandered about aimlessly. Atop her glass horse, the golden-haired woman looked even more beautiful than she had in life. Veronica walked over to her and touched her ankle.

"What's this?" Heather asked, bending down. She picked up a smooth round object, like a crystal ball or a paperweight. It was about the size of the snow globe in her pocket and seemed to glow slightly with its own light.

Turning, Veronica gaped at the thing in Heather's hand. "Don't touch anything!" she commanded.

Heather planted her hand on her hip. "You're not my boss," she said.

"Give me that," Veronica said, pointing to the crystal ball.

"Make me," Heather shot back.

Veronica took a deep breath. *I saved this girl's life, and she's acting like we're fighting over an ice cream cone,* she thought.

But she decided that she had to take a different approach. "Look," she said patiently, "I think I may know where we are. Can I just take a look at that for a minute?"

With a heavy sigh, Heather rolled her eyes. "Fine," she snapped. "Here." She tossed the crystal ball at Veronica.

I should take this moment to point out that Heather hated gym, and it was her lack of formal physical education that led to what happened next. You see, Heather hated sports of all kinds. She had convinced her mother to tell the school board that her horseback-riding classes should count toward her gym requirement, and—after months of letters and under threat of a lawsuit—they had finally agreed. That was why, when Heather threw the crystal ball, it flew high over Veronica's head, crashing into the golden-haired woman, shattering her into a million pieces.

Veronica stared dumbly at the shattered glass. Half the horse was still intact, but the glass woman lay strewn across the forest floor like glittering dew. Veronica's eye fell on a glass ear, which sent a shiver through her.

"Oops," Heather said.

"'Oops'?" Veronica repeated, wheeling to face Heather. "'Oops'? Do you have any idea what you just did?" Her voice rose to a hysterical scream.

For a moment, Heather didn't know what to say. "You know, my grandmother used to say that broken glass brings good luck," she pointed out at last.

"Well, tell your grandma that you just shattered Princess Arabelle!" Veronica shouted.

Heather looked confused. "Is that some kind of ghetto insult?"

"No, you moron!" Veronica cried. "Don't you get it? We're in the book!"

"What book?"

"*Queen of Twilight*! Jeez! Haven't you been wondering why there are Ookies and dwarves and magic wands? Look around you! We're in chapter two!"

"That's impossible." But as the words passed her lips, Heather remembered with a shudder the Ookie head she had kicked into the forest.

"It's impossible." Veronica craned her head, taking in the forest and the destruction around them. She looked Heather in the eye. "But it's true. And guess what, genius?" Veronica went on, her voice dripping with sarcasm. "I know you've never read the book, so I'll have to explain the situation to you. You've just shattered the heroine. Princess Arabelle. The One. Incidentally, she's probably the only person who could have helped us out of here." Reaching down, she grabbed the crystal ball and held it up, inspecting it. It was the Orb. The Orb of Inflation . . . or whatever. Well, at least it was in one piece. Veronica stuck it into the pocket of her hooded sweatshirt.

Heather's heart sank as she looked at the shattered glass, winking like diamonds in the pale light. She was starting to have the uncomfortable feeling that Veronica was right. Guilt washed through her. She hadn't meant to hurt anyone. "I'm sorry," she said.

"You're sorry?" Veronica snapped. "Great. We're stuck in a fictional forest full of Ookies and attacking hags, and you feel bad about smashing the only person who could have helped us. Ooh, that's so helpful! Thanks!"

"I said I was sorry," Heather replied. "What do you want from me? It's not like I carry Krazy Glue in my pocket or something. Besides, you don't even know for sure that we're inside your dumb book. It's not like you can prove it."

"Oh, yeah?" Veronica folded her arms across her chest. "Well, if we're in chapter two, then Princess Arabelle should be meeting an old man with a long beard just about . . ."

At that moment, a bush rustled. Veronica reached for the dead dwarf's battle-ax as two riders entered the clearing.

" . . . now," Veronica finished.

Sure enough, the rider in the lead was an elderly man. A long cottony gray beard flowed nearly to his waist. He wore a pale blue robe belted at the waist with rough cord and a hat resembling a stocking cap. His pale blue—almost white—eyes scanned the scene, taking in the destruction. Veronica watched as his concern turned to horror.

The other rider—taller than a dwarf but still shorter than Veronica—gasped when he saw the scene. "By the queen's nose!" he whispered, his large gray eyes wide. In front of him rode a large rodent, who chattered nervously, flicking his fluffy tail from side to side.

Veronica looked up at the old man. "Strathorn?" she asked in a quiet voice. She didn't dare say more.

The ice blue eyes flicked to her face and then to Heather's.

Strathorn sighed. "For a dragon's age have I searched the land of Galma for the One foretold by Landron the Sage—the One destined to rule as rightful queen of Talan Majeur, Garboleth, and the Eastern Isles," he said in a slow, rumbling voice.

Veronica cleared her throat. "Yeah, uh—about that—"

She fought the urge to run as, slowly, the old man dismounted his gray horse. *He's our only chance,* Veronica thought. *I'll just explain that Heather accidentally smashed Princess Arabelle and . . .*

And . . .

Oh, who am I kidding? We're dead. In five seconds, he's going to unleash a thunderbolt on our butts.

Strathorn walked over to the two girls and bowed down before Heather. Reaching up, he pressed her fingers in his own.

Heather cast Veronica a sideways glance. "This is weird," she whispered.

Veronica nudged her, indicating that she should go with it. Heather shrugged. So far, Strathorn was taking the smashed princess pretty well, considering he'd been searching for her for so long and all, she thought.

"I feared the Fragile Hag might do her work. Princess Arabelle"—Strathorn's voice caught in his throat as he gazed up at Heather—"thanks to the Weaver, you're alive."

For a moment, nobody spoke.

It took a beat for Veronica to realize the magnitude of their luck. *Oh my God, this could totally save us!* "Um—so—she's the princess," Veronica said hesitantly, pointing at Heather.

Strathorn scowled at her. "Of course she's the princess," he replied. "Who else wears the feathers of the sacred pink Quintarin bird at her neck?" The wizard aimed a finger at the hot pink trim on the collar of Heather's denim jacket.

"Oh," Heather said finally. "Oh, I get it. No, no—you're making a mistake—"

"Yes, the princess is right," Veronica agreed quickly. She

flashed Heather a meaningful glare. "What she means is that it's a mistake for us to stay here in the clearing. . . ."

Heather rolled her eyes. "That is *so* not what I meant," she snapped. "God, you're such a know-it-all." She turned back to Strathorn. "No—what I was going to say is—"

"That we should move on immediately," Veronica cut her off. "Yes, yes, good idea, Princess."

"Okay, would you quit insulting me?" Heather huffed. "I know you think I'm spoiled, but you don't have to keep calling me 'Princess' like that—and I'm trying to say something here—"

Veronica looked down at Strathorn, who was still kneeling in front of Heather. He looked extremely confused.

"Would you excuse us for one second?" Veronica asked.

"Ow!" Heather protested as Veronica wrapped her fingers around Heather's arm and yanked her to the other side of the clearing.

"What do you think you're doing?" Veronica demanded.

"I'm just—"

"Look, I've got to make this fast. Strathorn is a wizard," Veronica explained as patiently as she could. "He's been searching for Princess Arabelle. He thinks you're Arabelle!"

"But I'm not," Heather protested.

"Who cares? He's our only hope of getting out of this Ookie-infested forest! Besides, do you want to be the one to tell him that you smashed the princess to smithereens?"

Heather and Veronica looked over at the old man. He smiled hopefully, waving his stocking cap.

The girls waved back.

"If you don't pretend to be the princess," Veronica

warned, "I swear to God, I'll kill you myself. I won't wait for some Ookie to do it."

Heather hesitated. Even though she knew that Veronica had a point, she felt it was just wrong to give in to such a dork. It was the principle of the thing.

Sensing her reluctance, Veronica added, "Look, I have a plan, okay? I don't know how we got here, but I think I know how we can get back. Strathorn is a wizard, and at the end of the book, he grants Arabelle her heart's desire. If you fulfill Arabelle's quest, you'll get your heart's desire."

"Wow." Heather tugged thoughtfully at a strand of high-lighted hair. "Gosh, I don't even know what I'd choose. . . ."

"You'd choose to get us out of here!"

The images of designer handbags and dates with movie stars that had been tumbling through Heather's brain disappeared immediately. "Oh," she said. "Right." She sighed. She really didn't like Little Nerd's plan, but she couldn't come up with an alternative. "Okay," she whispered finally. "I'll do it. But only because I've always wanted to be a princess."

Veronica snorted. "Fine. Whatever."

Pasting bright smiles across their faces, the two girls walked back to where Strathorn stood beside the short guy on the pony.

Veronica nudged Heather.

"Uh—hi," Heather said.

"Princess," Strathorn said warmly.

The short guy took off his small green cap and held it over his heart. "Princess," he said. "My name is Doggett." He smiled softly. "Truly, your golden hair is as beautiful as it is in the songs they sing about you."

Heather touched her new blond highlights self-consciously. "Really? Because I'm not totally sure if I like it—"

"I knew that we would find you," Strathorn put in. "I'm so glad that you and your vassal survived the attack."

"Vassal?" Veronica repeated.

Strathorn's whiskers twitched. "Of course," he said, gesturing to Veronica's chest. "Unless my eyes deceive me."

Confused, Veronica looked down at her gray sweatshirt. VASSAR, it read across the chest in maroon letters—it was the college of Veronica's choice. But the sweatshirt was ancient and the letters faded. The R was half gone.

"What's a vassal?" Heather asked.

"A servant," Veronica snapped. She wanted to explain that she wasn't Heather's servant . . . but she knew that would lead to all sorts of other explanations that she didn't want to get into.

Heather's eyes grew round and she gave a little gigglesnort. "Of course, Strathorn," she said gleefully. "A princess always needs a servant!"

At that moment, the large rodent bounded over to Heather's feet, and she let out a scream and jumped back.

The rodent bowed low. "Princess Arabelle," it said. "Chattergee is at your service."

Heather shrieked again. "Ohmigod, it's a talking rat!"

The rodent fluffed out considerably—his poufy tail stood up straight.

"Uh . . . he's a squirrel," Doggett whispered.

"Whatever," Heather snapped. "He's a rodent."

Chattergee looked as insulted as it's possible for a squirrel to look.

"Well," Doggett pointed out to the squirrel, "it's true."

"Princess," Veronica said quickly, "we really must be going."

Doggett looked closely at Veronica. "You're rather tall for a dwarf," he told her. "If you don't mind my saying so."

Oh, crap, Veronica thought. She'd momentarily spaced on the fact that Princess Arabelle had been raised by dwarves. So—right, if she was the princess's vassal, she had to be dwarfish. *Okay, just play along,* she thought. "It's a curse," Veronica told Doggett. She sighed heavily, for dramatic effect.

"Pay no heed to anyone who says that you are too tall, my lady," Chattergee said gallantly. "You are in fine proportion." He looked her up and down, giving her a grin that was more wolf than squirrel.

"I'm tall too," Doggett volunteered. "But I don't mind."

"Tall?" Heather demanded. Doggett was a good three inches shorter than she was, although he looked older.

Doggett blushed. "For my kind," he said quickly. "The Kiblar elves."

"The Weaver has provided us with a fine beast," Strathorn said as he reached for the reins of the black-bearded dwarf's pony. He turned and gave Heather a somber look. "I'm sorry about your fallen guards," he said gravely.

Heather blinked blankly. "Who?"

"The dwarves," Veronica said through clenched teeth.

"Oh, yeah, right. Well, they were kind of annoying anyway," Heather said brightly. She patted Strathorn's white horse on the neck. "So—should I take the horse or what?"

"Yes, yes, of course," Strathorn said quickly. "Take my steed. I'll take the pony."

"I guess I'll walk," Veronica said as she watched Heather expertly mount the horse.

"Nonsense, my lady," Doggett said, holding out his pony's reins. "Franklin here is an excellent pony. I'll walk."

"Well, I—"

Chattergee bowed low. "Chattergee cannot allow such a fair maiden to walk through the Shadow Forest, oh, no." Veronica wasn't sure, but she thought she saw his tiny eyebrows waggle.

"Well . . . okay." Veronica had ridden a pony exactly twice before. Both times at county fairs. *It isn't hard,* she told herself. *It's like sitting down at the movies and having someone kick the back of your chair. Kind of.*

Doggett laced his fingers together and helped her into the saddle. The moment she was off the ground, though, Veronica's eye fell on the scattered shards of the real princess.

"Princess," Strathorn asked in a low voice, "do you have it?"

Heather looked blank. "Have what?"

"The . . . " Strathorn dropped his voice. "Orb of Neftalion."

"The Orb of Neftalion!" Veronica crowed. *Not the Orb of Inflation! Jeez!*

Strathorn looked at her quizzically.

Heather peered at Veronica. "Uh, I don't know—"

"It's safe," Veronica said. "I have it."

The wizard's white eyebrows flew up. "You?" But he recovered. "The princess trusts you indeed. May I . . . may I see it?"

Reaching into her pocket, Veronica held out the Orb. "You should keep it," she told him.

The old man shook his head. "Not I," he said in a hushed whisper. "I dare not touch it." He looked up at Heather. "The One must keep it."

"I don't know if that's—" Veronica began, but Heather cut her off.

"Fine," she said, swiping the globe from Veronica's hand. "I saw it first anyway." She tucked it into the inside pocket of her jean jacket.

Veronica sighed. *We've only been in this story for fifteen minutes,* she thought, *and already everything is going wrong.*

HREE

J eez, it's dim around here," Heather complained as the company rode farther into the forest.

Strathorn sighed sadly. "The Twilight Queen hates the sun,
Princess. Her powers grow stronger as the light grows dimmer."

Veronica had to keep from snorting. Strathorn had been
one of her favorite characters when she'd read *Queen of Twilight*
as a child. She had loved how dignified and wise he was. It was
kind of sad to see him this way—sitting atop a pony, his legs
reaching almost to the ground, and pinning the hopes of all of
Galma on someone like Heather instead of the true Princess
Arabelle.

"No light?" Heather repeated.

"The sun never comes up," Doggett said, anger simmering
in his voice. "Never goes down. Galma's all in twilight. Always
twilight."

"But you will bring the light," Strathorn told Heather. His
voice held absolute certainty, and Veronica felt even worse.

"Me?" Heather asked. She looked around the forest
appraisingly, as though she had just been asked to redecorate it.
"Well . . . I guess we could use some tiki torches or something."

Poor, poor Strathorn, Veronica thought.

Strathorn was clearly nonplussed by Heather's comment, but Doggett let out a deep laugh. Heather looked over at him, her eyebrows knit together. Heather hated to be laughed at. Nobody understood how frustrating it was when people started laughing and you hadn't even realized that you'd said anything funny. This happened to Heather all the time, by the way.

Chattergee hopped from Doggett's left shoulder onto the neck of Veronica's pony. Veronica felt the scratch of his claws as he scrambled up her arm and sat on her shoulder. "Ow!" Veronica shrugged her shoulder in an effort to dislodge the large rodent. "Get off me, you stupid squirrel."

"Many beautiful ladies have enjoyed Chattergee's company," the squirrel said in a suave voice. He wrapped his furry tail around Veronica's neck, and she batted at it.

"You're choking me," Veronica said. "Get off!"

Heather gave Veronica's new neck piece a haughty look. "Besides, nobody is wearing fur these days," she said. "Fur is murder."

"Chattergee sees the lady is ferocious." The squirrel rubbed his little paws together eagerly. "Chattergee loves a fierce lady."

"Oh, yeah?" Veronica snapped. "Well, if Chattergee doesn't get his tail off my neck, he's going to be looking for it in the bushes."

With wide eyes, Chattergee flicked his tail away from Veronica's neck.

"Chattergee, I think you'd better ride on my shoulder," Doggett suggested.

"Chattergee shall admire the lady from afar!" the squirrel said gallantly, hopping from Veronica's shoulder to Doggett's. Once he had landed, he gave Veronica an elaborate wink. "Grrowr," he trilled.

Veronica rolled her eyes. She didn't remember Chattergee at all from the book. Maybe Fabiella Banks had found him too annoying a character to write about, Veronica guessed. *But more likely we'll ditch him soon.* That was a cheering thought. *Maybe when we arrive at the elves' quarters . . .*

"The bloom fades from the fair ladies' cheeks," Chattergee said after a while. "I suggest we rest."

Strathorn looked around nervously, but eventually, he nodded. "All right," he said. "But not for long."

"So, can I just ask one question?" Heather asked as she stepped down from her horse.

Veronica winced. *Oh, please don't,* she thought.

"Of course, Princess," Strathorn replied.

"Where are we going?"

Jeez, Veronica thought, grimacing. *Doesn't this girl know how to play along with anything?*

For a moment, Strathorn seemed taken aback. But he recovered, saying, "Of course, Princess. I had forgotten that you have spent many years with the dwarves. It's natural that you are unfamiliar with the Shadow Forest."

"Yes," Veronica put in quickly. "In fact, the dwarves didn't tell the princess much about anything. So, you know, we may want to fill her in." Actually, Veronica was fairly proud of this lie. The dwarves were famous throughout Galma for their secrecy. Veronica remembered Fabiella Banks mentioning in the opening chapter that the princess had been the first "Outsider" allowed past the borders of the Dwarfish Lands in more than five hundred years.

The wizard's white eyebrows wiggled in perplexity. "What did they tell you?" Strathorn asked Heather.

Heather waved her hand dismissively. "Oh, this and that. You know. Whatever. Like—who's this queen that everyone keeps talking about?"

Strathorn's icy eyes grew wide. "By the Weaver," he said in a hushed voice. "I knew the dwarves were secretive, but I never thought they would keep you so thoroughly in the dark." For the first time, he actually appeared to be concerned.

"Well, you know how tight-lipped us dwarves can be," Veronica said lightly.

Everyone gaped at her. Below her, Franklin the pony snorted.

Veronica winced. "Um . . . sorry?"

"All right," Strathorn said patiently. He cleared his throat. "I suppose I must start at the beginning."

"That's where Chattergee always starts," the squirrel piped up. "And then I move on," he added, glancing suggestively at Veronica.

"Pipe down," Doggett told Chattergee.

"The Queen of Twilight is a witch," Strathorn said. He lifted his white eyebrows and leaned forward on his pony. "That much, surely, you know."

"Oh, yeah," Heather said. "I mean, I gathered."

"It is she who keeps the land of Galma in eternal twilight. She was your father's closest confidant," Strathorn told Heather. "And it was she who betrayed him. She murdered him and your mother and seized the throne. And she would have killed you too if your nurse hadn't got wind of the plot and carried you off to her people."

"The dwarves," Chattergee put in.

Heather looked seriously disturbed by the news. "But—why?" she asked. "What did they—uh, my parents—ever do to her?"

Strathorn shook his head. "Nothing," he said. "But at your birth, Landron the Sage, oldest of the elves, prophesied that you would usher in a new era in Galma. Two hundred years of light would begin when the crown is placed upon your golden head, Princess."

"And the queen doesn't like light, you see," Chattergee added.

"She's the meanest, evilest, most horrible witch in Galma," Doggett said through clenched teeth.

"So . . . so the queen is out to get the princess? I mean, me?" Heather asked. She glanced at Veronica.

"Not only you," Strathorn corrected. "She also wants the Orb."

"But we won't let her get you," Doggett said loyally, stabbing at the air with a stick. "She won't put one dirty paw on you, not while I'm around."

"She wants *this* thing?" Heather pulled the glass ball out of her pocket and glanced at it. It didn't look like anything anyone would particularly want. In fact, it looked almost exactly like the snow globe in her other pocket. "What for?"

"The Twilight Queen already holds the Orb of Archtelion," Strathorn explained, tracing his fingers thoughtfully through his long beard. "The light began to disappear the moment she stole it from the princes of the

Eastern Isles. But Galma wasn't plunged into twilight until she tricked the elves into giving up the Orb of Intarion. Now only the Orb of Neftalion keeps us from slipping into darkness altogether. When she controls all three, she will control the fate of Galma."

"Oh my God!" Heather gasped in amazement. "Am I seriously supposed to remember all of that?"

"She's sucking the magic from Galma," Veronica explained, ignoring Heather's comment. "She has almost all of it."

"But—wait a minute," Heather said to Strathorn. "You're a wizard, right? Why can't you just go in and blast the queen right out of the castle?"

"With two of the Orbs in her hands, even my magic is weakened," Strathorn explained.

"How weak is it?" Heather asked.

"Weak and unpredictable as that of a fledgling apprentice learning to cast his first love spell." The wizard's beard twitched, and his blue eyes twinkled. "But it has not entirely vanished. And I have other weapons, Princess, such as knowledge, that the Twilight Queen might find work to her disadvantage as well."

"So—that was her? That freak with the magic wand?" Heather asked. "She was the queen?"

"Oh, no, no," Chattergee said quickly.

"Yeah, you wish," Doggett agreed.

"That was her sister," Strathorn explained. "The Duchess of Breakable Objects."

Doggett slashed the air with his stick. "Or, as most of us call her, the Fragile Hag."

"She has another sister—the Countess of Uncomfortable Humidity," Strathorn added.

"That Drizzly Witch, she's no good neither," Doggett put in.

"All of them are dangerous," Strathorn said. "All of them would like to kill you. But the Queen of Twilight is the most desperate."

"She's the worst of the lot, all right," Doggett agreed.

"And now that the Fragile Hag has seen you—nearly killed you, from what I saw in the clearing—it won't be long before the queen unleashes the Galag Nur," Strathorn said. "That is why we must press on, toward the elves. Once we pass their borders, we will be safer."

Heather nodded, looking dazed. "Would you excuse me and my vassal for a minute?" she asked. She handed her reins to Doggett and pulled Veronica aside. "Hi," she whispered fiercely. "Okay, I think there are a few things you left out about being princess in this place."

Veronica winced as Heather's fingers tightened on her arm. "Don't worry, there's a happy ending. Anyway, nothing all that bad happens to the princess in the book," Veronica lied. Specifically, she was remembering a horrifying scene in which the entire company was attacked by a giant, drooling spider in a cave. In fact, that scene had haunted Veronica for many years of her childhood. It made the spider attack in the *Lord of the Rings* trilogy look like an afternoon playing Frisbee. It made the spider attack in *Harry Potter and the Chamber of Secrets* look like an ice cream social. It made the spider attack in *The Sea of Trolls* look like a game of patty-cake. You get the picture. Fabiella Banks's description was so horrifying that Veronica still had nightmares about it.

But *Heather doesn't really need to know about that right now,* Veronica told herself. *It isn't a real confidence builder.*

"So, nothing happens to the princess—except that she gets turned into glass and smashed to bits?" Heather asked.

"That wasn't supposed to happen," Veronica shot back. "But my theory is, as long as we stick to the actual plot, things should work out. And once Strathorn gets his full power back, he can totally zap us out of here."

"Just how long is this going to take?" Heather snapped.

A chill shivered across Veronica's shoulders. "I don't have any idea," she admitted.

There was a moment of silence as this information sank in.

"Are you trying to tell me that I could be stuck in this lame fantasy world for, like, days?" Heather demanded.

"Look, I don't like it any more than you do," Veronica said. After all, they had already been in this world for hours, and Veronica knew that her mother was probably freaking out. Ever since the day her father left the house and never came back, Carmen had been pretty high-strung about knowing where all of her family members were at all times. "But I can't think of any other way for us to get out of here. Can you?"

Heather huffed. "No."

"Okay, then." Veronica nodded. "The important thing is for Strathorn to get his powers back, so let's just try to follow the plot as much as we can."

"Fine," Heather grumbled as the girls turned back to rejoin the group. "Just wake me up when it's over."

Veronica, for the most part, enjoyed the ride through the

Shadow Forest. In the book, Fabiella Banks had made it sound gloomy and frightening. But Veronica found it surprisingly pleasant and bug free. Veronica was struck by the fact that Ms. Banks had chosen not to describe all of the colorful forest vegetation—the blue and purple vines that climbed possessively up the tree trunks, the gaudy orange flowers that sprouted among the smaller shrubbery, the brilliant blue birds that flitted anxiously between branches—in favor of focusing on the intimidating height of the trees and the way the branches moved like beckoning arms. In her attempt to create a certain mood for the story, Fabiella had left out a lot of the good stuff, in Veronica's opinion.

As she took in the dazzling flora, Veronica couldn't help wondering how Galma had come to be. Had Fabiella created it by writing it? Or had it existed on its own, before the writing? Had Fabiella visited it? Or were they, somehow, inside the mind of Fabiella Banks?

Oh, it was all too weird.

Veronica had a subscription to *American Science* and knew all about string theory and parallel universes. *The only thing I don't know,* she thought, *is whether or not I'm in one.* She wondered vaguely whether this was the kind of story where things happened and no time passed in the normal world. She hoped so. That way, her mother wouldn't be worried about her. *But what if time is passing at an even faster pace in the normal world? What if Heather and I go back to our world, and we discover that thousands of years have passed and everyone we know is dead and the Earth is ruined and apes have taken over the planet?*

There was so much to worry about.

Heather, for her part, wasn't worried at all. She was angry. She hated Galma and was busy coming up with a list of reasons she couldn't wait to get back home. It went something like this:

Reasons This Stupid Fantasy World Sucks,
by Heather Simms

1. No flush toilets. (Hel-lo! I had to use a leaf!)
2. No air-conditioning. (Ugh, I can feel the armpit stains forming)
3. No cute guys.
4. Some old guy thinks he's in charge of me.
5. No TV. (And it's sweeps week. Sweeps week!)
6. Am probably going to miss Walker's party Friday night. (Ooh, and I'll just bet Skylar is going to move right in on him!)
7. Can't get my ugly highlights fixed.
8. Dark makes me squint. (I can feel the wrinkles forming.)

And so on—you get the idea. It was a long list, and many things were listed two or three times, so I won't bore you with the whole thing. Heather was so preoccupied with forming the list that she didn't even notice her surroundings, which is why she didn't notice when they started to change.

After a few hours of plodding through the forest, Veronica heard a strange sound—almost like whispering. Overhead, the leaves were still. So it wasn't the wind. She turned to Doggett with wide eyes. "Do you hear that?" she murmured.

Doggett grinned, and deep dimples appeared in his cheeks.

"Indeed I do," he said. "We're pretty close now, I should think." He didn't seem frightened by whatever it was, which Veronica took as a positive sign.

She tried to imagine what it was that they were close to but couldn't come up with anything reasonable. She didn't remember any whispering in *Queen of Twilight*. *This must be a part that isn't in the book,* she thought. When she was small, Veronica had always been bothered by the small gaps in time that disappeared inside a story. *When do the characters go to the bathroom?* she would wonder. Or, *In the last scene they were in a forest; now they're in a cave—so what happened on the way from one to the other?* Nothing interesting, apparently. Still, who was to say what was interesting? Veronica liked details. She always wanted to know how the characters got from here to there.

So here I am, she thought as the whispering grew louder, *in a part of the story that didn't make it into the story. I'm about to find out what didn't make the cut.*

But the mystery was soon solved as the company arrived at a clearing. Through the center of the clearing ran a wide stream. The whispering was the sound of water running over rocks. Of course, Veronica had spent her life in Somerville, New Jersey. She had been to the beach, sure, but she'd never heard the beautiful sound of clear water running over stones worn smooth by time. Some of the oval stones clacked together as the water rushed over them.

On the other side of the stream was a line of trees even denser than the one they had just stepped out of. Veronica took a deep breath and was surprised at how happy she was to drink in the open air. Overhead, the gray sky twinkled softly with a few faint stars.

"Look!" Heather cried as she dismounted her horse. "The river is lavender!"

Veronica saw that Heather was actually right. The stones lining the bottom of the river were a pale purplish color—although in the twilight, of course, it was difficult to see. It was so lovely, Veronica marveled at the fact that Ms. Banks had chosen not to include the scene in her book. A serious omission, in Veronica's opinion.

"We should rest and water the horses before we cross Willbury Stream," Strathorn said. "There are still several leagues to go before we reach the elves."

Heather considered this for a moment. "How far is a league?" she asked.

Strathorn looked blank. His mouth opened, then snapped closed, and he shook his head. "Do you mean how many steps?"

"It's three miles," Veronica said quickly as she dismounted from Franklin's back. Taking in Strathorn's befuddled look, she added, "Dwarf measurements," by way of explanation.

Strathorn shook his head. "The dwarves are truly a mysterious people. I must spend some time studying their ways." He pulled thoughtfully at his beard.

"Pardon me, miss," Doggett said with a smile. He motioned toward Veronica's pony. "I'll take Franklin from here," he said.

"Oh. Thanks." Veronica handed Doggett the reins.

"Chattergee shall return!" the squirrel announced as he hopped from Doggett's shoulder. Nobody said anything as he bounded back into the woods.

Doggett patted Franklin on the neck, and the pony whinnied happily. "That's a good pony, Franklin. You've been walking all day. Time for some water and some nice green grass, lad." Doggett led Franklin toward the clear brook. Once the pony was drinking, Doggett took the reins from Heather and then from Strathorn. He led all of the animals to the water, then began to unpack one of Franklin's saddlebags.

Heather flopped down on a patch of grass near the stream and dug around in her pocketbook. Unzipping a small pouch, she pulled out a lipstick case and checked her reflection. She looked up at Veronica. "Thanks for telling me that I had a leaf in my hair," she said as she dislodged the offending green-and-white leaf from behind her ear.

Veronica sat down beside Heather and watched as she reapplied her lipstick, refreshed her mascara, and added a little squirt of perfume to her right wrist. "What are you doing?" Veronica asked.

Heather gave her a heavy-lidded look. "It's called grooming," she said haughtily as she pulled out a brush. "You should try it."

Veronica cast a glance at Strathorn and then at Doggett. Neither one was exactly heartthrob material. "Why?"

Heather looked shocked. "Um, hello?" she said. "You never know who you might meet!"

"We're in a fictional story," Veronica pointed out.

"Not for long," Heather shot back. Rubbing her lips together, she bared her teeth and checked her reflection one more time. She wiped some lipstick off her incisors and flipped the compact closed. "I want to be prepared for when we get zapped out of this geeky hellhole."

Just then, Chattergee reappeared, his cheeks bulging. As he

approached the girls, he spat the contents—what looked to Veronica like about a pound of nuts of some kind—onto the ground in a heap. "Chattergee at your service!" the squirrel said, bowing low.

"Ladies," Doggett said as he handed each of them a wrapped package. "An apple roll and a tree-baked fudge cookie for each," he announced.

Heather crinkled her nose. "Can I ask you something?" she said as she looked Doggett up and down. As already noted, he was about three inches shorter than Heather. He was rather stout and had a round face. His clothing was clean, but the fabric was rough and made of rather muddy shades of gray and green. "No offense, but . . . I thought that elves were supposed to be tall and gorgeous and, you know, mysterious and elegant and all of that junk. What's the deal?"

Veronica rolled her eyes. In her opinion, any statement that started out with the words *no offense* was better left unsaid. But Doggett didn't seem bothered by Heather's question. He guffawed as Veronica bit into her fudge cookie. "Mmm," she said. "Wow. This is delicious." The cookie was crisp, much like shortbread, with a rich fudge layer on top.

"Seriously," Heather went on. "Aren't you supposed to have long flowing blond hair done in some kind of crazy braided knots at the sides of your head?"

"You're thinking of the Sylvan elves," Doggett said with a good-natured shrug. "The Kiblar elves are different. We aren't as tall, for one thing. And we aren't elegant, as you can see." He motioned to his rough garments and smiled shyly. "The Sylvans are the heroes and warriors."

"But the Sylvans can't bake a cookie to save their lives,"

Chattergee said loyally. "Nobody bakes cookies like the Kiblars."

Doggett winked. "The secret is to bake them in trees. My father was a tree baker, as was my father's father and his father before him. Alas, I don't have the skill." The Kiblar's gray eyes clouded.

Veronica held up her cookie. "Who baked these?"

"My sister," Doggett explained, seeming to brighten at the thought of his family. "She gave 'em to me before we set off to find you. Norea's got the family gift—but it seemed to pass right over me. That's why I work for Strathorn. I don't like traveling much, but my father wouldn't let me near the cookie dough ever since the time I burned a batch of crackers and smoked up the magic oven."

Veronica wasn't sure how to respond to that, so she just said, "I'm sorry."

"Oh, I don't mind," Doggett said with a smile. "I like working for Mr. Strathorn. Least, I liked it better when he had his full magic. He's just not been himself ever since that witch got the second Orb." With a sigh, Doggett turned and walked over to Strathorn, who was sitting alone on a nearby boulder. Chattergee bounded behind him and spat a few nuts at Strathorn's feet.

Veronica watched him for a moment. "That sucks," she said finally.

Heather nibbled her apple roll. "What? The fact that we have to eat nuts that have been vomited up by a squirrel?"

Veronica rolled her eyes. "Okay, number one, they were just in his cheeks, and number two, you take them out of the shell," she snapped. Even though, silently, she had to agree that it was pretty gross. "But no—I was thinking how much it must suck to be a Kiblar elf. Basically all they do is serve the Sylvans. I never really thought about it before when I read the book, but it's kind of messed up."

"Why?" Heather shrugged. "Doggett seems perfectly happy."

"But it's wrong," Veronica pointed out. "I mean, to think that one class is a bunch of heroes and another is a bunch of servants. And it all just depends on what you're born into."

Heather thought for a moment. "Well . . . that's life, right?" Catching Veronica's glare, she added, "I mean . . . it's kind of the same in our world. You're either one of the beautiful people . . . or you're . . . you know . . . a Kiblar elf. Like the difference between me and you."

Veronica stared at Heather, who was blinking at her with wide blue eyes. Veronica didn't know what to say. It was one of the most honest things anyone had ever said to her.

At that moment, a wild screech cut across the sky, shredding the peaceful night. It was scary. Very scary. Trapped-in-a-coffin scary. Drowning-in-a-tidal-wave scary. Shark-attack scary.

And that was just the sound.

When Heather looked up, she saw a . . . thing . . . riding a . . . thing. It was a hooded figure, draped in black. Nothing was visible but a pair of glowing red eyes. It rode something that looked like a cross between a crow and a pterodactyl—the kind of crow that Godzilla would battle. Its talons were black as iron and looked like they could—and perhaps would—peel the flesh from its victims' bones. It had wide black leathery wings and its beak curved like a sickle. The duo looked to Heather like creatures that had recently escaped from hell.

"Make for the forest!" Strathorn shouted.

The words snapped the company from its trance, and in a moment, Veronica found herself splashing across the shallow stream, hysterical to reach the other side.

Doggett slapped Franklin's flank, and the pony darted toward the trees, the second pony at his hooves. The white horse had already galloped into the woods, led by Chattergee, who had been the first to flee.

On the far side of the stream, Strathorn stood motionless as the hooded thing unleashed another soul-shuddering screech. Then it plunged directly for Heather, who was almost in the far side of the stream. Suddenly her foot slipped on a smooth stone, and she found herself facedown in the water. It was cool and sweet, but she knew the Dark Thing was coming; she could tell because her back was cold, as though it had passed into shade.

Veronica reached for Heather's arm just as the old wizard held up what looked like a carved ivory dagger. *Don't look at it,* said a voice in Veronica's mind, and she didn't. She looked down at Heather.

In a moment, the clearing exploded in light.

The shrieking pounded through her head as though a thousand church bells were tolling in her skull, but Veronica pulled at Heather's arm, and at last she was on her feet, and they were running, running, running for the forest.

The Dark Thing reeled backward. The giant crow flapped wildly, temporarily blind.

Strathorn was on the move now, running faster than any old man should be able to. He was across the stream. He was halfway to the woods when Veronica and Heather plunged past the tree line.

"Keep going!" Doggett told them. "Forward—straight as you can. Don't look back. Don't stop until you hit the Great Oak."

Veronica didn't even process his words until later. She heard only *keep going,* and she did—dragging Heather by the arm.

In the clearing, the Dark Thing recovered. With another scream, it dove straight for the wizard. And Strathorn's magic was weak. There would be no second chance. The talons reached out, a breath away.

"Over here!" Doggett shouted, running out of the woods. He flapped his hands.

The Dark Thing caught sight of him, and the crow veered slightly—just enough. Wheeling, Strathorn plunged the ivory dagger into the outstretched talon.

The Dark Thing let out a scream like the end of the world.

Veronica felt her blood turn to ice, but she kept running. Deeper and deeper into the darkness—she couldn't see. She had no idea how she would find the Great Oak, but she didn't slow down, didn't let go of Heather. She didn't look back.

She just ran.

OUR

It turned out that Veronica needn't have worried about missing the Great Oak, because she ran right into it.

"Oof!"

A wall rose up and slammed her in the face, and she rocked backward. Then Heather stumbled into her, and the two girls sprawled across the forest floor.

For a moment, they didn't speak. There was only the sound of their breath.

Finally, Heather sat up. She blinked, letting her eyes adjust to the darkness. Beside her, Veronica stirred. She put a hand to her forehead. No cuts. Just a bruise.

"Are you okay?" Heather asked.

Veronica prodded her cheekbone tenderly. "Ah, I guess."

"What the hell was that?" Heather demanded.

"I guess it's the Great Oak," Veronica said. Reaching out, she felt the tree's rough bark. In the dim light, she could see that it was, indeed, Great. Capital *G*. Its trunk was like a wall—so large that at first, she couldn't even see it curve. The tree was massive. Veronica was reminded of being a little girl, standing at the foot of the Empire State Building and looking up—it was that massive. Golden leaves disappeared into the twilight sky above, and its stillness was awe-inspiring.

"Not that," Heather snapped. "I'm talking about the hell beast that just tried to kill us!"

"Oh." It took an effort, but Veronica managed to stand. She was a bit wobbly but upright. "It was a Galag Nur."

"A what?" Heather demanded. "Jeez, can't anything have a normal name around here? Why does everything have to be so hard to pronounce?"

"They're also called Shadowshriekers," Veronica explained.

"That's helpful, thanks." Heather waited for more. "And their problem is . . ." she prompted.

Veronica sighed, tucking a loose strand of hair behind her ear. "There are four of them. They used to be the princes of the Eastern Isles—until the Twilight Queen got hold of them. She twisted their souls and made them into horrible ghouls."

"Oh, well, that explains everything," Heather said sarcastically. "Okay, terrible ghouls." She folded her arms across her chest. "So. Whatever happened to 'nothing bad happens to the princess'? I mean, couldn't you have warned me that we were about to get attacked by a ghoul with a freaky giant mutant bird?"

Veronica leaned against the Great Oak. The bark was warm beneath her hand, almost as though the tree was a living mammal. For a moment, she thought she felt a tender *thump, thump*—like the heartbeat of the forest. Veronica took a deep breath. A warm feeling spread from her hand to her arm, like the tree was giving her strength. She stood up straighter. "Look," Veronica said, "I didn't mention the Galag Nur because they aren't supposed to show up this early in the book, okay?"

In fact, Veronica was right—the Shadowshriekers *weren't* supposed to appear this early in the book. But when she and Heather had appeared in Galma, Heather's screams had drawn the attention of the Fragile Hag. The Duchess of Breakable Objects had contacted her sisters, and the queen had unleashed her most formidable weapon—the Galag Nur.

So there you have it. This was the first evidence that Heather and Veronica's presence had already begun to change the world of Galma and the action of the story itself.

This realization was only beginning to dawn on Veronica, and it made her blood run cold. As I mentioned, she was a fan of science. She understood chaos theory, in which even an event as small as the flapping of a butterfly's wings can alter the future in enormous ways. Veronica didn't like chaos. And she didn't like the idea that the story might be changing in ways they couldn't control. Because if Strathorn didn't get his powers back . . .

Don't think about it, she commanded herself. *You are going home. Don't even let yourself think that you're not.* She did her best to push the thought away, but still it lurked in the depths of her heart. As frightening as the Galag Nur had been, this thought was worse.

"Okay." Heather took a deep, cleansing yoga breath. "Okay. Look. Is there anything else you want to tell me about? Now, you know—before we get attacked by lions or something? Just so I'll be prepared."

An image of the giant spider flashed in Veronica's mind, but she pushed it aside. There was no way she was going to tell Heather about that. Besides, it didn't happen until much closer to the end of the book. No need to get into that now. "No," Veronica said.

Overhead, the golden leaves rustled indignantly. Veronica stepped back and was about to apologize to the tree for telling a fib when a Jack Russell terrier–sized figure came crashing through the golden leaves and plopped to the ground.

Quickly hopping to his feet and brushing himself off, Chattergee bowed low. "Chattergee is pleased to see that the ladies bravely withstood the attack of the fearsome Galag Nur."

"Yeah," Heather said, "no thanks to you."

The squirrel puffed up. "Chattergee led you to the Great Oak, did he not?"

"Oh, yeah," Veronica said. "You led the way very well. You were running really fast."

Chattergee bowed again. "Chattergee is glad to have helped."

"My lady!" called a voice.

A few moments later, Doggett and Strathorn stumbled up. The old wizard leaned against Doggett. He gazed at Heather as though she was a precious jewel.

"Thank the Weaver you're safe," Strathorn said breathlessly. "Without the One, we're lost."

Veronica felt a pang. For the first time, she actually felt guilty for deceiving Strathorn. *Well—what choice did we have?* she asked herself stubbornly. *Besides, what would it help if he knew that Princess Arabelle was smashed to pieces? This way, at least, he has some hope.*

Utterly misplaced hope, but hope nonetheless.

Heather cleared her throat. "Uh, yeah. We're okay. But the horses have disappeared."

Doggett whistled, and in a moment, the group heard the friendly *clop-clop* of hooves. Franklin appeared first, followed by the white horse and the other pony. Doggett patted his faithful pony on the neck. "That's a good 'un, Franklin," Doggett said. "I knew I could count on you."

Franklin nuzzled Doggett's head.

"Princess," Strathorn said in a low voice. "The fact that the Galag Nur have found us is very, very bad."

Heather nodded. "You're telling me."

"I think the time has come," Strathorn went on, "for us to consult the Orb."

"Consult the Orb?" Heather snuck a glance at Veronica.

Oh, crap, Veronica thought.

You see, it wasn't really Veronica's fault that she kept forgetting to tell Heather important information about Princess Arabelle. She was under a lot of stress. When you're running from a giant attacking crow or fighting hideous troll-like Ookies, things can slip your mind. In her defense, Veronica tried to make up for it as well as she could.

"The princess has been under a great strain," Veronica said quickly, "I'm not sure that she can—"

Strathorn put up a hand. "She is the One. She must try."

Veronica's mouth clamped shut. Fabiella Banks had never mentioned how stubborn Strathorn could be.

Doggett and Chattergee looked at Heather expectantly. Even Franklin seemed to be looking at Heather expectantly. "Of course I'll try," Heather said, kicking in Veronica's direction.

Veronica bit back a groan as the blow landed on her shin. "Right, Princess. So—just do as you usually do. Take out the Orb and gaze deeply into it. Then we will be able to see pieces of the future." Veronica winced under Heather's glare.

The girls stared each other down for a few moments.

Finally, Heather's eyes flicked to Strathorn's hopeful face. She sighed. "Sure, no problem," she said.

Of course, Heather knew that she wouldn't be able to see the future in the Orb. *But what the hell?* she thought. *Maybe Strathorn will. Or maybe he'll buy that I'm tired. Who knows?* Reaching into her pocket, Heather felt a globe. Pulling it out, she held it up.

The wizard gaped at the orb in her hand as though it held the answers to the universe. "The Dark Tower," he whispered.

Heather looked down. There, without a doubt, was the image of a dark tower, surrounded by swirling snow.

She did it! Veronica thought in triumph. *This is better than the scene in* The Golden Compass *when Lyra first realizes she can use the compass to tell the future! My God, we're becoming part of this book. . . . Maybe, because we're here, Heather really has become the One. . . .*

Veronica looked carefully at the Orb of Neftalion. That Dark Tower looked awfully familiar. . . .

Is that a snow globe?

Strathorn gazed wordlessly at the small plastic Empire State Building.

"By the nose," Doggett said. "I didn't think we'd have to go there."

Strathorn's eyes met Heather's. "It is just as I feared," he said. "We must go by the northern route. It is a slower route. But if the Orb foretells—"

"Wait, wait," Veronica said slowly.

All eyes turned to her.

"Aren't we—shouldn't we go to the south?" Veronica bit her lip. In the book, Princess Arabelle never went to any Dark Tower. She took a different route. "Shouldn't we cross the Gorge of Fire?"

Strathorn stroked his long gray beard. "It's true," he said thoughtfully. "I had planned to use the magic of the Orb to safely cross the gorge."

Heather glanced over at Veronica. "Yes, good thinking, Veronica!" she said brightly. "Maybe we should use the magic of the Orb to cross the Gorge of Fire!" She fluttered her eyelashes. "That sounds like a great idea!"

Veronica swallowed hard. She had to admit, it didn't sound like a perfect plan. But neither did going off course. Still, she didn't see what choice she had. She couldn't insist on going to the south without blowing Heather's cover. Besides, there was no way that Heather could get any magic out of that Orb. Only the One could do that—and if there was one thing Heather wasn't, it was the One.

"Fine," Veronica said finally. "We'll go north."

꿍

Veronica wasn't sure how long it took to pass the Great Oak. About an hour, she supposed. The wall of bark went on and on, until she became so used to it that she was surprised when Doggett touched her ankle and said, "Bear left, my lady."

Veronica looked down at him, puzzled. "Why?"

The Kiblar elf smiled up at her kindly. "Because if we follow the tree, we shall go in a circle."

Veronica nearly laughed at herself. Of course! The tree was round . . . even though it was so large that it seemed like they were going in a straight line. She nudged Franklin to the left, and slowly, almost imperceptibly, the Great Oak began to inch away.

"Many have been lost in the Shadow Forest," Strathorn said. "Many have come to the Great Oak and never left."

Veronica shuddered slightly, imagining herself going around and around the tree, thinking she was following a straight wall. Suddenly, the warm feeling that she had felt emanating from the tree seemed less benign.

"It's getting darker," Heather said. Her voice was subdued. "Does that mean it's almost night?"

"It's never night," Doggett said. "Never light. Never dark."

"Twilight only," Veronica added through clenched teeth. *When is Heather going to get this?* "Queen. Of. Twilight."

"But it's getting darker," Heather insisted.

"The trees grow denser, Princess," Chattergee said. "Pity— it makes it so much harder for Chattergee to see the ladies' beautiful faces."

Veronica rolled her eyes.

Heather looked up. Overhead, the branches grew together, weaving a tight, verdant fabric and all but blocking out the feeble light. The trees also seemed shorter and closer together. Crowded. Heather swallowed hard.

She hated tight spaces.

She'd hated them ever since the time she'd made the mistake of rooting through her mother's shoe closet. As a small girl, Heather had been enchanted by the shelf after shelf of colorful shoes. Her mother didn't eat meat and often proclaimed loudly the sins of the fur industry. But she loved her shoes. She couldn't resist the supple leather, the slim crocodile straps, the soft suede. You have to realize that Charlotte Simms rarely wore her beautiful shoes. After all, she spent most of her time trekking through jungles or living in huts among impoverished natives in third world countries. But she collected shoes. Sandals studded with brilliant beads, strappy stilettos with silver clasps, colorful pumps, purple suede mules, red cowboy boots, delicate ballet flats. Shoes and shoes and shoes.

Sometimes, Heather would simply open the closet door and look at the shoes. She would take one off the shelf and touch it. Sniff it. Rub it against her cheek. When she was six, Heather had gotten locked in the shoe closet.

Once the door closed, the light clicked off. She was trapped in the dark.

Screaming and crying, she beat her body against the closet door. But nobody heard her. It was late afternoon when Heather locked herself in, and her father never came home before nine o'clock. Her mother wasn't in town at all. She was in Calcutta, helping lepers. The only other person in the house was an overworked Mexican maid, who was supposed to keep an eye on Heather.

The maid also had a daughter who was six. Because the maid had to work all day, in the afternoon, her daughter was supervised by her two older brothers—who were eight and ten. Isidora thought of six-year-olds as mini-adults, perfectly capable of taking care of themselves. So she didn't think anything of the fact that the little blond girl in the house, who usually spent the afternoon bothering her for a cookie or asking her to play games, was—for once—amusing herself quietly upstairs by herself for a good three hours.

When Isidora finally finished cleaning out the refrigerator, which she had been meaning to do for two weeks, she went upstairs to look for Heather. Heather had by then given up yelling. It was only when she heard Isidora calling her name that she began to beat savagely at the door again.

Hearing the hysterical thumping, Isidora opened the door to Mrs. Simms's shoe closet, and a terrified, bruised, and tearstained Heather tumbled out. The closet reeked of vomit and urine, where Heather's fear had overwhelmed her. Shoes torn from the shelves lay scattered across the floor. The little girl clung to Isidora's legs so desperately that the maid sank to the floor and wrapped her arms around Heather. Heather buried her face in Isidora's chest, and by the time Heather stopped crying, the front of Isidora's uniform was soaked through.

Patiently, Isidora held the crying girl until she stopped shaking. Then she took Heather to the bathroom and ran a bath for her. Once Heather was clean and dry, Isidora brought her downstairs and gave her a bowl of ice cream. Isidora tried to slip away in order to clean the closet, but Heather wouldn't let her out of her sight. She followed Isidora upstairs, and the two cleaned out the closet together.

Then Isidora tucked Heather into bed. But even after her father came home, Heather still wouldn't let her leave. Isidora lay on the twin bed next to Heather's until the little girl fell asleep.

Sometimes, Heather still dreamed of that shoe closet. And she hated the dark. She hated confined spaces. They made her feel sick. . . .

Now, in the forest, Heather started to sweat. "Is it hot? Is anyone else hot?" she asked.

"It is getting hot," Veronica admitted.

"It's not the heat," Doggett pointed out, "it's the humidity."

"We've entered the domain of the Drizzly Witch," Strathorn announced. "We must be on our guard."

Heather swallowed hard. The air was thick and hard to breathe. She felt like she was choking the oxygen out of the viscous air. Dark branches reached down toward her like arms, like fingers. . . .

She felt dizzy. An image of a silver stiletto sandal flashed in her mind. "I have to stop," Heather announced.

"Please, Princess, let us not pause," Strathorn insisted. "We're close. We must press on toward the safe haven of the elfin border."

Heather's body started to shake. Everything around her was darkness. She felt it pressing in on her. "I have to stop," she insisted, her rising panic making her voice higher than usual. "I need . . . " *I need some light,* she thought. *Light.* "I need to rest. I just need to sit by a fire for a minute," Heather explained. "Maybe have something to eat."

"It's not a good idea—" Veronica started.

"Would you shut up?" Heather snapped. "I'm the One, okay? And I. Need. A. Fire! Now!" Without another word, she dismounted her horse.

The leaves rustled overhead.

A moment later, Heather heard a sound, like two rocks being smashed together. Then there was a spark, and the spark flared slightly, revealing Doggett's face. He was bent at the ground, making a small fire. "That's all right, Princess," he said. "I was thinking I should cook up something for us. Still a ways to go before we reach the elves, right, Strathorn? A snack couldn't hurt?"

Strathorn sighed. But he dismounted his pony. "If we

must, we must," he relented. "But a short one."

"That's right," Doggett said. "Just a quick rest." His eyes flicked to Heather, and he smiled at her. "There's nothing like a nice fire to cut the darkness."

Heather couldn't reply. All she could do was shake her head. She had never been so grateful to anyone in her life.

Veronica and Doggett collected some dead wood—there was plenty nearby—and they fed the fire.

Heather would have helped, but she was still half frozen with fear. Her body ached, and she felt cold, then hot, then cold.

Above them, the leaves whispered.

"Seems like the wind is picking up," Strathorn said thoughtfully. Looking into the darkness, he added, "I do not like this place."

"I hope you don't think you can just make us do whatever you want," Veronica growled in Heather's ear as she tossed some wood on the fire. "Don't you go pulling this 'I'm the One, we have to do what I say' crap again." Veronica didn't mean to be rude, but she was beginning to feel afraid, which made her irritable.

Heather ignored her. She would have explained about the shoe closet, but she knew Veronica would probably just make fun of her. So she sat perfectly still and silent and focused on her yoga breathing.

Chattergee hopped around, "securing the perimeter," as Doggett dug in his canvas sack and came up with a frying pan. This he stuck in the fire. He unwrapped something from his pouch and put it in the pan, where it began to melt. A moment later, Chattergee came back with a few mushrooms. Doggett chopped them up and threw them in the pan, and a lovely smell began to waft up from the fire.

Doggett grinned with pride. "Right. A small snack, a quick rest, and we'll be right as—"

But he never finished his sentence, because the trees attacked.

Heather let out a wild scream as a branch reached out, grabbing Veronica by the waist. In a moment, Veronica was dangling above her head, only the whites of her eyes visible in the darkness.

"Aiee!" Chattergee cried. He leaped onto a branch—away from Veronica.

"No!" Veronica shouted as she kicked at the branch that held her. Her arm was pinned to her side.

Heather screeched as stems wound around her ankles, crawled up her calves. The earth parted, revealing a network of roots—some thick as a giant's thigh, some thin and spidery. Screaming, she tore at the plants as they sucked at her legs.

"Get back!" Doggett cried, lunging at the roots with his kitchen knife.

A long plant lashed out, striking the knife from his hand in a single whiplike slash. Still screaming, Heather disappeared into the dark earth.

Heather was surrounded by darkness. The earth was pressing on her, the trees clawing at her. She wanted to fight, but she couldn't move. She wanted to scream, but her mouth was stopped with soil.

"Save the One!" Strathorn shouted, and he and Doggett dove toward the place where Heather had been only moments before.

Strathorn beat at the branches with his staff, but the trees reached out for him, pulling him by the legs into their grasp. "You will not hold me!" Reaching down, the wizard thrust his staff into the fire. With a burst of flame, the end caught fire. Strathorn jabbed the flaming staff against the branch holding his legs. Squealing, the tree released its hold, and both Strathorn and Veronica dropped to the forest floor, where Doggett was clawing at the earth.

"I can't reach her!" he cried.

Strathorn jabbed his flaming staff at the ground. The earth shifted slightly, but the roots did not give way.

Plucking a long branch from the fire, Veronica helped Strathorn beat back the branches with the flames. Doggett took a hatchet from his belt and hacked at the roots. They shoved him back, and he landed face-first, only inches from the fire.

Reaching out, the Kiblar elf grabbed his frying pan. The mushrooms in hot grease sizzled as he turned back, pouring the grease on the roots.

The forest floor boiled, and the earth parted, revealing a white arm. Doggett reached for Heather, struggling with all of his might to pull her from the earth. Strathorn bent to help, and in a moment, her head appeared above the ground. Coughing, she spat the bitter soil from her mouth. Her eyes rolled, and she looked up at Doggett in terror. "Don't let go," she whispered. Her skin was white as chalk beneath streaks of black earth.

At that moment, a root lashed out behind him. Doggett screamed in pain as the root pierced his shoulder, but he didn't let go. Veronica shoved her flaming branch at the root, and it snaked backward, coiling back into the ground.

With a final heave, Doggett pulled Heather from the ground.

"Back!" Strathorn shouted at the trees. "Get back!" He motioned over the end of his staff with his hand, and the flames grew till they nearly touched the branches overhead. A quick gesture at the other end, and Strathorn's staff was now burning at both ends. "We will reach the elves!" he cried.

Just then, Heather screamed. "Doggett's fainted!"

Gently, Strathorn touched the place on Doggett's shoulder where the root had cut through his flesh. "The roots are poison," Strathorn said in a low voice.

Hot tears streamed down Heather's face, leaving white streaks through the dirt. "Save him!"

"We cannot tarry here," Strathorn said.

"We can't leave him," Heather said. "We can't."

"I will tend to him," the wizard pledged, "but we must reach the safety of the elves. I will need their help."

"We have to move!" Veronica shouted as a branch closed in on her. "Now!"

Strathorn and Heather struggled to throw Doggett, sack-like, onto Franklin's back. And in a moment, they were on the move. With an eerie crackling noise, the branches and roots retreated overhead and below as the company moved on.

Strathorn held his burning staff at the front, Veronica held her flaming branch at the back, but the rest of the forest was quiet and still as they plunged forward into the darkness.

IVE

It seemed to Heather like they had been running forever—like she had spent her entire life plunging headlong through the darkness of a forest with neither beginning nor end. No one spoke. Instead, the pounding of their feet seemed to take on its own voice: *Hurry, hurry, hurry.* Heather tried not to stare at Strathorn's torch. When she looked at the light too long, she was blinded and couldn't see her way. Then again, the light was the only comfort in a forest full of invisible dangers.

That was why it was so disturbing when the light blew out.

Strathorn stopped suddenly, and the entire company came to a halt. Doggett swayed—unstable—on Franklin's back, and Heather reached out to steady the pony. The feeble fire of Veronica's torch was the only light they had to see by. That was why it was the sound, rather than the sight, that alerted Heather to the fact that the line of trees behind them seemed to be closing ranks.

There was a hurried rustling and scraping as the branches grew together into a thick wall. With a scream, Heather thrust herself against the barrier, clawing to get out.

"Shh, Princess," Strathorn said gently as he took her arm. "Bravely now."

"No!" Heather screamed through her throat, which was almost closed. "Let me out! Please! I want to wake up! Let me out!"

"We're trapped!" Chattergee cried, hopping back and forth at Heather's feet. "We're dead! We're dead! Ooh, poor Chattergee— such an ignominious death for such a fine squirrel!"

"It's all right," Strathorn said. He took Heather firmly by the shoulders and looked her in the eye. "It's all right."

"Look," Veronica said. Heather followed Veronica's gaze— her face was tilted toward the branches above. The trees in this part of the forest were taller, slim with silvery leaves. The air was no longer thick but clear and sweet. Veronica knew where they were. This was a description she had read many times, but even the beauty of Ms. Banks's prose couldn't relate the loveliness of the slender trees, the lightness of the air, the perfect stillness that surrounded them. "We've reached them," she whispered.

Just as the words passed her lips, the pale limbs overhead parted slightly, letting in the fragile twilight. There was a quick zipping sound, and Heather looked up to see four figures descending quickly on ropes, as though they were rappelling down a mountain.

They dropped noiselessly to the ground before Strathorn and then stood, unmoving, waiting for the wizard to speak.

Veronica stared in awe, realizing that none of Fabiella Banks's descriptions had done these creatures justice. There were two men and two women—only they weren't men or women at all. For one thing, they were much taller than men. The shortest female elf stood a head taller than Strathorn. Also, they were slight and graceful in their movements. Veronica mused that if she passed one of these beings in the forest, she might actually have mistaken it for a tree, so absolute was their stillness. Their clothing, too, worked as camouflage. Richly textured and all in shades of brown, gray, and green, it was embroidered with intricate patterns that—from a distance—resembled bark. But when she looked more closely, Veronica could see that the embroidery actually held figures of the forest and seemed to tell a tale of its own. She wished that she could spend a century studying it.

What captured Heather's attention was the elves' faces. She had never read *Queen of Twilight* and therefore had an image in her mind based loosely on a combination of the *Lord of the Rings* movies and the Claymation *Rudolf, the Red-Nosed Reindeer*, Christmas special. But these elves were like nothing she had ever pictured. For one thing, they were about as far from Doggett as could be imagined. They were a good two to three feet taller than he was and slender where he was stocky. And their hair was white. Not platinum blond or ash blond or any kind of blond you've ever seen, but white as a page of fresh copy paper and luminous, like the fire in an opal. Heather could tell that there were two males and two females, but their hair was all cut short and stuck out around their faces like flower petals. And their skin—it was a rich, honeyed shade of brown that made Heather think at once of antelope and café au lait and many other things that were soft and sweet and wonderful. Their eyes were green, but not the green of a jewel. Instead, they were the shocking green of a pine branch in a snowy landscape.

They were so beautiful that Heather would have felt sick even if she wasn't in a strange forest and frightened and streaked with mud and dirt and pretending to be a princess she knew nothing about.

All in all, they were rather stunning, to say the least.

Finally, after what seemed like forever, Strathorn stepped forward. "Ibharn, Prince of the Elves, I have found the One," he said.

The tallest elf's green eyes flicked to Heather and hovered on her face for a moment. She held her breath. *He knows,* she thought as she met the elf's gaze. *He must know the truth.* She couldn't imagine that anyone as obviously magical as the elf before her wouldn't know that she was a fraud on sight. She lowered her eyes, and Ibharn turned back to Strathorn.

"I had heard that the princess was very beautiful," Ibharn said, bowing low. Straightening up, he shrugged, and his eyes flicked again to Heather. "But—to tell you truly—all of the daughters of men look the same to me."

Heather's eyes narrowed, and Veronica tried to beam her a silent message to be quiet. According to Fabiella Banks, Sylvan elves were touchy—everyone knew that. It was easy to set them off.

Doggett let out a low moan, and his eyes moved beneath their lids.

"It looks as though you have found more than the One, Strathorn," said one of the female elves.

"Linnea speaks the truth," Ibharn agreed. "Or else something found you."

"You have to help him," Heather said quickly.

Ibharn lifted the pale fire of his eyebrows and gazed at Heather haughtily. "I have to?" he repeated.

Oh, boy, Veronica thought. *Here we go.* But there was no way to stop Heather once she got rolling.

"Yes, you have to! We were attacked by killer trees and he saved me and now he's injured, but Strathorn says he can save him with your help!" Heather cried.

The corners of Ibharn's mouth curled slightly, like a sprout from a seed. "You're very dramatic," he observed coolly.

Heather gaped at him, unsure how to reply, but luckily, Strathorn stepped forward. "This is my Kiblar. He was wounded by an oak in the forest. We respectfully request your assistance in his care."

There was only the faintest movement of Ibharn's facial muscles to indicate that he had understood Strathorn's words. "We offer your Kiblar such medicine as we know and a place to rest that you may tend him," Ibharn said finally. "And we will welcome you with a feast in our tradition. Come."

He stood without moving, and Heather was just wondering how she was supposed to follow him if he wasn't going anywhere when ropes fell from the trees overhead. Before she had a chance to protest, the elves had tied an intricate knot around her torso, then her legs, and in a moment, she was zipping up, up, up into the green canopy overhead.

꙰

And the brave and true Siltarinn,

Son of the just and wise Favorajorn,

Daughter of the witty yet not overly loquacious Larandranon,

Who was very friendly with the great Princess Arion,

And once met the great King Melevedeh at a party—

But that is another story and not the one we are telling now.

Yes, I remember it well; it occurred on a Tuesday,

In the summer of the fullest moon,
When the corn was ripe and the air was clear.
It was then that Siltarinn felt slightly thirsty
And felt that he needed a glass of water
To quench this thirst of which he was not the master. . . .

Veronica couldn't help yawning as the elvish bard strummed her lute. At least, Veronica guessed it was a lute. She knew that the elves played lutes—or was it lyres? She'd never had a very clear image from what was described in the book—but the instrument was basically a guitar shaped like half of a giant avocado. She glanced over at Heather, who looked like she was about to die of boredom. Not that Veronica blamed her. In the book, Fabiella Banks had described the elves' songs as "dreamlike" and "hypnotic." Well, that was an overly generous description, Veronica was realizing. What they were was boring. The bard—an elf woman dressed in flowing silvergreen robes—could not seem to get to the point. They had been listening for an hour already, and the hero Siltarinn still hadn't taken a sip of water. And who knew where the story would go after that? Maybe he would scratch himself? Go to the bathroom?

Veronica knew that there were people who studied *Queen of Twilight*'s elvish songs and thought they were masterpieces in their own right. You see, Ms. Banks had—very intelligently, as Veronica realized now—chosen to write them in their original elvish dialect. People had been puzzling over the mysterious songs since the book's first publication, but Fabiella Banks had never offered a translation. There was a whole branch of scholarship dedicated to decoding the mysterious ballads.

However, because Heather and Veronica spoke only English, the elfin bard had offered to sing the song in the visitors' own language.

Maybe some of the magic is lost in the translation, Veronica mused. *Let's hope.*

Still, although their song was boring, the elves themselves were fascinating. Once they had brought the entire group into the trees, Veronica had gasped at what she saw. The ropes had led to the top of a lookout tower with a view of the treetops that stretched for miles. But after a moment, Veronica realized that what she was seeing wasn't treetops at all—rather, it was a vast city, a series of buildings built into the branches and made to resemble trees. And through the city, surefooted elves climbed from tree to tree, building to building. *Patrifice,* Veronica thought. The great elf city. She was so thrilled to see it, she actually managed to put her fear about getting home out of her mind for a while.

"I say," Chattergee had said in awe, "now this surely is a sight. Not even the squirrels can compare with the elves for climbing, that's certain." He bowed low to Ibharn.

"Thank you for stating the obvious," Ibharn said.

This was another thing that Veronica was realizing Fabiella had chosen to soft-pedal in her story—Ibharn, Prince of the Elves, was a major jerk.

"Where are you taking him?" Heather had asked as a Sylvan elf slung Doggett over his shoulder and started away. Strathorn had moved to follow him but stopped in his tracks at Heather's latest outburst.

"Lifkin is taking the Kiblar to the restful sanctuary," Ibharn said haughtily. "That he may be cured."

"I want to come along," Heather announced. Veronica could tell that she didn't want to leave him. It was almost as if she was afraid to leave him.

Ibharn laughed. "Really, that's quite touching," he said. "But it would take you hours to climb to the sanctuary. And I think the sooner we get him there, the better. Besides," he added with a sniff, "you need a wash."

Heather looked like she was about to claw out Ibharn's eyes, but Strathorn stepped in. "We all need a wash and a change of clothing, Prince," he said in his slow, kind way. His ice blue eyes rested lightly on Heather's face. "I will return in as short a time as I may," he promised. In a flash, the wizard had disappeared after Lifkin.

And in the next moment, the elves whisked them away, leading them slowly down rope ladders and across platforms. Veronica could tell that they were impatient with the slow humans. In fact, the only one who seemed to get along well with the elves was Chattergee. He chattered nonstop as he hopped from one branch to another.

"And then the Galag Nur attacked!" Chattergee cried dramatically. "I drew my sword, of course, but it was no use. I heard the screams of terror around me and realized that I had to help my friends, who, in their fear, could hardly find their weapons. . . ."

Veronica rolled her eyes, but the elves seemed to be eating it up, so she didn't bother to correct the story. Let them think Chattergee was a big hero—who cared?

The unusually quiet one was Heather. She barely said a word as the elves led them to their strange, shower-like contraptions that shot jets of water at them from every direction.

Even as Veronica exclaimed over the scented jasmine soap and moisturizer—and Veronica rarely noticed that kind of thing—Heather said nothing. She just kept her lips pressed into a firm line and her eyebrows knit together. Finally, Veronica gave up, and the two girls got dressed in their new elfin clothes—which were simple, green embroidered tunics over brown drawstring capri pants, basically (apparently the elves weren't going to waste their best stuff on a couple of humans, even if Heather was the One)—in silence.

Veronica was understandably thrilled to get rid of her Vassar/Vassal sweatshirt. It was bad enough that she had to pretend to be Heather's handmaiden—wearing a huge sign across her chest that proclaimed her servitude was a little too much. As for Heather, she didn't blink as she traded in her princess-pink jacket (now a mess of rags and ruined feathers) for a simple tunic. She didn't complain as she transferred everything from her pockets and leather shoulder bag to a plain cloth knapsack. Veronica had expected Heather to pitch a fit that her expensive Coach bag had been ruined, but Heather didn't seem to care.

In fact, Heather didn't care. She just hoped Doggett was okay. She wished she could go see him, but once Strathorn returned from the sick ward, or whatever it was called, he had said only, "I have done what I can. Now Doggett must rest, and we shall see."

So Heather was stuck at the feast listening to the boring elf song, like everyone else.

The meal wasn't bad, she thought now as she sat at the long table, as long as you liked vegetarian stuff. So that was okay. She'd been kind of meaning to become a vegetarian anyway because Guru Stacey said it was a good idea. Still, if someone had offered her a big, juicy hamburger and a plate of fries, Heather wouldn't have said no. The veggies weren't really filling her up, and she was hungry.

The bard droned on and on, and Heather fiddled with the food on her plate. She really wished she could make this story end. Not just the one she was listening to—the one she was in. But at least they had reached the elves now. *I think that must be somewhere near the end,* Heather decided. *It kind of feels like the end. I'll ask Veronica about it later.*

Heather looked around. She could not believe these people. They were staring at the bard as though she was reciting the text of the best Harlequin romance novel in the world instead of delivering the most deadly dull tale of a thirsty guy who discovers that the tap isn't working. Even Strathorn seemed into it. But maybe he was just being polite. You never could tell with that guy, Heather thought.

Still, the hall was nice enough. The plates were made of solid gold and had elaborate leaf-and-vine patterns etched into the rims. The goblet that held her wine—or whatever the sweet drink was—was set with a purple jewel as big as Chattergee's fist. The elves themselves were beautiful, of course, and Heather's freshly conditioned hair fell around her in soft waves, smelling faintly of jasmine. Still, she couldn't wait to get out of here. She kept thinking about Doggett, worrying about him. An image of him flashed in her mind—the look in his gray eyes as he'd pulled her out of the sucking ground that was trying to gobble her up. She could still feel his hand in hers, the strong fingers wrapped around her wrist, refusing to let go. Heather still couldn't believe he had saved her. He had gone near that ground, he had fought the roots . . . and all the while, Heather hadn't even been able to move, speak, or fight. The terror had taken over. If it wasn't for Doggett, she knew she'd be dead right now, dead and buried deep in the earth, wrapped in a shroud of roots.

Who would have thought such a little elf guy could be so brave?

As she shifted slightly, Heather's eye fell on a pedestal near her chair. It was against the rear wall, and on top of the carved wood was a golden box. The box was small, the size of a deck of cards. The perfect thing to slip into a pocket.

And these elfin capri pants . . . they had deep pockets.

What happened next wasn't even her choice, so don't bother getting angry about it. Heather's fingers acted of their own accord, and before she knew what had happened, the box was resting in her right pocket, the corner pressing against her thigh.

Finally, the song ended. For a moment, Heather feared that they had realized what she had just done, but no . . . the song was simply over. Automatically, Heather started to clap and then realized that all eyes were turned to her.

"Elves observe a moment of respectful silence after a performance," Veronica whispered in Heather's ear.

"Yeah—you know what?" Heather hissed as she sat on her hands. "Your information's good, but your timing is a little off."

Prince Ibharn cocked a white eyebrow, and his brown skin dimpled as a snarky smile spread across one half of his face. "What were you doing, Princess? Killing mosquitoes?"

The elves cracked up.

Elfin humor is even lamer than elfin music, Heather thought.

And this Ibharn guy was seriously working her nerves. "Where I'm from, we clap after a performance," she said haughtily.

"I have never heard of this strange dwarvish custom," Ibharn replied.

"Well, I guess you need to get out more," Heather snapped.

Ibharn narrowed his eyes at her. Heather could feel Veronica shooting her a look, but she ignored it. She didn't care.

"Your handmaiden, Princess, does hardly look like a dwarf," Ibharn said slowly. "She is very tall."

Veronica kicked Heather under the table, but Heather just kicked back. *Okay, so maybe Ibharn is suspicious,* she thought. *But if I can bluff my way into the hottest nightclub in New York City without an ID, I can certainly fake out this guy.* Heather sighed dramatically. "Please, Ibharn, she's sensitive enough about her height as it is," she said. "You don't have to go pointing out her flaws."

"I'm just saying—"

Heather leaned forward. "And I'm just saying that now I'm going to have to listen to boo-hooing and 'No dwarf will ever marry me' all night, and I really need some rest—so could you just zip it?"

Ibharn sat back in shock. "I have never heard anyone speak as you do," he said.

"Look, I'm a human princess raised by dwarves, okay?" Heather shot back. "I've got issues."

Ibharn's green eyes locked onto Heather's blue ones.

Not a chance, buddy, Heather thought as the elf tried to glare her down. *I can stare at my reflection for hours. You're going down.*

Strathorn cleared his throat. "Er . . . well. I, uh . . . "

Heather and Ibharn continued to stare at each other.

"Prince—what news of the Twilight Queen?" Strathorn asked finally.

Ibharn's eyes flicked toward the wizard.

"You blinked!" Heather crowed.

"No, I didn't," Ibharn protested. "I just—"

"You did," Heather shot back. "Don't even try it."

"Already the Eastern Isles have fallen," Linnea informed Strathorn, ignoring her brother as he sulked. "Her army is on the march."

Strathorn nodded, his face grave. "The Shadow Forest is almost fully in the grasp of the Fragile Hag and the Drizzly Witch," he said. "The time has come . . . to fight."

Veronica leaned forward in her chair. This was one of her favorite parts of the book—when Strathorn convinces Ibharn to march on the queen.

Ibharn folded his arms across his chest. "Who? Strathorn, who will fight? The dwarves"—and here he shot a nasty look in Heather's direction—"are too far to the west. And as long as the queen holds the Orb of Ichtelion, we are weak. If we stand against her forces now, we'll be slaughtered."

"There is a way . . . " Strathorn began. "The Twilight Queen can feel our fear. She feeds on it. She knows that we will defend ourselves, but she does not count on a direct attack. As long as the Orbs are in her hands, she feels invincible. Perhaps this, then, is the key to her defeat. If we were to seize the Orbs . . . "

"The queen's power would lie in our hands!" Veronica finished.

It took a moment for Veronica to realize that everyone was staring at her. *Did I just say that out loud?* she wondered.

Strathorn's white eyebrows shot up so far, they were practically in the middle of his forehead. "Er . . . that was, uh, exactly what I was about to say," Strathorn said.

Veronica sank a little lower in her chair. "Sorry," she mumbled.

"But how will we get the Orbs?" Ibharn asked.

"It's impossible. Even if someone got past her guards, no one can sneak up on the Twilight Queen," Linnea insisted. "Her powers of smell are too strong!"

"Not if we have the Helmet of Unsmellability!" Veronica shot out of her chair, getting carried away again. She cleared her throat. Her cheeks flaming, she sank back into her chair. "Sorry again."

"Uh, exactly," Strathorn agreed, tugging on his beard. "Deep in the cave of the dragon Karn lies the helmet, which makes its wearer odorless," he explained. He gave Veronica a strange look. "How is it that a dwarf possesses this secret?"

Veronica was saved from having to answer by Ibharn, who looked skeptical. "You'd have to kill the dragon to get it," he pointed out. "And for that, you would need the Sword of Defiance, which lies deep in the stronghold of the Drizzly Witch."

Strathorn nodded. "Precisely."

"How will you cross the Gorge of Fire?" Linnea asked.

"We shall not," Strathorn explained. "We shall take the northern route, across Mount Panic."

"It's a longer route to Talan Majeur," Ibharn said.

"Yes," Strathorn agreed. "But once the sword and the helmet are in our hands, we have hope. We shall travel to Talan Majeur and join the king's army. With those weapons and the Orb of Neftalion, we will face the queen on the field of battle and—"

"Victory!" Ibharn's green eyes glittered.

"Yes," Strathorn agreed, his face grave. "The task is daunting, true. But possible."

Heather rolled her eyes. "Yeah, but what idiot would be willing to do all of that?" she asked.

The hall was silent.

"Why are you all staring at me?" Heather asked. "Do I have something on my face?"

Veronica stomped on her foot, and finally, Heather understood. "Oh, no way." She shook her head. "No way am I going on some kind of crazy—"

"What the princess means," Veronica said quickly, grinding her heel onto Heather's foot, "is that of course the One must accept such a task. The only question is who will go with her."

"I will go," Ibharn said.

Oh, jeez. Heather lifted her eyebrows. *Like it's not bad enough to be stuck in this stupid fantasy story—now I have to hang out with Prince Un-charming? He and Veronica will probably spend the whole time talking about magic jewels and crap like that.*

"The One should not travel without a warrior at her side," Ibharn added.

"I will go too," Strathorn volunteered.

Veronica nodded. Great—the story was finally getting back on track. Ibharn would slay the dragon Karn, and Strathorn would lead the army at the end of the story. And then, with the destruction of the Orbs, his power would return, and he would un-weave the web of night that had fallen over Galma. So—that was everyone they needed: the warrior, the wizard, and the One.

"And, of course, I must accompany the princess," Veronica announced. "Unfortunately," she added under her breath.

"Chattergee would not miss such an adventure!" the squirrel announced, giving Veronica a lurid wink.

Veronica sighed. "Great."

Linnea stood, smiling softly. "This is a great and terrible journey," she announced, "and it will carry many dangers. For this, the Sylvan elves offer the travelers certain gifts."

"Gifts?" Heather asked, sitting up straighter.

"The first is for you, Princess," Linnea said as a Kiblar elf appeared at her elbow and opened a long wooden box. Linnea pulled out a golden dagger. "This is made of gold and tempered with steel, crafted by our finest smiths. The handle is carved from a single giant black pearl found in the depths of the Sea of Hope. Its sheath is made of the hide of the king peacock. May it help you in desperate times," she added as she offered the blade to Heather.

"Um . . . thanks," Heather said. Nobody had ever given her a knife as a gift before. It wasn't really the kind of present she'd been hoping for. Still, it was the thought that counted.

"For your handmaiden," Linnea went on, "the Sylvans offer this crossbow. It holds bolts made from the branches of the silver willow."

"Yeah, but what are the arrows made of?" Heather asked as

Linnea held up a quiver full of silver arrows set with blue feathers. "They're pretty."

"Crossbow arrows are called bolts, Princess," Veronica explained.

Strathorn tugged his beard. "Those secretive dwarves," he said to himself. "The princess's lack of knowledge is lamentable."

"The bow is self-guiding," Linnea said, handing the quiver to a rosy-cheeked Kiblar elf. "Once you look at your target and pull the trigger, the bolt will find its mark."

"Wow!" Veronica exclaimed as the Kiblar delivered her present. "Great gift!" Of course, there wasn't a handmaiden in Fabiella's book, so, although Veronica had known that the princess would receive a golden knife, she hadn't been sure that she would get a present at all. But this was a very practical item for someone who would soon be fighting a giant spider.

"For the valiant squirrel," Linnea said, "we have this sword." In her hand was a tiny blade—almost a toothpick, really—which shone with silvery light. "This weapon is small, but its core is diamond, and the blade cannot be broken. Use it well, Chattergee."

"That's a waste of some diamond right there," Heather muttered as the squirrel chattered happily over his gift.

"And for Strathorn, the Sylvans offer this." Linnea held out a small tool no longer than an elfin finger. It looked to have a small set of shears at one end. "It is made of finest gold, lightweight and easy to carry."

Strathorn seemed intrigued. "What is it, my lady?" he asked.

"It is something entirely new—a multiuse blade made by the inventive and self-reliant people of the north," Linnea explained. "It has two small knives, a pair of shears, a corkscrew, and a nail file. And it all folds up into a tiny package."

The wizard nodded. "A most ingenious device, and I shall use it often," he pledged as he put the knife in his pocket. "It is decided," he announced, looking around. "We have a Comradeship of the Orb, a company of five."

"Five . . . plus Doggett," Heather said quickly.

Strathorn's mouth snapped closed. "Doggett?" he said.

"Who's that?" Ibharn asked.

"The elf who saved me," Heather said.

"Do you mean the Kiblar?" Ibharn asked. He burst into laughter. "We can't take a Kiblar along on a trip of this kind."

Heather narrowed her eyes. "I'm not going without him."

"I won't go if he goes," Ibharn hissed.

"Like I care," Heather shot back.

"Whoa, whoa, wait a minute," Veronica said. "Let's not be hasty."

"Doggett comes with us," Heather insisted, slamming her fist on the table. "And that's final!"

Ibharn considered this for a moment. "Fine," he said at last. "The One has made her choice. Our Sylvan scouts will guide you to the edge of the forest, toward the domain of the Drizzly Witch. But I will not join the company." He stood, and all of the other elves followed suit.

"Wait!" Veronica cried. "Wait!"

But they didn't wait. She stared in horror as the elves filed silently out of the hall.

‍⁘

Heather stood outside the door for a moment, hesitating. She couldn't tell whether or not this was a bad time to come in.

Strathorn had said that it was all right—Doggett was feeling well enough for a visitor. But it seemed like someone in Doggett's room was in the middle of an argument.

"No, no, no!" said a female voice. "You call that pillow plump? It could be twice as fluffy. Let me have it."

"I'm telling you, Freda, I know what I'm doing," complained another—younger-sounding—female voice. "You're a scrubber, anyway. What do you know about linens?"

"Really, it's quite plump," Doggett's voice said.

"Gersha, you know perfectly well that I was in linens for three frigts before I moved to scrubbing," Freda said, ignoring Doggett's comment. "I was plumping pillows before you were born!"

"He doesn't need any more pillows, ladies," said a third voice. "He needs more cookies. Fresh from the tree!"

"Oh, Malag, you and your cookies," Freda's voice complained.

"Really, I'm fine," Doggett insisted.

"Listen to him," Gersha said, her voice thick with emotion.

"A true Kiblar hero," Freda agreed with a sniffle. "He says he's fine after all he's been through—can you imagine?"

"Now, you just sit back and have a cookie," Malag cooed.

Finally, Heather decided that these voices were likely to go on in this manner forever, so she knocked gently at the door and poked her head in. "Excuse me," she began.

"By the nose, it's the princess!" Malag cried, dropping the platter of tree-baked cookies.

"Oh my goodness, I never thought I'd live to see the day," Freda breathed as she frantically dusted Doggett's footboard.

"Your Holiness." Gersha, who was twice as plump as the pillow she was holding, gave a low bow, which was made rather awkward by the pillow still in her hand.

"Um," Heather said, "really, that's okay—"

"What are you doing, you crazy Kiblar?" Freda demanded. "Call her Your Majesty! Oh, who is training the servants these days?"

"Your Majesty." Malag bowed so low that his long pointy nose practically touched the cookies he had spilled on the floor.

Freda launched into a low bow as well, which set off an impromptu bowing contest in which all three Kiblar servants tried to outdo each other with the number and depth of their bows.

Heather looked at Doggett helplessly.

His gray eyes danced. "They can't help themselves," he explained.

"Okay," Heather said as the servants kept bowing. "Okay, really, that's—that's enough. Enough!"

Straightening up, Freda flicked her feather duster at Gersha. "See? Now you've annoyed her."

"Um, could I talk to Doggett?" Heather asked.

"Oh, of course," Freda said, motioning to Doggett, who was propped up on a massive mountain of white pillows. He looked pale and weak, but there was a pink bloom in his cheeks, and his eyes were twinkling.

"Speak away!" Gersha added.

Malag nodded eagerly.

Heather stood there for a moment. None of the servants moved. "Actually," she said after a moment, "I sort of meant alone."

"By the nose, of course you did!" Gersha cried. "What else would you mean?"

"The hero and the princess need to confer," Malag said quickly. "Quite right, quite right."

"Don't be too brave," Freda called as she backed out the door. "Call us if you need us, Doggett, sir!" The three servants bustled out of the room, leaving it feeling strangely silent and empty.

Heather smiled at Doggett. "Wow," she said finally. "I guess you're some kind of big deal around here."

Doggett chuckled. "There's never been a Kiblar hero before. One of the servants overheard what you said at the council—about how I saved you from the trees—and now I can't get them to leave me alone."

"Well, sorry about that." Heather sat on the edge of his bed.

Doggett sighed. "Oh, I don't mind," he said. "It's just . . ." Laughing softly, he shook his head. "I don't really feel like a hero. To tell the truth, I feel kind of like a fraud."

Heather looked out of the window. Doggett had a wonderful view over the treetops. A few stars glimmered faintly in the twilit sky above. "I know what you mean," she said at last.

"Do you?" Doggett's gray gaze was penetrating, and Heather shifted beneath it. "In my culture, you know you're doing your job well when you become invisible. You anticipate others' needs and fill them before they even have a chance to realize what those needs are. This—being so visible all of a sudden . . . it's strange. For the first time, I feel like I don't know what people want from me. . . ." The Kiblar shifted against his mountain of pillows. "Princess Arabelle," Doggett said finally. "Are you sure you're doing the right thing?"

Heather felt a shiver—the kind when you step from the hot, sticky summer city air into an air-conditioned store. *He knows,* whispered a voice in her mind. *Give it up.*

"About what?" she hedged.

Doggett blushed. "I mean . . . wouldn't you rather have Ibharn along on the journey?"

Heather felt her muscles relax under the wave of relief that poured through her body. "So you heard about that too," she said.

"Servants hear everything."

Heather sighed. She couldn't deny that there were a lot of appealing things about Ibharn. He was gorgeous, for one thing. And he did seem brave and strong and quick and all of that junk. But . . . but Doggett had saved her. Besides, he was the only one Heather could really talk to. Veronica was a geek, Strathorn was old, and Chattergee was vermin. She just didn't have much to say to any of them. "I won't leave you behind," she said finally.

Doggett looked down at the white blankets that covered him, but he couldn't hide his smile. "Well . . . good," he said finally.

"Besides," Heather added, "Ibharn is kind of a jerk."

Doggett laughed. "Tell me about it. I know his personal assistant. The guy doesn't even want to wipe his own bum."

Heather giggled. She and Doggett smiled at each other, and she couldn't help thinking that he looked rather proud. Not in a haughty way, but in a nice way. His eyes were glowing with a new sort of confidence.

They sat in silence for a few moments until Doggett finally turned his eyes to the window. The dim purple haze was lovely . . . but unending, unchanging. "I only wish the sun would rise," he said softly.

"I'm sure it will," Heather heard herself say. She wasn't sure where the words were coming from—only that she couldn't not say them. They had to be true. Even she needed them to be true. "Soon."

IX

"This totally sucks," Heather muttered as she lurched forward along the rocky, uneven road. She was carrying her small pack, and the straps cut into her shoulders. Strathorn's back had already disappeared around the curve ahead again. Doggett and Chattergee trotted along behind him. "Jeez, you'd think the old man could slow down a little. Doesn't he know that he's old? He could fall and break a hip."

"Would you shut up?" Veronica snapped. "You've done nothing but complain for the past five days."

"Oh, and you've been a total joy to be around," Heather griped. She was silent for a moment. Then she announced, "I have another rock in my shoe."

Veronica pressed her lips together. *I will not lose it,* she told herself. *I will not give her the satisfaction.*

Then, even though she told herself not to, even though she had been giving herself strict commands to the contrary, Veronica glanced up. There was nothing but a sheer gray rock face that seemed to stretch into eternity, interrupted here and there among the cracks with small, drab white flowers.

"When does this damn mountain end?" Heather demanded, reading Veronica's mind.

Veronica gritted her teeth, wishing she was reading about this mountain pass instead of crossing it. Of course, thanks to Heather, they were taking a northern route to Talan Majeur instead of the southern one. So Fabiella Banks—whom Veronica was starting to think of as "my friend Fabsie"—had never had to describe the treacherous pass leading across Mount Panic. If she had, though, she would have made it seem way more glorious than it was; of that Veronica was sure. She would have focused on the view of the mountain as the company stepped out of the forest. She would have noticed the dramatic precipices, the veil of clouds shrouding the last third of the steep ascent, the brilliant purple of the twilit sky behind the dark, hulking rock. Fabsie wouldn't have bothered talking about how much one's thighs started to ache after three days of trudging up a steep incline. She wouldn't have bothered mentioning how hard it is to fall asleep when you're lying on ground that seems to be covered with spiny rock. She wouldn't have included Heather's whining or Chattergee's lascivious chatter or mentioned how hard it was to suck oxygen from the thin air. No—it would have been all noble toil against impossible odds and dramatic vistas. Not this crap.

And then there was the worry. Veronica kept pressing herself forward, terrified to stop or to even slow down. Now that they were on the quest, she wanted to get it over with as soon as possible. She had taken too long already. If time actually was passing in her home world, her mother would probably have given up on her by now. Veronica could picture Carmen's face, pale and patchy from weeping. She could picture the worn black dress, shiny with age at the shoulders, that Carmen would have pulled out of the back of the closet to wear to the funeral. She could see her sitting there on a folding chair, watching as the empty coffin was lowered into the hole in the ground.

And after the funeral, once the neighbors had left and the casseroles stopped coming, Veronica knew how the house would feel then—quiet, empty. Even Luz's chatter would have stopped for once. She would be lying on her bed, perfectly still, unable to move. That was how she got when something bad happened. And Esteban—he would have disappeared, gone off to forget his sadness with his friends.

It was all too familiar, and Veronica could only hope that it wasn't happening.

"It's clammy up here," Heather pointed out, snapping Veronica out of her thoughts. "I'm cold."

They turned the corner and found Strathorn waiting for them, eyes narrowed in thought. "We must be careful from now on," he announced. "The mountain holds many dangers. For this reason, we must be on our guard and as silent as possible. We have re-entered the domain of the Drizzly Witch."

"Is that why it's so clammy?" Heather asked.

Strathorn nodded. "It's going to be very damp and uncomfortable from now on," he warned. "Very. Damp." With a dramatic flourish, he whirled and strode away.

Heather and Veronica exchanged glances. "Whatever that was about," Heather said.

Veronica wished she was back with the elves, that she didn't have to go on this quest at all. They had stayed there three days while they waited for Doggett to get better, and in that time Veronica had explored the trees and watched the elves as they went about their daily lives. She had practiced with her crossbow and had found it remarkably lightweight and simple to use. Linnea had also shown Veronica how to use the battle-ax she had taken from the real Arabelle's dwarf servant. "It's a right and good weapon for a dwarf such as yourself," Linnea had said approvingly.

Veronica had tried to get Heather to learn some weapon skills also, but the fake princess had refused. Heather had said it was because she didn't want to leave Doggett's side, but Veronica didn't believe that for second. She thought about the excuses Heather always made to get out of gym class. This was exactly the same thing. Whatever. She was actually much happier to have those days to herself.

"Whoa!" Doggett cried as he pitched forward. The pots and pans in his pack clattered. "I'm okay!" he called. His voice was a little muffled because he was facedown in the dirt. He'd been a little absentminded ever since they left the elves. Heather suspected it was because he was sad over having to leave Franklin, the pony, behind.

Veronica glared at the Kiblar as he rolled over, turtle-like, and scrambled to his feet. "God, he's such a klutz," she muttered.

"Shut up," Heather snapped. "This road is rocky."

"He shouldn't even be here," Veronica pointed out. "We're supposed to be traveling with Ibharn . . . you know, the hero? Not Doggett and his stupid squirrel sidekick." It wasn't that Veronica didn't like Doggett. She did. It was just that waiting for him to get better had put them even further behind schedule. She was starting to feel the weight of the wasted time like a stone on her heart. She wanted to get back home. And there was something else. . . .

Now that they didn't have Ibharn, who was to say that they would even be able to finish the quest? Without him, they might never make it home.

Don't think it, she told herself. *You can't go back. Only forward.*

Heather's face burned. "That guy Ibharn was a jerk," she said. "If he was here, he'd just be making rude comments about your hairstyle, so don't even start." The truth was, she was feeling a little defensive. After all, Doggett was here because she had insisted. But she was starting to wonder if she might have made a mistake. Veronica seemed so sure that they needed Ibharn. . . .

Well, it's too late now, she told herself.

A chill wind blew, driving a mist against Heather's face. *Great,* she thought miserably, *now I'm going to frizz.* Shivering slightly, she dug her hands deep into her pockets. The fingers on her right hand traced along the edge of the golden box. She had forgotten about it, but on touching it, she was seized with the desire to look at it again. But she didn't want anyone else to see it. Heather could just imagine the lecture she'd get from Veronica if she found out that Heather had taken the box from her precious elves. *Blah, blah, blah.* That girl never shut up as it was.

She wanted to see the box, but she didn't want to share it. *Maybe later,* she told herself. *I'll look at it later.*

For hours, Heather heard nothing but the sound of her own breathing and the scratch of her feet scrambling over rocks as she followed Strathorn up, up, endlessly up the mountain path. No one spoke, and the silence seemed to increase the volume of their beating hearts. Heather kept one hand on the golden box, tracing and retracing the tree pattern inlaid into the top.

At every step, the clouds seemed to thicken until they were almost blinding. Heather was sure that at any moment, she would take a wrong step and plunge off the side of the mountain. She fought the closed-in feeling that pressed against her, reminding herself that she was surrounded by open space. But she couldn't see the open space, so telling herself that it was there only helped a little.

Then, without warning, the haze lifted. In the sudden light, Heather saw Strathorn step out farther than should have been possible. She was about to scream at him to stop when he turned and faced her with serious eyes and nodded.

"Cloudside," Strathorn announced, as though that meant something.

"By the nose," Doggett said breathlessly as he appeared behind Heather. "I never thought I'd see the day."

Veronica stopped and stared. She closed her eyes slowly, then opened them again—her face was almost awestruck.

Heather had to admit, it was a nice view from up here. She found herself standing on a wide outcropping—a long shelf of rock that jutted out of the side of the mountain. They were above the clouds, and one could see the entire line of mountains poking above the gray haze, their snowy peaks brilliant against the blue sky. The sun was warm on her face, and she felt her scalp heating up.

"Now I'm too hot," she said.

Veronica gaped at her. "That's because we're standing in the sun," she pointed out.

It took Heather a moment to realize what Veronica

meant—and then it dawned on her. The sun. The sun! They had actually climbed out of the twilight and into the blue sky. Heather felt her clothes drying out, warming. It seemed like she hadn't seen the sun in years, and she had forgotten its friendly light, its brilliance.

She heard a slight sniffle and was surprised to find Chattergee weeping. "How beautiful," the squirrel said.

"That it is," Doggett agreed. "A sight for sore eyes and a balm for sore limbs, that's for sure."

"These are the remains of Tilbran-Al-Aleh, High Temple of the Air," Strathorn explained. "It was once a holy place for men and elves alike. But since the Dark Times, the magic of this place has gone feral. I fear it no longer knows any allegiance."

"What's feral?" Heather asked.

"Wild," Veronica said, shuddering slightly. She could almost feel the wild presence of the magic of this place, as though it was another being among them, watching.

Heather took a deep breath and felt like she was breathing in the light as well as the fresh mountain air. For the first time since she had come to this crazy country, she felt safe. The light was warm and comfortable. She wanted to sit here, sunning herself on this flat rock, forever.

The wizard inspected a pile of rocks—what looked like it might have been the remains of a wall. Gingerly, he prodded a depression in the stones with his staff, frowning. He looked down a long line of similar depressions, as though the sight was not what he expected. "Strange . . . " the wizard said in a low voice. Then he looked up at the sun and shook himself.

Heather drank in another breath. "It's wonderful up here."

"Yes," Strathorn agreed. "But we cannot tarry. It is only a

little farther to the top. With haste, we can be halfway down the mountain before tomorrow."

A fist of dread seized Heather's heart. "Halfway down?" she repeated. She didn't want to move on. She wanted to stay here, where it was warm and she felt safe.

But Strathorn began to move on, and the others followed.

Heather started to shuffle her feet, hoping that the others would pass her, move ahead, go away, whatever. All of a sudden, she was gripped with the desire to look at the golden box. *I need something to cheer myself up,* she thought as she rubbed her index finger along an engraved edge. She was glad that she had taken it from those stupid, stuck-up Sylvans. The box was a very precious thing. And it was hers now. *Mine,* she thought. *My precious treasure.*

"Why are you slowing down?" Veronica asked.

"I have another rock in my shoe," Heather lied.

Veronica heaved a sigh. "Fine," she said, leaning against a sheer rock wall.

Oh, great, Heather thought, rubbing the box. *She isn't leaving.* "God, you don't have to hover over me all the time," she spat.

Veronica threw up her hands. "Whatever," she snapped.

Heather smiled at Veronica's back as it retreated up the path. Strathorn and Doggett (with Chattergee on his shoulder) were several paces farther along. Turning her back slightly, so that no one would see what she was doing even if they turned back suddenly, Heather pulled the box from her pocket.

The golden box reflected the brilliant sunlight. The lid was engraved with an elaborate tree, inlaid with milky white moonstones at the leaves—this was the pattern Heather had traced over and over with her fingers. As she looked at it, the intricate tree seemed almost to sway gently, as though a breeze was blowing through its branches.

Heather took a moment to wonder what could be inside. A precious jewel, maybe? A secret scroll? Fairy dust?

Very, very carefully, she pulled open the hinged lid.

The box was empty.

The would-be princess stared at the inside for a moment, but she barely had time to register her disappointment because a high-pitched scream cut through the air, seeming to slice its way deep into her skull.

"Heeeeeeeeeeeeeeeeeelllpp meeeeeeeeeeeee!" screamed the whiny voice. "Oh, heeeeeeeeeeeelp meeeeeeeeeeee! This kleptomaniac stole me! Put me down, you klepto!"

"Close it, you fool!" Strathorn shouted, running toward her.

Heather looked up in confusion. She didn't actually connect the noise with the box in her hand, but as it let out another piercing, "Heeeeeeeeeeeelp meeeeeeeeeeee!" she dropped it as though it was on fire.

"Now I'm in the dirt!" the box screeched. "She threw me in the dirt!"

Heather lifted her foot to stomp on the box, but Strathorn caught her hand.

"I'm diiiiiiiiiiiirteeeeeeeeeee!" the golden box shrieked just before Strathorn leaned down and snapped shut the lid.

Heather's blue eyes met Strathorn's frigid gaze. "What have you done?" he whispered. His face had gone pale. He looked like a vision of death.

"I didn't mean to," Heather said quickly, but before she had time to explain that sometimes her fingers did things she didn't want them to do, there was a horrible, hideous flapping of wings. Looking up, Heather saw three things swooping toward them. They had twisted, troll-like faces and huge bat wings. And they seemed to be made of stone—as though they were gargoyles come to life.

Strathorn cast a glance at the depression in the stone. "It is just as I feared."

"Granite specters!" Doggett shouted, reaching for his sword.

Almost reflexively, Veronica pulled her bow from her back and took aim.

Ziip!

Just as the first specter lunged at her, the arrow hit its mark. Sparks showered, scattering across the rocky ground as his skull shattered under the blow. Rock chips flew as a long granite arm clattered down the mountain. The gargoyle's stony body flapped and flailed. Pulling a fresh bolt from her quiver, Veronica stabbed the being in the heart, and the way the arrow sank into the stony flesh made her shudder. Ms. Banks had never bothered to describe how horrible it was to kill something—even when that something was a hideous gargoyle bent on killing you.

The granite specter staggered back. He slammed into the side of the mountain and was still as his two brothers swooped in for an attack.

"Somebody do something!" Chattergee shrieked as he leaped atop a nearby boulder. "Oh, they're horrible!"

"Get back, Princess," Strathorn shouted. Heather cowered against a sheer rock face as Strathorn stepped forward, pointing his staff at a specter.

"An drahal meh nolante draknath!" Strathorn chanted. "Masne saptimal findrenthia mista!"

The gargoyles paused on the air, flapping and hovering before him as though hearing a voice they recognized, perhaps from far away.

"What's he saying?" Heather whispered.

"I don't know," Veronica admitted. "I think it's Elvish."

"Not Elvish," Doggett corrected. "It's the Ancient Tongue. I think he's reminding them who they are—gargoyles carved to defend the temple."

"Masne tantal naneveh oblinga!" cried the wizard. He hurled the words at the specters, and one of them froze in midair. His wings stopped flapping, and his mottled gray skin became even grayer. A crack ran down his face, and he dropped from the sky, landing before them with a rocky crash.

"Ooh, a rock chip almost hit Chattergee's ear!" the squirrel cried as he retreated into a rodent-sized cave.

The other specter screamed, lunging at the company. Doggett stabbed at it with his sword, but the specter reached for the weapon. With a mighty yank, the gargoyle swung the sword sideways. But Doggett refused to let go. Grinning evilly, the specter yanked the sword in the other direction. Doggett pitched forward, and his pack came undone, spilling pots and pans across the road.

Heather let out a scream as two more gargoyles appeared from beyond the edge of the cliff. One of them lunged for Doggett. Strathorn swung at the other with his staff, sending the gargoyle reeling as the other reached out. . . .

Clang!

Doggett clocked the specter with a frying pan. The specter

swayed for a moment . . . and then his head fell off.

"Get back!" Veronica shouted at the wizard as she launched a crossbow bolt at the final specter. It darted away, but not quickly enough. The bolt shattered its leg.

Seeing his comrades lying still and broken, the final gargoyle flapped and fled, disappearing into the clouds.

The silence after the specters were destroyed was absolute. Heather couldn't hear anything but her companions' breathing. They stood ready to fight, but the mountain remained quiet—eerily so.

After a few moments, Doggett slung his pan back into its pack. Then he started to gather the others. Veronica bent to help him.

Chattergee peeked out of his tiny cave. "What happened?" he asked.

Ignoring the squirrel, Strathorn reached out a hand to Heather. She opened her mouth to apologize, but Strathorn's glance silenced her. "I believe this is yours," he said to Heather, holding out the golden box.

She took it wordlessly.

"Princess, I beseech you not to open it again," Strathorn said. His voice was gentle but firm.

Heather nodded as the old wizard turned away.

"We must press on and quickly," Strathorn announced. "More granite specters are undoubtedly on the way. They will come in greater numbers . . . and they may bring something worse with them next time."

But before his final word had ceased to hum on the warm air, a hideous shriek tore through the sky, sending a wave of terror down Heather's spine. She looked out over the sea of gray cloud just in time to see a giant black crow burst through, trailing streams of mist from its wide wings.

"Galag Nur!" Doggett shouted, just as the first crow was followed by another, then two more. The hooded figures leaned forward, urging their steeds, and, although she couldn't see their faces, Heather felt their eyes on her, pinning her to the mountain.

"Run!" Chattergee shouted, but it was no use. They could never make it down the mountain in time, never.

Before she realized what was happening, Veronica had once again pulled her crossbow from her back and sent a bolt flying toward the first Galag Nur. The crow hurtled toward them, and the bolt met its mark. With a hideous scream, the crow bucked—its throat pierced by Veronica's silver arrow. The enormous bird flapped limply, then plunged. But the Galag Nur leaped, lynx-like—an impossible leap, farther than any human—and landed at the edge of the outcropping. The other three crows wheeled behind him.

Strathorn raised his staff. "Come no farther," he shouted.

An inhuman hiss emanated from the black hood.

"You shall not take her," Strathorn warned. "The magic of the temple protects us."

The tallest of the Galag Nur snarled, almost in scorn, Veronica thought. He lunged forward, and with a flash, Strathorn swung his staff. But the Galag Nur flicked it away, as though it was nothing but a bothersome gnat or fly, knocking the wizard to the ground. The Shadowshrieker stepped forward, toward Heather.

One of the three crows wheeled and dove, and Veronica unleashed another bolt. It whistled past the crow, missing by a hair's breadth. The Galag Nur dropped from the crow's back, landing on the shelf of rock, and Veronica took aim. Her arrow zipped into his shoulder. He shrieked, then yanked the bolt from his shoulder and tossed it on the ground.

Strathorn brought his staff down on the first Galag Nur. The hooded figure stumbled back, and the wizard pressed forward. A crow wheeled behind him.

With a desperate heave, Doggett flung his small hatchet.

Screech!

As the hatchet hit its mark, the crow plunged and the Galag Nur flailed. The two fell, head over wing, down the side of the mountain.

Veronica unleashed another arrow into the side of the fourth crow. The beast pressed on, and she shot again, this time piercing its red eye as Doggett darted forward, driving his sword into the bird's side. The Galag Nur riding it kicked him away, and Doggett stumbled backward. Heather let out a scream as he teetered at the edge of the cliff.

Swinging his staff, Strathorn reached out to Doggett, and the Kiblar clung to the rod for dear life. But just as he regained his footing, two dark hands appeared at the edge of the rock. The Galag Nur that had fallen through the clouds with his crow climbed over the lip of Cloudside.

Strathorn and Doggett hurried to Veronica's side as she unleashed bolt after bolt against the four dark figures. She let out a shriek of rage as she shot another. She knew it was useless, but she couldn't give up. In a line, the four figures advanced. Their bodies were flecked with bolts—quilled, like porcupines—but they did not falter as they advanced.

Heather felt the warmth of Veronica's arm against her side

as the company huddled together to fight. They were backed against the side of the mountain. There was nowhere to run.

One of the Shadowshriekers drew a long blade from the belt at his side.

"Aah!" Veronica cried, shooting a bolt into the place where his heart would have been.

The hooded horror did not waver. He stepped forward.

The Galag Nur were only an arm's length away.

If Heather had reached out, she could have touched them.

This is where something should happen, Veronica thought desperately. *If this was a normal fantasy book, someone would appear now to save us. Ibharn—a company of dwarves—someone—*

The Galag Nur reached up, their long fingers flickering at the edge of their hoods.

"Don't look!" Strathorn shouted. "Don't look!"

But Heather couldn't turn away as the Galag Nur pulled back the dark fabric.

She gasped in shock.

"Oh my God," she whispered, staggered by what she saw. "The Galag Nur . . . " Her head was swimming. She felt sick and faint. "They're *hot!*"

"Don't look at them!" Strathorn shouted. "Princess, shut your eyes!"

But Heather couldn't—no more than she could pass by *People*'s Sexiest Man Alive issue on the newsstand and not buy a copy. Heather remembered something about how the Galag Nur used to be the princes of the Eastern Isles. Well, the Twilight Queen might have twisted their souls, Heather thought, but she sure hadn't twisted their chiseled cheekbones.

Okay, so their eyes kind of glowed and their skin had a sort of waxy tint to it, but still . . .

They were four flavors of gorgeous.

One was tall and slim, with blond hair and blue eyes. *He'd be the preppy type,* Heather thought, *if he ditched that black robe for some tennis whites.* One was a dark Latin lover type. Hot salsa. The third had dark hair and green eyes. . . . He had sort of a hot Irish thing going. He flashed Heather a killer smile. The fourth Galag Nur—the one with dark cocoa skin and a shaved head—reached out a hand.

"No!" Veronica screamed. *"No!"*

But Heather didn't even hear her as she stepped forward . . . into the arms of the Galag Nur.

EVEN

This isn't supposed to happen.

Veronica could scarcely believe that it had. She stared at the vacant stretch of blue sky—the empty space where Heather had been only a moment ago. But the fact remained that Heather had gone with them. She had stepped forward, and the Shadowshriekers had swept her away. Now they were moving down the mountain—the four ghouls and Heather—descending into the twilight below.

Still, Veronica couldn't accept it. *We never should have left Ibharn behind,* her brain raged. *We never should have taken the northern route. We should have followed the plot! "Follow the plot!" Isn't that what I said from the beginning?*

But how could we have? asked another voice. *Simply by appearing here, we changed the story. From the very beginning, we destroyed the One and tried to put a fake in her place. How could I have expected the usual rules to apply?*

Someone was sobbing gently behind her. Veronica didn't need to turn to know that it was Doggett. He would have fought to the death to keep the One safe. But he didn't get the chance.

"They took her," Strathorn said. His voice was empty.

"We're lost," Doggett said sadly. "All of Galma. Everything." He looked down at the lake of clouds below them. "She'll keep us in darkness forever now."

Lost. We're lost, Veronica repeated to herself. Her head spun. *It's all over.* "I'm never going home," she said softly.

Doggett put a gentle hand at her elbow. "I'm sure the dwarves will send for you, miss," he said kindly.

In all of her years reading fantasy, Veronica had never read one that ended suddenly with the heroine's capture. Sure, sometimes characters were taken by the enemy. Like Frodo, for example, when he was stung by Shelob and taken to the Orc tower. Or like Dorothy, when the Wicked Witch of the West trapped her in the castle. Or like Edmund, when the White Witch took him. Or like twenty other examples that zipped through her mind, one after the other—*click, click, click, click, click.*

Chattergee peeked out of the cave in which he had been hiding. "Are they gone?" he asked.

Strathorn looked down at him, expressionless. "They have taken the One."

No, they haven't, Veronica thought. *They've taken the imposter. There is no One!* She wanted to shout it, to hear it echo back at her across the mountaintops. But she feared that Strathorn would never go after Heather if he knew she wasn't Arabelle.

And that's what we have to do, Veronica realized. *It's the only way to get back on track—to make the plot come out the way it was supposed to.* Besides . . . although Heather could be unbelievably irritating, Veronica couldn't imagine leaving her behind in Galma. It just wouldn't be right. They were going back to their own world together or they weren't going at all.

"We have to save her," Veronica announced.

"Save her?" Chattergee laughed bitterly. "My dear beautiful lady, the Galag Nur have taken her! The Galag Nur! This isn't some Ookie with a sharpened stick. These are four evil creatures with hearts as black as night and the strength of ten bulls. They can't be killed. They can't be reasoned with. They do not tire. And they will not stop until they have brought the princess to their Queen of Twilight!"

"I know, but . . . " Veronica replied, "we've got to go after her." She looked at Strathorn, who was staring at her with surprise.

"Yes," the wizard murmured.

Doggett picked up his hatchet and stuck it into his belt.

"Doggett, Doggett—surely you don't think this is a good idea?" Chattergee asked.

"I'm sure I don't know," Doggett told the squirrel. "But I don't see where there's any reason not to go. The only other choice is to give up and go home."

"Exactly!" Chattergee nodded. "Yes! Let's give up and go home, Doggett."

One side of Doggett's face curled into a wry smile. "Ah," he said slowly. "But how can we go back to the dark after standing in the sun?" Closing his eyes, he lifted his face to the light and took a deep breath. When his eyes flicked open, there was steel in them. "I'm ready," he announced.

Strathorn glanced at the Kiblar, then at Veronica. "All right," the old man said finally, tucking his long beard into his belt. "We'll have to double our pace. The Galag Nur travel quickly."

"They won't go that quickly if they've got the princess with them," Veronica pointed out.

"We may have a chance," Doggett said.

"This is insanity!" Chattergee insisted. "Chattergee isn't going." He sat down on a rock.

"Good," Veronica told him.

"It's your choice," Strathorn told the squirrel. "But I wouldn't want to be alone if the granite specters return." He turned and headed up the path.

Veronica followed him.

"Good luck, Chattergee," Doggett said, casting a last glance at his friend.

Chattergee folded his arms across his chest. "All right, go ahead!" he shouted as the rest of them disappeared between two large rocks. "Let the Galag Nur kill you! See if Chattergee cares! You'll be sorry that you left Chattergee behind! Just you wait!"

⟡

"Ow! Would you slow down?" Heather griped. "I'm getting a cramp in my leg."

The Galag Nur whom Heather liked to think of as Hot Salsa snarled and shoved her forward.

"Okay, it is totally not necessary to resort to physical violence," Heather said. "You guys could use some sensitivity training."

Dark Chocolate hissed at her.

"See?" Heather stopped in her tracks. "This is what I'm talking about. You think you can just hiss at people and everyone's going to do what you want. But I'm not moving. How about that, smart guy? If you want me to go somewhere, you can ask me ni—ow!" Paddy O'Hotcakes had just picked her up and tossed her over his shoulder.

Mega-prep growled.

Jeez, I wish these guys would say something, Heather thought. The way they just hiss and snarl is seriously creepy. It totally ruins the hot-guy effect.

The Galag Nur pressed on.

"Would you try not to bounce so much?" Heather complained. "Your bony shoulder is punching me in the gut."

Paddy O'Hotcakes ignored her.

Heather sighed, wishing she had never come along with these guys. She hadn't meant to. It was as though—for a moment—her whole body had suddenly come under the same spell that her fingers often suffered from. She'd told herself to stand still, to fight—but the Galag Nur's gorgeousness had taken her in a surprise attack. And now she couldn't even appreciate their beauty. Sure, they looked good. But they acted like major zombie pigs.

"I'm getting hungry," Heather announced. She raised her head. None of the Galag Nur were paying her any attention. "Hello?" she shouted. "I'm hungry!"

A bush rustled nearby. Without even pausing his stride, Mega-prep reached down and grabbed a gray rabbit from between the green leaves.

"Oh, look! You found a bun—!"

With a twist, Mega-prep pulled off the rabbit's head. Blood poured over the limp fur, and he held out the rabbit to Heather.

"Ohmigod!" she shrieked. "You killed it! I'm going to throw up!"

The Galag Nur shoved the bloody rabbit toward her face, his nostrils flaring.

LISA PAPADEMETRIOU

"Get that thing away from me!" Heather screeched. "I'm not eating that!"

With a low snarl, Mega-prep took a huge bite out of the bunny's carcass. He chewed twice, then spit out a pile of bones and fur in Heather's face.

"Eww!" Heather shrieked, reaching up to wipe the goo from her face. "Ohmigod, you're disgusting!" *I'm never going to feel clean again,* she thought. *Never!*

The other Galag Nur chuckled softly. A chill skittered down Heather's spine, and she realized that she liked them even less when they were laughing than when they were growling.

Hot tears blinded her. *How can these guys be so awful?* Heather wondered. *Why are all of the good-looking people in this world such jerks?*

It was a backward world—totally the opposite of the way things should be. And so unfair!

And the worst part of it was . . . she was alone. And she had no idea how she was going to get out of this mess.

As Paddy O'Hotcakes plowed on, Heather felt something sharp dig into her pocket. That stupid box, she realized. That stupid, shrieking box. That stupid, shrieking, talking . . .

Suddenly, Heather had an idea. With each bouncy step that Paddy took, she shifted slightly until finally, she could reach her hand into her pocket. As subtly as she could, she reached in and pulled out the box. Then she dropped it.

There, Heather thought, feeling slightly better. *If anyone comes looking for me, at least they'll have a clue.* Suddenly, her appetite returned.

"Uh, hello?" she said. "I'm still hungry."

Snarls.

"Look, you can starve me if you want, but I think the queen wants me alive, right?" Heather demanded. At least, that was what she assumed—otherwise, she figured, she'd have been dead by now. Heather, by the way, was not as dumb as most people thought.

Dark Chocolate looked at Hot Salsa.

"Good," Heather said. "So why don't you just suck it up and make me some dinner? Something cooked."

Paddy O'Hotcakes grunted, and all four Shadowdowshriekers changed course.

Ooh, these guys were not nice at all.

꿎

"The trail ends here," Strathorn announced. "I can't find any traces of them after this point."

"How?" Doggett asked, searching the rocky ground for clues. "How can they have just disappeared?"

"We've been following the princess's tracks only," Strathorn explained. "The Galag Nur leave no trace."

"So what happened?" Veronica asked. Suddenly Heather wasn't leaving any footsteps? That didn't sound like a good sign. Her stomach twisted.

Strathorn's face went gray. "I don't know," he whispered.

"There has to be a clue," Doggett insisted. "We just have to look for it."

Veronica scanned the ground. The terrain here was dusty and rocky. Only a few sparse bushes dotted the landscape, growing out of cracks in the rock. There was a natural path down the mountain, but the Galag Nur did not seem to have taken it. Instead, they chose the harder route, full of steep descents and scrambling slopes. It was hard enough to follow them when they did have Heather's footsteps to go by. . . .

"Mrgraphergree har rurgrund!"

Veronica looked up to see Chattergee standing triumphantly atop a boulder. He gave her a smug smile. His left cheek bulged.

Oh, crap, she thought. *He's back.* "What is it?" Veronica asked.

"Mrgraphergree har rurgrund!" Chattergee repeated, his tail twitching.

"Would you just take whatever it is out of your mouth and tell me what you want?" Veronica asked.

Sulkily, the squirrel pulled a golden box from his cheek. "I said, 'Chattergee has returned!'" he snapped. "Has the lady missed her faithful squirrel?"

"We only left you an hour ago," Veronica pointed out.

"I missed you," Doggett said loyally. His eyes fell on the golden object in Chattergee's hand. "The princess's box!" Doggett cried. "Chattergee, you're wonderful!"

"Where did you find it?" Strathorn demanded.

"Half a league yonder," Chattergee replied. "I took a shortcut to catch up with you. Ahem." He kicked at the ground. "I really did expect you to come back for me, you know," he added in a hurt voice.

"Would you quit sulking and open the box!" Strathorn commanded.

With a flip of his paw, Chattergee snapped open the box.

"I've been swallowed by a squirrel!" shrieked the box. "I've been dropped in the dirt and held in the mouth of a rodent! Oh, my, oh, my! If only my maker knew what had become of me!"

"Quiet, you," Doggett said.

"You be quiet, Kiblar, and learn your place!" cried the box. "I'm a Sylvan box, and I deserve a little respect."

"Most excellent and beautiful box crafted by the Sylvans," Strathorn said in his most patient voice, "we humbly request that you please tell us which direction the princess went."

"I most certainly will not," snapped the box. "That girl is the rudest, most vile creature I've ever encountered in my long existence. She stole me!"

"Look," Veronica said as patiently as she could, "we're going to the castle of the Queen of Twilight. Once we get there, Strathorn will get his magic back, and he'll be able to grant wishes."

"So?" the golden box demanded.

"So?!" Doggett cried. "So, he'll be able to give you your heart's desire!"

"I don't have a heart's desire, you cretin, I'm a box!"

"Look, you," Doggett snarled. "If you don't tell us where she is, you'll find yourself full of boiling hot tea."

For the first time, the box was silent.

"Well, since you put it that way," it said finally, "I think they were headed southeast."

☙❧

"What now?" Veronica whispered as the company stared at the Galag Nur. Heather was propped awkwardly against a large stump while one of the Shadowshriekers grilled something over a fire. Whatever it was, it was giving off a foul smell that infected Veronica's nostrils.

"I'm ready." Doggett narrowed his eyes and pulled out his hatchet.

"Peace, Kiblar," Strathorn said, putting a gentle palm over

Doggett's hand. "We cannot face the Galag Nur that way."

"Not unless we want to be killed," Chattergee piped up. "Which this squirrel does not."

"But how will we reach the One?" Doggett asked.

Strathorn raked his fingers thoughtfully through his beard. He tugged off his stocking cap, then put it back on again. "I don't know," he said finally.

"Are you saying they can't be defeated?" Veronica asked. In the book, in fact, the Shadowshriekers never were defeated. So she had no idea whether it was even possible.

"They cannot be killed, if that is your question," Strathorn said. "Their physical bodies can be imprisoned—for a while—but it would take a force far greater than . . ." Strathorn paused, looking up the mountain. Veronica felt almost like she could hear the wheels turning in his mind.

"What?" Chattergee demanded, peering after the wizard. "What is it?"

"Give me the box," Strathorn told Veronica. His voice left no room for questions. She handed it over.

In a flash, Strathorn flipped open the box and tossed it toward the Galag Nur, where it flipped end over end, then landed—open—on the ground.

"Aiiiiiiiiiiiiiiiiiiiiiiiiiiiiiiiiiiiieeeee!" The screech was inhuman, only slightly less horrifying than the noise of the Galag Nur themselves, and loud enough to be heard all over the mountain.

"Help me!" screeched the box. "The wizard just tossed me in the *dirt!*"

Hot Salsa turned toward the noise, his eyes flaming.

"Down here, you imbeciles!" screeched a voice. "What am I, invisible?"

"What are you doing?" Doggett asked the wizard, who merely held up a hand, palm flat, indicating for him to wait.

Mega-prep stooped down and picked up the golden box; it lay open between two perfectly male manicured hands.

"They've come for the princess!" the box screeched. "Look behind—"

There was a sound, a noise like a heartbeat or flapping wings.

Veronica looked up just in time to see the first granite specter wheel overhead.

"Take cover!" Strathorn cried, and Veronica, Chattergee, and Doggett hurried to obey as another granite specter joined the first. Chattergee raced up a tree as another appeared. Then another. Then three more. And soon, the air around them was full of the sound of flapping wings as the sky turned gray with a hundred gargoyles.

"Nambratha multalenta givinarch garenterech!" Strathorn shouted, and in an instant, the specters dove at the Galag Nur.

The Shadowshriekers rent the sky with their cries as the granite specters swarmed them. Hot Salsa tore the head from one of the gargoyles, but it was no use—the monsters kept coming, overwhelming them, covering the Galag Nur like a stone blanket.

"Veronica!" Doggett shouted as one of the gargoyles reached for Heather.

Ziip!

The specter's head exploded as Veronica's bolt shot through his open mouth. Heather screamed as the closest Galag Nur fought his way through the gargoyles holding him, only to be overwhelmed by another two.

"Save the One!" Strathorn shouted as he planted his feet and held out his hands. "Bron, sith mahala!" the old wizard chanted. "Bron, migdaral! Bron, didruviel et mektannen chargront!"

The mountain began to rumble beneath her feet as Veronica shot bolt after bolt at the gargoyles that approached Heather. Doggett ran toward the ersatz princess, stumbling as the ground shook.

Ziip!

Screeching, a gargoyle flapped feebly, struggling with the wing Veronica had just shattered.

Finally, Doggett reached Heather. She looked up at him with huge eyes as he reached for her.

Veronica marveled at how lucky it was that Doggett had spent his life carrying heavy packs as he struggled back, shouldering Heather.

"Look out!" Veronica cried as one of the Shadowshriekers threw off his granite specter and grabbed for Heather. But a crack formed in the ground beneath his feet. He fell, and the ground shifted again, trapping his leg.

"To the tree!" Strathorn cried, gesturing toward a wide oak with several low-hanging branches. "Haste! Haste! There is no time!"

Veronica hurried to the lowest branch, and Strathorn pulled her into the tree just as the ground roiled and bucked beneath her feet.

There was a sound like rolling thunder, and the rocks on the mountain began to twitch. The gargoyles let out a collective shout, a sort of "Hai! Hai! Hai!" and in a moment, the air was filled with the creatures as they flapped away frantically.

The Galag Nur reeled at their release, but in a moment they were standing. Then they were running with speed beyond human.

Doggett was only steps away from the tree. He reached out.

The Galag Nur were so close, he could hear their breath, but in the next moment, strong arms reached out and pulled him into a tree, and before he could even wonder what good that would do, a crossbow bolt zipped past his head directly into the face of the closest Shadowshrieker. He stumbled and the ground shifted, and then the noise took over, a roar like a tidal wave and a deafening crack, then a groan, and the tree was tilting, falling.

"Don't let go!" Strathorn shouted as the ground bucked and the tree fell and the stones rained down. And in a moment they were falling, riding the tree, and Heather thought she would be crushed by the strength of Doggett's grip around her waist and Veronica thought that she could never hold on as the mountain slid down, swallowing the Galag Nur and sweeping the tree before the crushing tide of an avalanche.

IGHT

Veronica's arms ached, but she gripped the branches with every bit of strength she had. Bits of rock rose up and met her in the face as the massive tree slid down the mountain. Her knee dragged, and she felt the cloth rip from her elfin capri pants; then she felt the flesh rip from her kneecap as gravel dug into her flesh.

"Aieeeeee!" Heather screamed as the trunk bucked and wove over the rocky ground. "Aieeeeeyieeeyieeeyieeeeeechhh hcchh hcchh!" She coughed, then started screaming again.

"Look out!" Doggett cried as the tree drove straight for a stand of pines.

How can I look out? Veronica wondered, watching the trunk plunge forward. After all, it wasn't like she was driving the thing.

The top branches caught the trunks of the pines and held, but the root end of the tree kept going. It slid sideways, then forward, until the tree was completely turned around, and then—miraculously—it stopped.

Plink, plop, plink. A few remaining rocks bounced down the mountain after them as the company rolled off the log and onto their backs, panting.

Veronica did a mental check of her body parts. Head? Still attached, apparently. Same with arms and legs, although she had been banged around pretty badly. She bent her knee, wincing. It hurt, but not too much. At least her leg wasn't broken.

Rolling over, Doggett hurried to Heather's side and untied her bonds.

"Princess?" Strathorn asked gently. "Are you all right?"

Heather sniffled. "Well, what do you think?" she demanded, snuffling. "My manicure is a mess!"

Strathorn sighed.

Doggett sat straight up and looked around. "Chattergee!" he called, panic rising in his voice. "By the nose, where's Chattergee?" He scrambled to his feet and stared up the mountain, which had been completely rearranged by the wave of rock and dirt that had swept down its face. "Oh, brave and noble squirrel! How could we have left you behind?" He raked his fingers through his hair and burst into sobs.

Veronica felt a pang. Even though she had found Chattergee annoying, it wasn't like she'd wanted anything bad to happen to him. . . .

There was a rustling from the topmost end of the branches, and a fluffy tail appeared, like a periscope, above the green. "By the fur of the Great Squirrel," said a voice.

"Chattergee!" Doggett cried, diving in among the leaves.

Chattergee's tiny head popped up, and he grinned as Doggett wrapped him in a hug. "Chattergee faced the wrath of the mountain and lived!" cried the squirrel.

"We all faced the wrath of the mountain and lived," Veronica said, even though she was relieved to see the rodent again.

"Yes, but it was Chattergee who first ran up the mighty tree," the squirrel replied.

Veronica was just about to point out that running first was not really something to be proud of when Strathorn stood up, saying, "We must hurry." Bending down, he retrieved his staff, which was—amazingly—unbroken.

"Hurry?" Heather repeated, taking a break from her snuffling sobs.

"I called upon the rocks of the ancient temple to recall their old allegiances," Strathorn explained. "They have answered. But they will not save us again."

"You mean—the avalanche was magic?" Veronica asked.

"No, no." Strathorn wagged his head impatiently. "My magic is too weak for that. But I still speak the Ancient Tongues. I know the language of the rocks. The gargoyles have gone completely wild—only one of them still heard me. But the rocks of the temple itself were older, and they remembered themselves. They came when I called."

"Wow," Doggett said. "I'd call that a form of magic."

"Oh, nonsense." Strathorn waved his hand. "My mother insisted that I learn a foreign language." The wizard planted his staff firmly. "Enough. The Galag Nur have been delayed—we must use this to our best advantage."

"Whoa, whoa, whoa." Heather held up a hand. "The Galag Nur aren't delayed. They're dead." She looked from Strathorn to Doggett, then back again. "I mean, they're dead . . . right?"

"We must hurry," Strathorn repeated.

"But even with the gargoyles and the avalanche . . . " Heather's voice trailed off.

Doggett gathered his pack as Veronica rose, painfully, to her feet.

Swallowing hard, Heather forced herself to stand. And in moments, the company found themselves hurrying—on foot, this time—down the mountain.

ᚸᚷᚠ

Doggett hummed quietly as he dropped one ingredient after another into the black pan. Heather watched his thick hands as they sliced and stirred, dusted a pinch of this or a dash of that, and sent a delicious aroma wafting her way. They were strange, Heather thought, those hands of Doggett's. They were wide and strong and looked like they were made for heavy tasks—chopping wood, hauling water, digging dirt, crushing rock. But when set to the task of cooking or straightening or even sewing—as Heather had seen him do when he tore a hole in his jacket elbow—his fingers were as graceful as dancers. Doggett himself was like that. Wide and sturdy but quick and gentle, Heather mused.

They had hurried through the night, straight down the mountain until they passed again from darkness to twilight, and still they hurried on for hours until Strathorn had finally said they could stop. They had taken a winding path, and Strathorn had used his weak magic to cover their tracks. "It should be enough to confuse them," he'd said, and Heather hoped he was right.

Now they were resting, getting ready to eat something. The others had wandered off and left Doggett to prepare the meal, as usual. Chattergee was "on the lookout," although Heather suspected he was really making a nuisance of himself to the female squirrels in the forest. Veronica hadn't said a word to

Heather since her rescue. Not that Heather really blamed her. She'd done something terrible and stupid and had put them all in danger.

In fact, part of Heather still couldn't believe that they'd actually come to rescue her after she betrayed them. *I wouldn't have,* she thought, *if someone did that to me.*

But they had. And even more amazingly, Doggett seemed to have forgiven her. Strathorn too. Even Chattergee.

Only Veronica couldn't get over it.

It was ironic that it was Veronica's response that made the most sense to Heather.

Now Veronica was off with Strathorn somewhere. *Probably planning how to take the most pain-inducing, complicated path to wherever it is we're going,* Heather thought.

Doggett pulled the cover off the pan and peered inside. He took a sniff and frowned at the bubbles. Without looking, he groped for his stirring spoon. It was three inches to the left of his grasp. Reaching out, Heather placed the spoon in his hand.

Doggett's gray eyes met her blue ones, and he smiled.

"Well, now," he said, "isn't that something? Imagine, me being waited on by a princess!"

Heather blushed as Doggett dipped the spoon into the thick brown sauce and stirred. It was amazing, how he carried the heaviest packs and handled all of the cooking—not to mention the fact that he had saved her twice—and yet he never complained.

"Can I . . . can I help you?" Heather asked.

Doggett burst out laughing. "Hoo-hoo! Oh, Princess!" He shook his head. "That's a good one." He wiped a tear from his eye, giggling.

"I can help," Heather insisted stubbornly. "I could . . . I could chop something."

Doggett was overcome with fresh giggles.

"Stop laughing!" Heather snapped. "I'm a good cook." This wasn't exactly true . . . that is, she could cook a few things. But most of them required equipment that she didn't have here—equipment like a bag of fat-free popcorn and a microwave. Still, she could help. She wanted to help, if only Doggett would stop laughing.

"Doggett, I mean it," Heather said. "Nobody ever helps you. *I* never help you. Please—let me do some of the work for a change."

Something in her tone stopped Doggett's chuckles, and he turned to look at Heather more carefully.

For a moment, neither of them spoke, and Heather found it difficult to meet his gaze. It was weird, having this short guy with the big nose stare at her like that. In her old life, whenever she caught a guy like that at school looking at her, she stared him straight in the eye and demanded, "What are you looking at?" Then she snorted and rolled her eyes to show him just how stupid he was to think that he had a right to look in her direction.

But Doggett—well, he does have a right to look at me, Heather thought. *If it weren't for him, I wouldn't even be here. I'd be buried underground or on my way to the Twilight Queen's castle on the backs of the Galag Nur.*

"I didn't mean to hurt your feelings, Princess," Doggett said quietly. "I appreciate the offer. But I couldn't possibly let you do any work. Princesses don't do work of this kind. I'm a Kiblar, and this task is my task."

"I thought princesses got to do whatever they wanted."

Heather looked away, sighing. "I don't seem to get to do anything I want to do."

Doggett nodded and turned back to his pot. "It's a heavy burden," he said thoughtfully.

"Maybe I don't want to be a princess anymore," Heather said.

Doggett smiled. "Ah . . . but who would take your place? You are the One."

Heather laughed softly, bitterly. "Yeah," she said after a moment. "Right. I forgot."

"You must fulfill your destiny," Doggett said.

"And what about your destiny?" Heather asked.

Doggett crumbled three dried green leaves into the pan, one at a time. "I suppose my destiny is to help you fulfill your destiny."

Heather sighed. "Okay." She leaned back against a tree trunk and thought for a moment. "Doggett—what if you could choose your own destiny? What would you do? I mean, forget about helping me and the quest and all that. What would you do with your life?"

Doggett shook his head, and his eyebrows drew together. "I am a Kiblar. We are bakers and servants. That is the way it ever was, is, and shall be."

"Okay, yeah," Heather said straightening up, "but let's say you could be anything. Forget the whole Kiblar thing. What would you be if you could?"

"Ah." Doggett inhaled deeply, and his eyes took on a faraway look. "If I could do anything . . . I've heard such wonderful tales about the sea."

"The sea?" Heather repeated.

His face broke into a smile. "I met one of the water folk once. He said that when the sun slants over the water, it looks as though there are diamonds dancing on the waves. He told me about the boats, about the foam shooting up over the side, the wind against your face. And the way he described it, well . . . " Doggett's voice was quiet, almost as though he was talking to himself. "I felt it, in my chest. I felt as though I was there. And I thought, *Ah. Ah, I could be a sea captain.*" He laughed softly and turned back to his sauce, giving it a stir.

Heather half expected him to say more, but when he was silent, she asked, "Why don't you?"

Doggett shook his head. "Oh, Princess. I'm a Kiblar. Serving is my vocation, not sailing."

Heather wanted to fight with him, to tell him that it wasn't true—that he could be anything he wanted to be. But she knew he wouldn't believe her.

She wasn't sure she believed her either.

⁊ɔɾ

Veronica stood at the edge of a rock shelf, looking out into the purple twilight. Descending back into the dim world of Galma had been harder than she had thought it would be. Even now, she had to fight the urge to claw her way back up the mountain, back toward the sun, the light . . .

"The sky grows darker," Strathorn said behind her. "And the path harder to see."

Veronica looked up at his lined face. His gray eyes, too, scanned the depths. Veronica wondered if he could see more than she could. She waited for him to speak.

"Now the queen and her sisters know of our plans," Strathorn said thoughtfully. "No doubt she suspects that we will press toward the east, seeking the Sword of Defiance from the stronghold of the Drizzly Witch. No doubt the battlements have been reinforced with an army of Ookies and trolls.

Veronica sighed.

"It's a blow," Strathorn continued. "But we'll just have to make do without the sword. We will not move east until we pass the Caves of Terror."

Veronica shook her head. They couldn't move on without the Sword of Defiance. They needed it to defeat the dragon Karn. Then again, they needed Ibharn for that, too. There were a lot of things they needed and didn't have—like the real Princess Arabelle. Besides, just beyond the Drizzly Witch's castle, they were supposed to come across some giants. The giants were important. For one thing, they helped seal the venom-spewing giant spider in its cave. For another, they played a pivotal role in the big battle scene—heaving rocks at the queen's battlements. *We need those giants,* Veronica thought. *We need that sword.* "Strathorn," she said, "I think we should go east sooner rather than later."

Strathorn looked at her out of the corner of an ice blue eye. "We stand no chance against the Countess of Uncomfortable Humidity."

"But how will we defeat the dragon without the Sword of Defiance?" Veronica asked.

"I have been wondering the same thing," Strathorn said, folding his arms across his chest. His mustache wiggled as he blew out a heavy sigh. "At first, I simply thought that the Orb foretold a journey to the north. But now I suspect that we must actually go to the Dark Tower itself. We are meant to take the Fragile Hag's wand."

Veronica frowned. "And use that on the dragon instead of the sword?"

"Perhaps," Strathorn said, tugging on his gray beard.

It might work, Veronica thought. *It might. . . .*

But what about the giants?

"What would you say," Veronica asked slowly, "if I told you that I thought the future of our battle with the queen depends on meeting some giants?"

"I would say that the future is hard to read," Strathorn replied. "And is, no doubt, unfolding exactly as it should."

Veronica bit her lip, but she couldn't argue. After all, Strathorn was right about one thing—the Drizzly Witch knew they were on the way. She'd have her entire fortress defended and scouts spread out around her for miles. Heather's capture had made it impossible for them to sneak in and take the sword. And they'd probably never make it to the giants', either.

Stupid Heather. Now that the "princess" was safe again, Veronica was realizing just how angry she was with Heather for being captured by the Galag Nur. *Doesn't she know how important she is?* Veronica thought. *Doesn't she know how much depends on her? So she screwed up, and now we're stuck, improvising as usual.* Veronica hated not knowing how things were going to come out. And here she was—pitched into uncertainty, with everything on the line.

An image of her mother popped into her mind. Ever since she had arrived in Galma, Veronica had been sure that if she could do the right things, play along with whatever was happening here, she and Heather could get out. But with every change of plans, her confidence slipped away.

Veronica remembered the day, years before, that she had

kissed her father good-bye at the breakfast table. She had breathed in the comforting, spicy smell of his aftershave and watched as he hugged her mother and left for work in his blue uniform. She had been so sure that she would see him again that she never even said good-bye. But he never came home.

That day, Mr. Lopez had responded to a call about a liquor store robbery and had been shot in the head. The suspects had fled on foot. Never been caught.

That was why Veronica liked things she could count on. Predictable things. Like empanadas for supper on Wednesday night. Like classes ending fifty minutes after the bell. That was why she liked reading the same books over and over. She already knew how they would come out.

"The Black Tower is of vital importance," Strathorn said suddenly. "I am convinced that is why the Orb will show nothing else." He planted his staff firmly in front of him. "It is clear that we must steal the wand of the Fragile Hag instead of the Sword of Defiance from the Drizzly Witch."

"Yeah . . . " Veronica said slowly. She thought for a moment. Maybe it was time to come clean. To tell Strathorn the truth.

But if he knew Heather wasn't the One, wouldn't he abandon the quest? And if he gave up, then she and Heather would definitely never get home.

Never.

It was just too big a risk.

Veronica bit her lip. "Did you ever think maybe that's not what it means? I mean, maybe the Orb is out of whack?"

Strathorn smiled wryly. "No," he said, "I didn't."

Veronica sighed. It was clear that Strathorn had made up

his mind. "Okay," she said finally. "I guess we're off to the Black Tower."

It took another full day for the company to pick their way down the mountain. Veronica was in a foul mood and vented her anger by spending the entire trip downward cursing under her breath. "We (expletive)-ing killed ourselves on the way up, and now it's just as (expletive)-ing bad going down!" she muttered over and over. Veronica had grown up in a rough neighborhood, and her vocabulary included many interesting new words that Chattergee had never heard before. It included some that Heather had never heard before. In addition, Veronica was very creative and often came up with new expletives of her own.

"My, you dwarves have such cultured phrases," Chattergee told Veronica as he listened to her, wide-eyed. "Would you teach Chattergee some of your foreign tongue?"

At that, Veronica unleashed some of her most creative and colorful expletives, which caused the squirrel to gasp in admiration and burst into applause.

Once they reached the bottom of the mountain, they made a happy discovery. The northern terrain was mostly grassy and lush and made for leagues of wonderful, easy walking. Veronica couldn't help thinking that, if only the twilight would lift, the scenery around them must be beautiful. Tall trees with long trailing tendrils swayed on a light cool breeze, and the grass underfoot had an almost reddish-purple cast that would have been amazing in light. But in the twilight, it was hard to see.

Spotting something silver glinting between the blades, Heather bent down for a closer look. Gently, she pressed the grass away from the silver object and peered at it closely.

It was a violet.

A silver violet, Heather thought, plucking the tiny flower from the grass. *Amazing.* She stared at it in wonder.

"Would someone please tell the princess to hurry up?" Veronica demanded from up ahead. "We can't keep stopping because of her."

Heather rolled her eyes. This was Veronica's new game. She hadn't spoken a word to Heather since the incident with the Galag Nur. In fact, she often went out of her way to make it clear that she wasn't talking to Heather by relaying messages through Doggett. This left the poor Kiblar constantly confused and uncomfortable.

"Um, Princess," Doggett said now, "the lady Veronica has asked that you slightly increase your speed."

"Fine," Heather snapped, tossing the violet on the ground. It didn't seem so amazing anymore. She trudged toward the company.

"Would someone please ask the princess to try to keep up with the others?" Veronica demanded as she stalked ahead. "She's the slowest of the group."

Doggett winced. "Er—Princess," he said, "the lady Veronica—"

"Look, I have ears, Doggett, okay?" Heather snapped. "I heard her." She deepened her stride to catch up with Veronica. "You're going to have to talk to me sometime," she said.

"Doggett, would you kindly inform the princess that I don't have to do what she says?" Veronica asked.

Doggett looked confused. His mouth opened, then snapped closed again.

"This is exciting," Chattergee put in.

"Great, now you've got the squirrel interested," Heather pointed out.

"Well, why don't you just quit talking to me, and then nobody will care?" Veronica suggested in an icy voice.

"Ha!" Heather cried. "You just did it! You just talked to me!"

"That didn't count!" Veronica shot back.

"You did it again!" Heather crowed.

"Would you two please shut up?" Strathorn shouted.

The two girls looked up at him in surprise. He was standing at the crest of the hill before them, scowling down at them like a stern schoolmaster. "I can't listen to this bickering anymore!" Strathorn growled. "Grow up, both of you, and do it quickly." He turned and looked ahead. "We've reached the Black Tower."

Heather followed his glance to where the dark building hovered on the horizon, a single column with a tall spire rising to the clouds.

"Are you (expletive)-ing kidding me?" Veronica asked.

"My God," Heather breathed. "It looks just like the Empire State Building."

It was true. In the distance the hulking tower was the evil twin of the small plastic building in her snow globe.

"What did you say?" Strathorn asked. "Entire state?"

"It's a big monument," Veronica explained quickly.

Strathorn looked dubious.

"In, uh, Dwarf . . . York . . . City," Heather added, trying to make the story more believable. "Huge with the tourists."

Strathorn's eyebrows crept together like caterpillars, but he didn't ask questions.

A low, mournful howl swept out from the base of the tower. The note was fierce but sad, and Heather felt the pain of it in her own heart. The Galag Nur had sounded inhuman, and this did too. But the Shadowshriekers were unearthly, while this noise—it sounded primal, animal.

Unconsciously, Heather gripped Strathorn's elbow. "What is it?" she whispered.

"Moat Beast," Doggett replied.

"Am I the only one who doesn't like the sound of that?" Veronica asked as the company moved forward.

Nobody bothered to reply.

꠲

"Tell me that smell isn't coming from the tower," Heather said as she and the rest of the company peered at the Black Tower from a nearby rocky ledge.

"It's coming from the Moat Beast," Doggett informed her.

Heather eyed the half-submerged creature as it swam back and forth beneath the drawbridge leading to the castle. It was enormous and apelike, with long, muscular arms. Imagine King Kong dipped in a vat of brown goo. "It looks . . . sludgy," Heather said.

"He feeds on the dirt and filth discarded into the moat," Strathorn said. "The more refuse thrown into the water, the larger he grows, a vile guardian of the vile spirit of the Fragile Hag."

"It's sort of poetic, really," Doggett pointed out.

"If you think stench is poetic," Heather shot back.

"So—how do we get by the thing?" Veronica asked.

"He will attack anyone who comes near," Strathorn said. "Rip their limbs from their bodies and leave them to rot in the sun until they, too, become the dirt and filth that feeds him."

"Well, maybe we should just forget the whole thing, then," Chattergee suggested. He started to hop away from the castle.

Veronica grabbed him by the tail. "You're not going anywhere. I'm not going to waste time rescuing anyone else."

Chattergee cleared his throat. "Well," he squeaked, "not when asked by such a gracious lady . . ."

"So what's the plan?" Heather asked, turning to Strathorn. "You're a wizard. Can't you just magic us inside the castle or something?"

"My magic is not that strong," Strathorn replied.

"Look, what is the point of having a wizard along if he can't even do anything?" Heather demanded.

"His magic is weak right now," Veronica snapped. "Strathorn can't just beam us over there, okay?"

"Don't flip that attitude over here," Heather shot back, snapping her fingers.

"Perhaps . . . perhaps I could do something . . . " Strathorn said slowly as he gazed at the beast. His blue eyes were clouded in thought.

"What?" Doggett whispered.

Strathorn snapped his head up, as though he had made a decision. "The twilight—perhaps it is our friend after all. I believe I can make us invisible."

"What?" Heather cried. "Why didn't you mention this before? Um, hel-lo—that might have come in handy a few times."

Strathorn shook his head. "We won't really be invisible. But the Moat Beast isn't a very intelligent creature. I can make us appear dim to him—gray—so that we'll blend in with the twilight around us. But I can't hold the spell for very long. We'll have to move quickly."

"What are we waiting for?" Veronica asked. "Let's go."

🙟

"Make no noise," Strathorn whispered as the company prepared to start across the drawbridge.

Heather squinted at him. Actually, his invisible spell was working pretty well. She could barely see him. He looked like nothing but a ripply shadow of gray on gray.

Moving as quickly as they could, the five gray shadows crept across the bridge. Heather placed each foot carefully. After a few moments, she realized she was holding her breath. Exhaling, she looked down at the giant pool of sludge that guarded the castle.

The Moat Beast stood perfectly still, cocking his head. Brownish goop oozed from his shoulders, and Heather noticed with a start that he could easily crush her in a single giant hand.

And he just heard me, Heather realized. She paused for a moment, keeping perfectly still. She sensed—rather than saw—the others pausing too. After a moment, the Moat Beast moved on.

Heather was tempted not to move from her spot. But she knew she didn't have a choice. She couldn't just stand there on that rickety bridge forever. *He can't see me,* Heather reminded herself as she took a step forward.

Behind her, Veronica watched the planks on the bridge carefully. Some of them were rotten or half worn away. She tried to only step on the solid-looking ones.

Only five steps more, she thought, glancing up. *Only four. Only three.*

Creak.

It took only a moment for Veronica to realize what she had done. In looking up, she had taken her eyes off the wooden bridge. And now . . .

With a deafening roar, the Moat Beast rose from the water. Chains fell from a yoke at his neck, and Heather had just enough time to think, *Oh, good, he can't follow us inside. . . .*

"Run!" Doggett cried as he sprinted past Veronica into the castle.

The Moat Beast continued to rise until he was impossibly tall, almost fully half as tall as the tower itself. He unleashed another roar and brought his fist down onto the drawbridge. Splinters poured from the sky as a hunk of wood was blasted from the side of the bridge, but Heather didn't see it. She was running, running; they were all running, and now the Moat Beast had taken another chunk from the bridge. *But he can't see us,* Heather thought. *Thank God, he can't see us.* And it was only then that she realized that Doggett was flickering before her—there he was, then gone, there, then gone.

"We have to close the gate!" Veronica shouted as she— there, then gone—ran to the gate. Doggett joined her, and with desperate fingers they lowered the iron gate with a crash. The Moat Beast let out another roar just as Strathorn collapsed against the flagstones, and suddenly the entire company were visible.

The Moat Beast let out a shriek of fury as Veronica brought down another door, this one of solid iron. The roar turned dull behind the metal.

Heather crouched beside the wizard. "Strathorn!" she cried.

His eyelids fluttered. "I'm all right," he muttered. "Fine, just . . . help me up."

"The spell exhausted him," Doggett said.

"I'm fine," Strathorn insisted. He looked up at Heather, and she helped him to his feet. He leaned against her heavily as they made their way farther into the castle. They stumbled down a long hall, finally reaching a door.

"Is that . . . an elevator?" Veronica asked.

As if in answer, Strathorn pressed the button beside the door, which lit up, with an arrow pointing toward the ceiling.

Bing!

The elevator door slid open. Cautiously, the group skulked into the elevator.

"Which floor?" Heather asked.

"There's only one button," Veronica pointed out, pressing it. Noiselessly, the elevator door slid shut. Veronica felt her stomach drop as the elevator rose up, up, up.

Everyone stared straight ahead as Chattergee hummed nervously.

"Would you stop humming along to the elevator music?" Heather snapped at the squirrel.

Chattergee pouted. "It's catchy."

"Now it's going to be stuck in my head," Heather complained.

Bing!

The elevator came to a stop, and the door opened. The company piled out onto a wide terrace.

Have you ever been to the top of a tall building? Then you know that the air blows your hair around. Heather's highlighted blond locks whipped into her face as she stepped outside, and the air seemed vacant. Heather could tell without looking that it was a long way down. In the twilit distance, purple trees stood dark against the violet sky.

"Such a lovely view," said a voice.

It was the Hag. She wasn't wearing her gray cloak, and Heather was surprised at just how pretty the Duchess of Breakable Objects was. She looked almost like a china doll. In fact, there were rumors that her mother actually was a china doll and that the queen was only her half sister. I can't substantiate these rumors, except to say that the fact that the duchess's body seemed to be made of glass did make one wonder.

Her skin was white as porcelain, and her hair was dark, almost black. She was slender and wore a flowing white dress. The whole effect was rather Snow White meets Nicole Kidman at the Oscars, except that the Hag's right arm was tied up in a gauzy white sling, thanks to the fact that Veronica had bashed her with a branch in the Shadow Forest.

The duchess was seated on a white iron café chair beside a glass-topped table. Veronica's eyes traveled around the terrace, taking in all the life-sized glass statues in various poses. Of course, all of these people had been turned to glass by the Fragile Hag. Several of them were Ookies, and Veronica even spotted two large trolls. But most were men and women, and a few were elves or dwarves. Some seemed terrified. Some seemed merely surprised. Some seemed to be in the middle of saying something. And some seemed to have turned their backs.

"We have come for your wand, Duchess," Strathorn announced. "It is our destiny."

The Fragile Hag gazed at him coolly but did not reply. She

sipped from a delicate teacup. A small smile curled like a wisp of steam at the corner of her mouth. "Welcome to the Dark Tower, Princess," she said.

"Um, thanks for having me," Heather mumbled, suddenly self-conscious. "Ow," she added as Veronica stepped on her foot.

The Hag's eyes slid to Veronica's face. "Yes, I remember you," she said slowly. "You did this." She held up her arm.

Veronica cleared her throat. "Well . . . it was an accident."

"It was such a nuisance, really," the Hag went on as she placed her teacup daintily on its matching saucer. "You see, my right arm is my wand arm." She sighed as she pulled her magic wand from a pocket at her left hip. "It really put me out of sorts for days . . . until I realized I was ambidextrous." Lifting her wand, she aimed it right at Veronica.

"No!" Heather cried, shoving Veronica out of the way.

Zap!

The magic struck a glass troll, which cracked down the middle. With a horrible crash, it shattered to either side, scattering glass across the terrace.

"Get down!" Heather shouted as she yanked Veronica behind a statue of a dwarf leading a pony.

The Hag turned toward Strathorn, and in a flash, Veronica reached for her crossbow.

Ziip!

But the duchess was too quick. With a flick of her wand, the she turned the bolt to glass. It halted in midair and fell, shattering across the floor. By the time she turned back toward Strathorn, the wizard had ducked behind a statue of a woman holding a large snake.

"Don't let her get Chattergee!" Chattergee cried as he hopped from one statue to the next.

Zap!

She missed. Chattergee had darted frantically to the next statue, hopping onto an Ookie's shoulder. "Aiee!" he screeched when he saw the monster's expression.

"Shut up, you stupid squirrel!" the Hag cried, taking aim again. She blasted the glass Ookie, but Chattergee had jumped again. This time, he sent a troll smashing into an elf, which in turn smashed into something that appeared to be a cross between a leopard and a falcon, which smashed into a woman with roots for feet. . . .

Doggett let out a war cry as he flung his hatchet toward the Hag.

Zap! The hatchet turned to glass. *Crash!*

Strathorn made his move. With a deft stroke, he brought his staff down on the Hag's left arm. *Crunch!*

"You've shattered me!" shouted the Fragile Hag, her wand dropping to the floor.

Strathorn dove for it.

"Strathorn!" Veronica cried as the wizard and the witch struggled on the floor.

"Aha!" Strathorn cried. He came up with the wand. "Oof!"

The Hag—who had just kicked him in the face—plunged after the wand.

"Ooh! Look out!" Chattergee cried as a line of statues went down one after another, like dominoes, toward Strathorn. "Look out! Look out!"

Strathorn rolled out of the path of the crashing statues. Staggering, he managed to knock over another.

The Hag gripped the wand in her teeth. Jerking her head forward, she sent a bolt from her wand toward Doggett, who dodged it just in time. The statue beside him exploded.

The Hag struggled to her feet. "Ow I've ot oo!" she shouted through a mouthful of wand.

"What?" Heather asked from behind the statue.

"She said, 'Now I've got you,'" Veronica translated.

"Like hell," Heather said, grabbing Veronica's crossbow. "Strathorn!" she shouted. Quickly, she stood and took aim at the statue beside the Hag.

The duchess nodded frantically at the bolt that was about to explode the glass statue—which was why she didn't see Strathorn's staff as it landed with a hideous crack against her neck, shattering her collarbone.

The Hag's mouth opened in shock as her head twisted and the wand dropped to the floor with a clatter.

Slowly, almost as gently as a scarf in the wind, the Hag fell backward, over the edge of the terrace. There was a sickening sound of breaking glass as she dropped into the moat below.

The glass wand glittered darkly and Strathorn reached for it, but before his fingers made contact, the wand exploded in a flash of light. Strathorn rubbed his hand, which had been singed by the heat of the burst.

"What just happened?" Veronica asked warily.

"This is very bad," Strathorn said, staring at the place where the wand should have been.

"What? What is it?" Heather gaped at him.

His blue eyes met hers. "The wand was enchanted. I fear that the Twilight Queen herself has it now. Now she will wield her sister's power as her own."

"That is bad," Doggett agreed.

"But why would the Orb lead us astray?" Strathorn demanded. "It isn't possible!"

Just then, a pounding roar shook the castle.

"That moat thing is still chained up, right?" Heather asked.

"Unless the chains were magic bonds," Strathorn said. "Then they would have disappeared along with the rest of the Fragile Hag's magic."

The company digested that for a minute.

"Okay," Veronica said finally, "just how the hell are we going to get out of here?"

NINE

"G et behind me," Strathorn ordered when the group reached the drawbridge's iron gate. The walls shook, and Heather smelled the scent of burning rock as chips of stone fell like hail from the ceiling above them.

"Strathorn," Veronica said, "you're exhausted. Do you really think you can—"

The old wizard wheeled on her with a sudden ferocity. "I said, get behind me! I'm sick of your arguments—we have no time!"

As if to punctuate his point, a stone as large as a football fell at Chattergee's feet, which set the squirrel to screeching like a baby.

Heather cowered behind Veronica as another roar and a blast tore a hole in the wall behind Doggett.

"The bonds that hold this castle together are breaking," Strathorn said. "Soon the Moat Beast will leave this place nothing but a pile of rubble."

"Naturally," Veronica said dryly. Of course, she thought, villains in fantasy stories were always doing that—putting some kind of "self-destruct" charm on their homes and castles. If only she'd remembered that before they destroyed the Fragile

Hag. Taking a deep breath, she wound up her bow.

"Doggett," Strathorn commanded, "raise the gates."

The Kiblar gave a quick nod and then turned to yank the pulleys that operated the gates. With a series of clanks and groans, the iron door lifted, leaving only the cage-like gate behind it. When the Moat Beast caught sight of them, it blasted them with a roar.

"Jeez, would someone give that thing a breath mint?" Heather said.

"Now!" Strathorn shouted, and in the next instant the iron gate had been raised.

The Moat Beast reached an enormous, slimy hand toward Strathorn, but the wizard sent a blast from his staff. It landed on the beast's shoulder with a sizzle, and in a moment the air was heavy with a burning stench that was a mixture of tire fire and excrement. The Moat Beast howled in rage and pain.

"I'm going to be sick!" Heather shouted. She clung to Veronica as they followed Strathorn across the rickety bridge.

Heather could see that it would have been impossible for them to try to sneak back across—even if Strathorn had been strong enough to hold the invisibility spell. Much of the bridge had been blasted away, leaving nothing but a creaky mass of planks that made tiptoeing impossible.

The monster staggered in pain, and Veronica took aim, shooting him in the belly. With a bellow, he reached for Veronica.

Heather screamed as the beast's huge fingers wrapped around Veronica's waist. "Let her go!" Heather screeched, stabbing the hideous monster in the wrist. Her short golden dagger sank into the thick, rubbery skin and stuck there, but the creature didn't even seem to notice the wound. Heather pulled the knife out again.

"It's horriblehorriblehorriblehorrible!" Chattergee shouted frantically as the monster opened his maw, revealing three rows of massive razor teeth. Veronica took aim with her crossbow, shooting him in the mouth, but the Moat Beast merely coughed slightly, then swallowed. Her looked at her sharply with orange eyes, then lifted her toward his open mouth.

"No!" Doggett shouted, hurling a hatchet at the creature, but it bounced off his thick hide, falling into the moat.

Veronica screamed as the beast shook her like a maraca.

"Don't! Don't!" Heather shouted, fearing for a moment that the beast might fling Veronica to the ground.

But she needn't have worried. In the next moment, the beast opened his mouth again and brought Veronica to his lips.

"Let her go!" Doggett shouted, but his weapon was gone. Without thinking, he grabbed the first thing he could—the bag at his side—and hurled it with all his might at the beast.

The pack landed in the creature's mouth, and he coughed in surprise. He looked down at Doggett, then began to munch happily. Gently, he put Veronica down on the far end of the moat. Then he turned back to Doggett and opened his mouth wide.

"He's going to eat you!" Chattergee screamed, and fainted.

But the beast didn't lunge at Doggett. Instead, he stood immobile, mouth open, waiting expectantly. The Kiblar stared, wide-eyed, at the enormous creature.

"Toss him something else, Doggett," Heather said through clenched teeth.

"Oh!" Reaching into his pack, Doggett pulled out a

wrapped package and tossed it at the Moat Beast. The beast caught it in his mouth and chewed, smacking loudly.

"Back away slowly," Doggett told Heather as he reached into his pack.

Heather reached down and scooped up Chattergee; then she and Strathorn backed toward Veronica. "Hurry!" she urged.

Doggett tossed another package at the beast, which caught the snack and stepped forward.

The company reached the far side of the moat. The line of trees was only a few yards away. Doggett tossed the beast another wrapped package, and the beast sat back on his hind legs and roared.

"Run!" Doggett shouted, tossing the whole pack at the beast.

The beast growled and snarled as he ripped apart Doggett's pack, but none of the company saw it. They were too busy running for the trees.

They ran until their thighs ached. They ran until the sweat poured into their faces, stinging their eyes, until they were gasping for oxygen, until their bodies called out "No more!" They ran until Chattergee woke up, and then they stopped, collapsing in a small clearing beside a stream.

"What happened?" Chattergee asked. "Is this heaven?"

"Doggett saved us," Veronica told the squirrel.

"How do we know that thing isn't following us?" Heather asked.

Doggett glanced over his shoulder. "Well," he said, "I don't hear anything. I don't smell anything, either."

"Well done, my boy," Strathorn said, clapping Doggett on the shoulder.

Doggett blushed.

"What was in those packets you kept tossing at the beast, anyway?" Heather asked.

Coughing slightly in embarrassment, Doggett smiled shyly. "Well, those were just some tree-baked cookies, that's all," he said.

Heather laughed. "Saved by the Kiblars once again," she said, flopping backward on the grass.

⟁

They rested by the stream for a few moments, and Heather bathed her face in the cool water. Chattergee ran off to collect nuts while Strathorn leaned against his tree, smoking his pipe.

"Oh, you should go dip your toes in the spring over there," Heather said when she returned from the water.

Veronica looked up at Heather, who was smiling. It was strange—she looked different somehow. And not just because her makeup had worn off and—for once—she hadn't bothered reapplying it. It was almost as though her face was rearranging itself—the lines around her eyes were softer, but the set of her jaw was firmer. Veronica still couldn't believe how hard Heather had fought to save her at the Dark Tower. She didn't know what to make of it. "I'd love to go get clean," Veronica said finally. "Unfortunately, it involves getting up."

Strathorn continued frowning, chewing on the end of his pipe, and Heather gave him a little nudge with her foot. "You should go too, Strathorn," she urged.

"Hmm?" Strathorn looked up at her and a fog seemed to lift from his eyes. "Sorry. What?"

"What's bothering you?" Veronica asked. "You haven't said anything for the past hour."

Strathorn sighed. "I just don't understand it."

"Understand what?" Heather pulled a butter-yellow dandelion from the grass at her feet and tucked it behind her ear.

"Why would the Orb direct us to the Black Tower?" Strathorn asked.

Heather and Veronica exchanged a glance.

Strathorn pulled his pipe from his mouth. "Do you have it?" he asked Heather suddenly. "May I see it?"

With a sigh, Heather pulled the snow globe from her pocket.

"It still shows the Black Tower," Strathorn said in a whisper. "It shows nothing else." He shook his head. "I was certain that it was our task to take the wand. But once we failed, the Orb should have ceased to direct us to the tower. Perhaps we did not achieve our task there. Perhaps . . . perhaps we should go back."

Veronica bit her lip. There was no way she was heading back to the Black Tower and that horrible Moat Beast. *We never should have gone there in the first place!* she thought. "But . . . but don't you think it's destroyed by now?"

Strathorn frowned. "I don't know. But I can think of no other reason for the Orb to show the tower."

"Well," Veronica improvised, "maybe whatever we did there will turn out to be important later on."

"Yeah," Heather chimed in. "Maybe the Orb is just saying, you know, good job!"

Strathorn stroked his beard thoughtfully. "Perhaps," he said. "Perhaps we should press on to the Caves of Terror."

Veronica's heart stood still. The Caves of Terror. That was where the giant spider lived. She felt the hot blood in her veins turn icy.

"The what?" Heather asked.

Strathorn pulled out a map and smoothed it over the ground. "We are somewhere in here," he said, pointing to a thick forest with the stem of his pipe. "The dragon Karn lives on the other side of the Caves of Terror."

Heather looked at Veronica, her blue eyes hard. "Can I speak to you in private for a minute?" Turning quickly, she strode off between the trees.

With a heavy sigh, Veronica hauled herself off the comfortable grass and followed Heather. "What is it?" she asked, even though she knew what was coming.

"I'm not going into anything called the Caves of Terror," Heather hissed.

Veronica shrugged. "What choice do we have?" she asked miserably. Truthfully, she didn't want to go into the caves either. She wasn't in any hurry to meet that giant spider. In the book, it had taken Ibharn, the Sword of Defiance, and three giants to kill it. And they didn't have any of that. "At least we'll be heading back into the real plot of the book."

"Like I care about the stupid plot!" Heather snarled. "Look, I think we should tell Strathorn the truth."

Veronica shook her head. "And then what?"

"And then what? And then he won't expect us to head off after a dragon and fight a witch and go into some smelly caves, that's what!"

"No," Veronica said slowly. "I mean, and then—what? How will we get home? If he doesn't get his power back, I mean."

Heather looked over at Strathorn, who was still sucking on his pipe, deep in thought. Her eyes moved and came to rest on Doggett's form. He was washing his hatchet in the stream. "Can't we tell Doggett, at least?"

"What would be the point?"

"I don't know. . . ." Heather ran a hand through her hair. "I just . . . I just want someone to know the truth."

"Do you really think Doggett could keep a secret from Strathorn?" Veronica asked doubtfully.

"Not this kind," Heather admitted finally.

Veronica touched Heather on the shoulder. "Okay," she said, "I'll try to figure out a way to avoid the Caves of Terror. I think I have an idea."

The girls trooped back to Strathorn, who was poring over his map. Veronica's eyes scanned the various routes to Galma. "What if we were to go this way?" she suggested, tracing the path with her finger. "Around the Lake of Woe."

"It is surrounded by a foul bog, full of unknown dangers," Strathorn said. "And the Lake of Woe is ruled by the Drizzly Witch."

"What is with these names?" Heather demanded. "The Lake of Woe, the Caves of Terror. Has it occurred to anyone that maybe they're self-fulfilling prophecies? Like, maybe if they named it the Lake of Deliciousness, it wouldn't be so awful?"

Veronica shook her head. She knew they'd never make it through the Caves of Terror. Not with that spider. "Few make it through the Caves of Terror alive," Veronica said at last. "The Lake of Woe holds unknown dangers, but those of the caves may be greater."

"I don't know about you guys, but I want to hit the Mall of Fabulosity," Heather put in. "Forget these caves and lakes and all that crap."

Ignoring her, Strathorn stared at the map. "Mayhap you are right," he said finally.

Veronica breathed a sigh of relief. Okay, so now they were losing the plot . . . again. But they were also avoiding that spider. And keeping their secret. That was really all she cared about.

✶⊙✶

"This is so not the road to the Mall of Fabulosity," Heather said with a sigh as she sludged through the thick mud that clung to her feet as though it wanted to steal her shoes. The bog around the Lake of Woe, as Heather's businessman dad would have said, "exceeded expectations" in that it had turned out to be even worse than Strathorn had described it. For one thing, the principal vegetation was something known as a "slime fern," which reminded Heather of the tofu and seaweed sludge that was left at the bottom of a bowl of miso soup . . . but not in an appetizing way. It slapped against one's ankles at every step. And then there was the smell. Think week-old tuna fish sandwich meets rotting fungus. It was so pungent that Heather thought she could feel the smell seeping into her pores, polluting her body. "Ugh!" She slapped at her arm. "Oh my God!" she cried as the bug dropped to the ground, dead. It was the size of a lemon and had long spidery legs that were now sticking straight up in the air. "Did you see that thing?"

Doggett slapped at his neck and hacked at the vegetation with a kitchen knife. "Massive mosquitoes," he explained.

"Do you mean this place is swarming with giant bugs that want to suck my blood?" Heather demanded, her eyes wide with horror.

"Well, luckily they're very slow and easy to kill," Doggett

said cheerfully. "Just don't fall asleep, or they'll suck you dry."

Heather narrowed her eyes at Veronica. "This is the last time you get to pick the route."

Veronica didn't even bother to reply. She'd take an easily killed mosquito over a giant warehouse-sized spider any day. Besides, the bog wasn't that bad. It was gross, sure, but it was populated with trees hanging with oblong orange fruit. Veronica pulled one from a tree and gave it a sniff. It smelled a bit like orange with a hint of apple but was shaped like a banana. Peeling one end, she took a careful bite. *Not bad. Bananorange,* Veronica thought. *Okay, so that's one good thing about this place.*

"We should be through the bog in a matter of hours," Strathorn announced. "Then we must round the lake."

"What's that?" Chattergee cried as something swooped overhead, screeching loudly.

"Just a viper bat," Strathorn said. "Perfectly harmless. Unless they bite you, of course, in which case you'll be dead in five minutes."

"Wait—I think maybe I don't know what 'harmless' means," Heather said, "because you're using it in a really weird way."

"Oh, viper bats are shy and they can hardly see anything." Strathorn waved his hand, as though brushing away a fly. "They aren't interested in humans. They feed exclusively on the fruit of the bog. The smell, however, drives them into a frenzy, in which case you don't want to get in their way."

Veronica looked down at her bananorange and tossed it away. *Okay, so we're back to zero good things about the swamp,* she thought.

"This knife is getting dull," Doggett said, looking at his blade. "I wonder if we'll find a clearing soon. Chattergee, could you go have a look?"

"At your service," the squirrel said, dashing up a tree trunk. The leaves above rustled for a moment, dislodging a snowball-sized lump of sludge onto Heather's head.

"Oh, ewewewewewewew!" she cried, wiping the green slime from her hair.

"I see one!" Chattergee cried from a high branch. "Not twenty paces to the right!"

Doggett lifted his eyebrows at Strathorn in a silent question.

The old wizard nodded. "We'll rest," he said. "For a few moments, while you sharpen your blade. But the sooner we press on, the better."

It took longer than Heather would have thought possible to hack their way through to the clearing, and once they had, she almost wished they had decided to keep going. For one thing, it wasn't a true clearing. It was more like a heap of rotting leaves. And the odor it was giving off made the stench of the swamp seem like Chanel No. 5. But at least they weren't slime ferns, Heather thought as she flopped down onto the leaves. And they were actually kind of comfortable.

Doggett reached into the small pack that remained and pulled out a sharpening stone. He got to work on his blade.

Reaching into her elfin pack, Heather pulled out a compact and checked her reflection. Atrocious. Simply atrocious. She couldn't believe how awful she looked. Her face was caked with dirt, her hair was thick with rapidly hardening slime, and her mascara was running. "Some princess," she muttered, attempting to at least control the rebellious mascara. She shifted on her haunches to get some better light, but she found herself sitting on a weird rock, so she moved a bit to the left. *Another rock,* she thought.

"Is anyone else's seat kind of . . . lumpy?" Veronica asked, frowning.

"Now that you mention it," Strathorn said.

"Chattergee doesn't feel anything," the squirrel said from his place in a nearby tree.

"Mine is too," Heather said, reaching down into the pile of leaves. She felt around and pulled up a white object. It was perfectly round and about the size of a volleyball. "Soccer, anyone?" she joked, holding it up.

Veronica's face went pale. "I don't think that's a soccer ball . . . " she said slowly.

A hiss rattled from the tree just behind Heather.

Nobody moved.

Strathorn lifted his eyes to the place where the hiss had come from. "Put down the egg, Princess," he said in a low voice, "and back away."

Heather's breath caught in her throat, but—very, very slowly—she placed the egg down on the pile of leaves. Then— very, very slowly—she turned and looked behind her.

She instantly wished she hadn't.

"The Bloodsnake of Nithral," Strathorn whispered. "There are those who say it is only a legend, but I had feared otherwise."

Heather barely heard the words. Her mind could hardly take in what she was seeing. It was a snake. A huge, reddish-brown snake, coiled around the tree behind her. Its body was as thick as the tree itself, and it stared at her with yellow eyes, its tongue flickering in and out. Heather didn't realize it, but she let out a low moan of fear as she watched the snake watching her.

"Whatever we do," Strathorn said slowly and calmly, "we must not fight it—"

At that moment, the snake lunged, and so did Doggett, driving his kitchen knife into the snake's jaw.

With a scream, Heather backed away from the snake and stood with Veronica, watching as Doggett attacked.

"Run! Run!" Chattergee cried, hopping onto the next tree and disappearing into the bog.

The snake hissed and flailed, uncoiling its long tail from the tree. Doggett let out a wild cry and hacked at its neck.

"No!" Strathorn cried. "No!"

But Doggett was an elf possessed, and he hacked and hacked, spewing blood until the leaves were slick with it, wet with it.

"Stop!" Strathorn cried.

But Doggett wouldn't stop. He hacked until the snake's head was severed from its body, and even then the jaws snapped, the tail flickering wildly. Finally, the tail gave a final shudder and lay still, and even then, Doggett stood over the head, breathing heavily, as though daring it to move again.

"Doggett," Heather said. "That was . . . "

But something was happening. The leaves at Doggett's feet fluttered, then squirmed. He looked down in time to see the snake's blood . . . congealing. In a moment, a small pool had come together to form a mass, and a moment after that, it was whipping back and forth—a small snake.

Doggett backed away, but there was a hiss behind him. Turning, he saw that the blood behind him had congealed as well, forming another snake.

"Fool!" Strathorn shouted. "Didn't I tell you not to fight?"

But even as he spoke the words, the blood was doing its work, and soon the leaves were roiling with a web of blood-snakes. Doggett lunged at one with a knife.

"No!" Strathorn said. "By the Weaver, don't you understand? You'll only make more!"

Just then, the enormous head of the slain bloodsnake moved backward and forward. Then the giant tail.

"What's happening?" Veronica shouted.

"It's growing a new body," Strathorn cried, and in a moment, Veronica could see that he was right. The head was springing a new tail, and the tail was sprouting a new head. "Get behind me!" Strathorn commanded Heather and Veronica as he held out his staff.

"Doggett!" cried a voice from above. It was Chattergee—he was directly over Doggett, clinging to a long branch. "Reach!" Wrapping his tail around the branch, Chattergee leaped, lowering the branch toward his friend. Doggett jumped, but his fingers missed.

Strathorn used his staff to beat at the web of snakes at Doggett's feet. "Run!" he shouted as the two giant snakes—now fully formed—reared to face him. "Run, all of you!"

Doggett darted along the path Strathorn had cut for him through the snakes, and Chattergee leaped from branch to branch behind him. "Come on!" Heather shouted, pulling on Veronica's hand.

But Veronica couldn't move. She could only watch in horror

as the web of snakes grew before Strathorn and the two giant snakes hissed, ready to take their prey.

The old wizard began to chant. His voice had a deep, rich, musical quality, and Veronica guessed that he was trying to magically hypnotize the snakes.

"Come on!" Heather screamed. "Run!"

But Veronica was rooted to the spot.

Strathorn held up a hand, and the snakes began to quiet down. His chanting grew louder, and Veronica could see him trembling with the effort. *He's exhausted,* she realized.

Still, the snakes were quieter. The smaller ones were mostly still, and the large snakes' eyes drooped.

"It's working," Veronica whispered.

Taking a deep breath, Strathorn turned as though to follow them.

"Come on!" Heather shouted again.

But at that moment, one of the giant snakes blinked, and with a whip-crack motion, it lurched forward and bit Strathorn on the neck.

"No!" Veronica screamed, but it was no use—the other snake had moved forward and coiled its body around Strathorn. It looked down at the old wizard with yellow eyes and opened its mouth with a horrifying hiss.

Veronica didn't see what happened next, because something seized her arm in a viselike grip and gave it a vicious yank. She was dimly aware of voices around her, a voice above, but her mind was a blank as she retraced her steps, back and out of the bog.

TEN

"This has to be a psych-out," Veronica announced.

Still breathing hard, Heather looked up from where she was lying on the ground. Once they had reached the edge of the bog, the company had collapsed, overcome with fear and exhaustion. Doggett was lying belly-down beside Heather, his cheek pressed against the soft, damp ground. Chattergee was curled in a ball, his tail wrapped around him and tucked beside his head, house cat style. Heather was spent—too exhausted to cry for Strathorn, although she felt like a dam with a spiderweb of cracks across the front, ready to break at any moment.

Doggett, at least, was managing to do enough crying for the both of them. Tears dripped from his eyes and snot streamed from his nose, watering the grass below his head.

But Veronica was still standing. Staring. Gazing into the bog behind them, her face blank. She looked like she was expecting something to appear.

"What did you just say?" Heather asked, propping herself onto her elbows.

Veronica's brown eyes flicked to Heather's face, then turned back to the bog. "I said, 'This is a psych-out.'" She straightened her ponytail and folded her arms across her chest. "It has to be."

Doggett turned his tearstained face to hers. "What do you mean?"

"Strathorn isn't dead," Veronica explained, almost impatiently. "He can't be."

Flopping back on the grass, Heather barked a bitter laugh. "Yeah, okay."

"I'm telling you, this is a psych-out," Veronica insisted. "It's a standard story device, right? The most important character seems to die, it looks like all hope is lost, then he shows up again. It's in every fantasy book ever written. All we have to do is wait."

"That isn't going to happen," Heather said.

"Yes, it is." Veronica planted her feet a bit wider and continued to stare at the edge of the bog. She thought about Aslan in *The Lion, the Witch and the Wardrobe*. She forced herself to remember how she had cried, wailed, when she'd come to the chapter with the Stone Table. But he'd come back. Just as Gandalf had come back. Just as Tinkerbell had come back. Veronica conjured these characters in her mind and held them close around her, like a blanket. "He's coming," she said. "Any minute, he'll walk out of that bog."

Slowly, painfully, Doggett sat up. "But this isn't a story," he told Veronica in a gentle voice. "It's real."

Veronica swallowed hard. She knew better than anyone that real life didn't always play by the happy-endings rule. But this story—Fabiella Banks's story—wasn't supposed to be like real life. That was the whole point! But there was no way to explain that to Doggett. "Okay, Doggett," she said. As she spoke, she seemed to deflate a little, and hot tears welled in her eyes. "But you'll see that I'm right."

"So—what else is new?" Heather demanded, propping herself onto her elbows again. "You always think you're right, Veronica. That's why we went into the bog in the first place, remember? Because of you."

Veronica didn't tear her eyes from the bog. "Strathorn agreed—"

"Because you convinced him!" Heather screeched. "You're always so sure you know the answers, Veronica. Well, this time you didn't, okay? Strathorn is dead!" Those words shook the dam of Heather's heart, and in a moment, the spiderweb had widened, and the dam burst, and she was crying, crying, and she couldn't stop. "He's dead," she said again.

Chattergee didn't say anything, but he hopped over to Heather and curled up beside her. Her throat was closed, and tears spilled down her cheeks, wetting her face, dripping onto her neck. She hadn't cried like this in years, not since the first time her mother left home for three months to help build mud huts in Africa. She felt like tears were coming out of her very pores.

Veronica continued to stare at the edge of the bog, but something inside her was wavering, and a cold chill spread from her toes up her legs, clawed its way to her torso, her heart. "He'll be here any minute," she whispered.

"I hope you're right," Doggett said. But his voice didn't hold much hope.

❧❦❧

Once the company had eaten and the small fire that Doggett had managed to coax from the damp boggy branches had died down, the tired company did their best to fall asleep. All except for Veronica, who sat with her chin on her knees, staring toward the edge of the bog, still waiting for the wizard to appear.

With a huff, Heather rolled onto her side and pulled her cloak around her, trying to ignore the wet ground that chilled her skin. She had cried so much that she felt hollow and strangely clean. The tears had lightened her, made her calm, and returned a sense of clarity to her mind. And as she lay there, struggling to fall asleep, the thoughts started flowing thick and fast. *How long are we going to have to wait here before Veronica will admit to being wrong?* she wondered. *And then what? The Caves of Terror?* It didn't sound too appealing. *None of our options do,* Heather realized.

We should have told Strathorn the truth.

But now it was too late. She simply couldn't imagine confessing to Doggett now. Not now that their lie had cost Strathorn his life.

She shifted slightly, and something poked her in the ribs. Reaching into her pants pocket, Heather's fingers trailed over the Orb. The real Orb, the Orb of Neftalion. She hadn't pulled it out, not even to glance at it, since she had first tucked it away. The truth was, she didn't like having it. It made her hands clammy to know that so much rested on such a small thing. Its power made her uncomfortable. For one thing, its mere presence would expose her as a fraud. Only the One could look into it and see the future. And anyone would discover immediately that Heather wasn't seeing anything.

Then again, whispered a small voice, *how do you know?*

The Orb must have been trapping the heat from her fingers because its smooth surface slowly began to feel warm instead of cool as a glass marble. Without quite realizing what she was doing, Heather found herself pulling the Orb from her pocket. She held it before her in her open palm and was surprised to see that it was glowing slightly with a golden light.

Look into the Orb, Heather's mind whispered. *Maybe you will see something. . . .*

The light of the Orb brightened slightly, and Heather felt its golden glow against her skin as she pulled the round glass ball closer to her face. The light began to shimmer, and after a few moments, it looked like the Orb was filled with a thousand tiny fireflies, all signaling desperately for mates. The fireflies swirled, dipping and diving, separating and coming together until finally, they formed a scene. . . .

Heather squinted, trying to focus. *It's a green hill,* she thought, *a mountain*—but no, it was moving, as though it had a life of its own. Its surface was rough, covered with boulders and craters, and it pulsed, almost with breath. At the base of the mountain were two dark stretches of forest, and they, too, pulsed with life as a wind rippled through their branches and trees. Suddenly, the mountain moved upward, and Heather realized that no, it wasn't a mountain at all, and no, those weren't strips of forest—they were nostrils. It was a nose. A giant, horrifying nose. A green nose, and it was sniffing, sniffing, sniffing. . . .

Heather felt sick as the image adjusted, and now she saw the bottom half of a face, a pointed chin, muddy green skin, dark lips, black and frog-like, turned into a scowl. The top half of the face was hidden by a dark hood, and even that was frightening, for Heather knew this was the face of the Twilight Queen, and the nose was her nose, and she was sniffing . . . for her. Trying to smell her out . . .

Heather woke with a start and stared out into the twilight.

The Orb still poked her in the ribs. *I never took it out,* Heather realized. *It was just a dream.* Still, the Orb was warm, and Heather shuddered at the thought of her vision.

Taking a deep breath, she looked around. Veronica was still staring toward the bog. But the dim orange glow of the fire gave enough light to show the tear trickling down the side of her face.

"Are you all right?" Heather asked.

Veronica placed her cheek against her knees. "I don't think he's coming," she said.

Thanks for finally admitting that you screwed up, Heather thought. But she couldn't make herself say it. She just didn't have the heart.

"It's my fault," Veronica whispered, her voice catching. "You were right." She looked up at Heather, and Heather noticed that the tears made Veronica's dark eyes look soft, like melted chocolate. "Strathorn is dead . . . and we're never going home."

Heather's head felt light. "I know," she whispered. It was a thought that she hadn't even let herself think until this moment.

"What are we going to do?" Veronica asked. Her face was pale, her eyes huge, and Heather could easily imagine what she had looked like as a child.

"I don't know," Heather admitted. "I think . . . maybe . . . we should tell Doggett."

"We can't," Veronica whispered, desperation in her voice. "I can't. I can't tell him that we lied to Strathorn, and now he's—"

Heather put a hand on Veronica's shoulder. She wished that she were as wise as Strathorn, that she had something deep and meaningful to say. But she didn't. "It's okay," she said at last. "It's not your fault."

And then Veronica did something completely unexpected. Reaching out, she wrapped her arms around Heather in a stranglehold and started weeping, crying uncontrollably, wetting Heather's shirt with her tears. Heather racked her brain for something to say, something to do. What was it that her parents had done when she skinned her knee?

But nothing came to her. Her parents had never been there when Heather cried. Or else . . . they had been . . . but when Heather cried, they handed her off to someone else. Someone like Isidora.

Suddenly, Heather found herself singing softly. "Dormite, angelito; no tienes miedo; la lluvia no durará."

Slowly, Veronica's breathing grew regular and even. Loosening her grip, she looked up at Heather, who went on, "Las nubes despedirán antes del alba; y la luna plata brillará."

When she had finished, Veronica was silent for a moment. "Where did you learn that?" she asked.

Heather shook her head. "I . . . my maid used to sing it sometimes. She was Mexican."

"Guatemalan," Veronica corrected. "That lullaby is from Guatemala."

Heather felt herself blushing and wondered how she could have known Isidora for so long and never even have known where she was from. "Oh. Maybe I wasn't singing it right—"

"You were singing it right." Veronica sighed.

"I don't even know what it means," Heather admitted.

"It means, 'Sleep, little angel, don't be afraid. The rain won't last forever. The clouds will part before the dawn, and the silver moon will shine.'" Veronica cleared her throat, which felt thick. "My mother used to sing it too." *My mother,* she thought as hot tears streamed down her face. *Who I'll never see again.*

"Oh." Heather didn't know what to say.

Veronica swiped at her tears and took a deep breath. "I guess we'd better go to sleep," she said.

"Okay," Heather said.

A half smile crept up Veronica's face. "Thanks."

Heather nodded and went back to her place on the ground. Then she stared up at the sky, wishing that she was a baby in a crib and that the twilight would lift so she could see the silver rays of the moon shining down on her.

✵

Heather awoke to the sight of Veronica poking at the ground with a stick and muttering to herself. "What are you doing?" Heather asked.

Veronica's head snapped up, as though she had forgotten that anyone else was nearby. She laughed a little and jabbed the ground again. "Just trying to figure out which way to go next," she admitted, chucking away the stick.

"Aren't we . . . ?" Heather's voice was thick. "Are we going back?"

Veronica looked at her seriously. "We can't. That Moat Beast is still out there, and I'm not going past him again. Besides—no matter what, we have to make sure that the Orb gets to King Rellett."

"But what's the point, Veronica?" Heather asked.

Veronica knew what she was asking—what was the point,

now that they couldn't go home? Part of her wanted to give up too. To simply lie here, curled up in a ball, forever. But she just couldn't. "If we're going to live in this world," she said finally, "I don't want it to be a world of darkness."

Heather sighed. "Okay," she said finally. "Okay—so which way are we going?"

"Aren't we going to have to go through the Caves of Terror?" Doggett asked, walking over.

Heather rolled her eyes. She was seriously over these dark and depressing names. "Look, if I'm going on this trip, I want everyone to start thinking positive," she scolded. "From now on, they're the Spa Caves."

Veronica ignored her. "I can't see any other way," she said to Doggett. "If we want to get to Karn, our only other options are to try to go over the Impassable Mountains or cross through the Thousand Mile Forest." Veronica sighed, thinking of the spider. She did not want to go into those caves—how could she, knowing the danger? Then again, look at what had happened beside the Lake of Woe. *The truth is,* Veronica realized, *all of these places have their dangers. All we can do is pick a route and try our best. And Strathorn said from the start that we should take the caves.*

"Chattergee votes for the forest," said the squirrel as he scampered up Doggett's leg and up to his shoulder.

"But it will take too long, Chattergee," Doggett said earnestly. "For one thing, we're nearly out of supplies. And that Moat Beast ate my cook pots—I can't make much of anything. Besides, we have to get to Talan Majeur before the queen leads her army against King Rellett's stronghold. I think Strathorn would have wanted us to go through the Caves of Terror."

"So do I," Veronica admitted.

Everyone turned to look at Heather, who swallowed hard. She didn't really like the idea of caves. They were dark . . . and narrow. Then again, the Thousand Mile Forest and the Impassable Mountains didn't sound so great either. And they had lost so much time already. . . . "Whatever you guys want," she said.

An expression flashed across Veronica's face—was it gratitude? Heather wondered—and was gone in an instant. "Okay," Veronica announced. "We make for the Caves of Terror today."

꠸ꕥ꠸

"Come on, Princess," Doggett pleaded from inside the cave. "It isn't narrow at all."

Heather stared at the jagged black hole that formed the entrance to the Caves of Terror. "I can't," she whispered. The others had already gone inside. Veronica had been the first to plunge in, and Chattergee had followed close behind her, vowing to defend her from whatever lurked in the darkness (but always letting Veronica go first, Heather noticed). Doggett had entered the cave somewhat more reluctantly. But Heather—well, she just wasn't sure she could face it at all.

Doggett poked his head out of the entrance and smiled at her. "It's not bad," he said in a reassuring voice, as though he was speaking to a small child or to Chattergee. "Come on." He held out his hand.

Heather looked at the hand, at the strong stocky fingers and the wide palm. She took it and was surprised by Doggett's firm, gentle touch—by the warmth that radiated from his skin. "It's not bad," Doggett repeated quietly. "I promise." The corners of his eyes crinkled in a smile, and Heather felt instantly better.

"Okay," she whispered. And in the next moment, her foot had passed into the deeper shadow, and she ducked into the entrance of the Caves of Terror.

They walked along a low, wide corridor, crouching slightly to keep their heads from scraping against the rocky ceiling. For a moment, Heather felt sick—desperate to go back the way she had come, back into the air. But after about twenty paces, the ceiling lifted and the room opened up into a large cavern.

"Oh my God," Heather gasped as she looked around. "It's . . . it's beautiful!" The cavern was so large that being in it seemed almost like being outside. The feeling wasn't claustrophobic at all. The walls were made of some kind of iridescent rock, which lit the room with a pinkish glow.

Veronica turned, giving her a dubious glance. "Beautiful? Are you serious?"

"I just wish I had a mirror right now," Heather gushed. "This pink light is so flattering to the complexion! Veronica, you wouldn't believe how good your skin looks. Like you just had a facial!"

"We're in the Caves of Terror," Veronica pointed out.

"Potato, po-tah-to, that's just a name." Heather waved her hand impatiently. "The people of Galma, I swear, they have overactive imaginations. I'm telling you, this place is perfect for a destination spa. Look!" Striding across the cavern, she came to a small passage. "It's a little room! And there's tons of them! Perfect for massages or pedicures—whatever you want. All we need to do is clean this place up, and Galma will have a whole new industry." Smiling, Heather clapped.

"You sound seriously crazy right now," Veronica informed her. "Nobody is coming for a pedicure in the Caves of Terror."

"The Spa Caves," Heather said through gritted teeth.

"Um, shouldn't we be trying to get through the caves?" Doggett asked cautiously. "Rather than planning to remodel them?"

"Whenever Her Highness is ready," Veronica said.

Giving her a tight little smile, Heather brushed past Veronica and started toward the main passage. "You know, it *is* a bit stinky in here," she said lightly as she brushed away a cobweb. "I suppose we'll have to air the place out before we open it to the public."

Veronica rolled her eyes, but she didn't do anything to try to stop Heather's seemingly endless stream of babble about the Spa Caves. The truth was, the place gave Veronica the creeps. She couldn't stop thinking about the spider. The way Fabiella Banks had described it—with enormous, drooling fangs and legs thick as telephone poles, covered in hair like barbed wire, a stinger the length of a limo and sharp as a razor . . . She shuddered.

"I'm thinking reflexology," Heather was saying to Doggett. "People around here are way too tense—"

"Aiee!" Screaming, Chattergee jumped onto Heather's shoulder just as a spider the size of a grapefruit dropped onto Doggett's head.

"Doggett!" Veronica cried. She reached for the spider, but before she could swat at it, the spider hissed and spat.

Doggett cried out in pain as venom sizzled against his shoulder. He batted at the arachnid, which dropped to the floor and scampered toward the nearest wall.

"Squish it!" Heather shouted, reaching for her golden elf dagger. She lunged at the spider, but it hopped onto the wall and hissed again. Heather dodged its poison and stabbed again, but the spider crawled onto the ceiling, out of reach.

"It'll kill us all!" Chattergee shouted, drawing his sword.

"Shut up!" Veronica shouted, aiming her crossbow at the spider. But it was too dark, and the pinkish-gray fur that covered the spider's bulbous body blended into the rock above. "I can't see it!"

"It's here!" Heather cried, right before the spider launched a silvery web at her wrist. She cried out as the sticky web wrapped around her hand, enfolding the golden dagger in a soft cocoon.

In the next instant, the spider let down a silver rope and dropped toward the floor. It skittered toward Chattergee and the rodent screamed.

"Chattergee can't take anymore!" the squirrel cried, holding out his sword. "We surrender!"

"Nobody's surrendering!" Veronica cried. She unleashed a silver bolt, but the spider jumped aside, bounding onto a rock. The bolt sliced through the air and clattered—useless—against a wall of rock.

Doggett let out a fierce grunt as he chased the spider with a hatchet. *Clang!* The hatchet bounced off the rock floor as the spider leaped away. With another hiss, it spat a sticky gob at Doggett's feet, tripping him. The Kiblar muttered curses under his breath while Veronica got off another shot with her crossbow.

The spider let out a horrible, metallic screech, and two of its legs shattered under the weight of the bolt.

Heather flung her dagger against a rock, and the elfin blade sliced easily through the cocoon. Sticky spider residue clung to her weapon as she lunged toward the arachnid.

"No, no!" Chattergee whimpered from where he cowered on the floor. His tiny paws were still wrapped around the handle of his elfin blade, but the squirrel was tucked in a tight ball of fear.

"Die, you stupid bug!" Heather shouted as she leaped at the spider.

Hiss!

Venom landed on Heather's shin, burning like acid. "Damn it!" she screamed, dropping her dagger.

Doggett launched his dagger at the bug, but the spider bounced aside and then lunged at him, clawing at his face with its six remaining legs.

"Doggett!" Heather screamed as the Kiblar wrestled with the hissing spider. "Shoot it!" she hollered at Veronica.

"I can't!" Veronica cried helplessly—she didn't dare risk shooting Doggett by mistake.

"Kill it, Chattergee!" Heather shrieked. "Chattergee—get up off your lazy ass and kill that *bug*!"

The squirrel was right beside Doggett, but he couldn't move. He trembled in fear as Doggett writhed beside him.

"Get! Off!" Doggett screamed. He flailed left, then right. He screamed as the spider hissed again, and with a final, desperate move, he rolled, clawing at the bug.

With a frantic push, Doggett managed to dislodge the spider—planting it squarely on Chattergee's blade-up sword.

The arachnid let out a vile hiss, and its legs jerked and fidgeted, but they could go no further. They twitched and fought and finally were still.

Doggett stared at the spider, catching his breath.

"Doggett," Veronica whispered, "you killed it."

"Chattergee killed it, more like," Doggett said as he struggled to his feet.

"Hmm? What?" Chattergee opened one eye and let out a shriek when he saw the dead spider stuck to the edge of his sword.

"Calm down," Heather told him. "It's dead."

"You've saved my very life, valiant squirrel," Doggett said, bowing low. "You have my eternal gratitude."

"Chattergee slew the Great Spider," the squirrel said in awe.

"Let's not get carried away," Heather said as the rodent reverentially pulled his sword from the belly of the slain spider. "Your shoulder," she said to Doggett.

Gingerly, Doggett touched the spot where the spider's venom had landed. "It's not bad," he said. "No worse than a slight burn from the magic oven. Nothing to worry about."

Veronica breathed a sigh of relief. That spider attack had not been as bad as she had feared.

But . . . was that even the same spider? Veronica wondered. She was starting to realize that Fabiella Banks had an amazing gift for embellishment. *I mean, okay,* Veronica thought as she stared at the spider pinned to the ground, *this spider is big, sure. And ugly. And it spits poison.* But it certainly wasn't "the size of a warehouse," the way it was described in *Queen of Twilight.* And one didn't need an elf prince, three giants, and the Sword of Defiance to kill it.

Veronica actually let out a little giggle, remembering how frightened she had been of the spider—for years. She'd had nightmares in which the giant spider had sucked her blood down to dust and bone. And here it was . . . the size of a softball. She nudged it slightly with her toe, and its legs curled up.

"That's gross," Heather said, watching Veronica kick the spider. "Do you think there are more?"

"It's the only one," Veronica said.

"Good." Heather scowled at the spider. "Because a bug like that is bad for the spa business."

Hissss . . .

Everyone heard it at once. The sound wasn't loud so much as it was . . . large. As though whatever was making it was big. Very big.

Chattergee whimpered.

"Don't make me turn around," Heather begged.

But, of course, they had to. Even though what they saw made them wish that they hadn't.

It was a bug. A giant bug. It had a tiny black head with a curved, scythe-like proboscis. Its massive black body had two white spots, like eyes, on its haunches, and its form ended in six black-and-yellow-striped legs covered in spikes. Its scaly wings rattled, and drool dripped from its black beak. Smoke rose from the place on the ground where the drool fell.

"Okay, for this whole spa idea to work, that thing has got to go," Heather said.

"It's a cockroach," Veronica whispered.

"It looks more like an assassin bug," Heather corrected. "They hold down their prey and suck the blood from their bodies. Very common in Latin America."

Veronica gaped at her.

"Oh, right," Heather snapped. "Like I'm the only person in the world who watches the Nature Channel."

"Princess, could we stop arguing?" Doggett asked nervously as the assassin bug's antennae twitched inquisitively. A striped leg the size of a cement truck stepped forward with a disgusting crunch.

Letting out a screech that sent Veronica's blood running cold, the assassin leaped at Doggett. The Kiblar howled in pain as the bug pressed his shoulder to the ground with a spiny foot.

Shouts rang in the rock cavern and Veronica pulled a bolt from her quiver. She didn't even bother loading the crossbow—she stabbed the assassin in the hind leg. The bug squealed, viscous green blood gushing from its wound.

"Don't get near it!" Heather shouted, pointing to where the blood had landed on a rock. Smoke rose from the stone as the blood ate into its surface.

Veronica stared in horror as her silver bolt melted in the bug's blood. The insect kicked its enormous leg, spewing acid across the floor.

"Run!" Doggett screamed, beating at the insect's leg with a rock. The bug flinched, moving just enough for Doggett to roll away from its pressing grasp.

"Not that way!" Heather shouted as Veronica hurried toward a narrow passageway.

Veronica didn't break her stride. "It's the only way!"

Fighting the dizziness, Heather plunged into the darkness after Veronica. Doggett was right behind her.

"Wait for Chattergee!" cried the rodent, bolting past them all.

The assassin disappeared into a cave overhead and out of sight.

Heather's blood pounded in her ears as she raced down the narrow passage. It was close and dark, and she could touch rock on either side of her with her outstretched arms. Suddenly, she felt like the entire mountain was pressing down on her, ready to crush her. . . .

Hiss!

Veronica screamed as an antenna snaked in from an opening to the left, knocking her to the floor. A spiked leg reached in.

"No!" Heather cried, smashing it with a rock.

With a shriek, the insect withdrew its leg and antenna, and the company hurried on.

Even though it didn't seem possible, the dark got darker and the air got thicker. Heather thought it was like running through a sponge. The dank, rank air seemed to absorb all of the light and sound around them.

Suddenly, Doggett stopped. Veronica crashed into him, and both of them tumbled to the rocky ground.

"What is it?" Heather whispered, stopping. She felt Chattergee's fluffy tail flicker at her feet, as though reaching out to make sure she was still there.

"The air," Doggett said, scrambling to his feet. "It feels different."

"I think we're in an open space," Veronica agreed.

Heather took a deep breath. The air did seem drier, lighter, although it still held a foul taint. A breeze blew past her face. "We must be near an exit," she murmured.

"Chattergee, you have the best night vision of all of us," Doggett said. "Can you see anything?"

"Chattergee sees nothing," the squirrel said quickly.

Heather sighed. "Chattergee, if you can't find us a way out, we're going to be stuck in here with that giant bug . . . which is only going to get hungrier and hungrier."

Veronica swallowed hard. She knew that Heather was right—and that she was just trying to get the squirrel to help out a little—but she didn't like the idea of the assassin bug lurking in the dark, feeling for them with its antennae, oozing acid blood at every step.

The squirrel hopped tentatively forward. "The breeze comes from this direction," he said. "The air behind us is foul, but the wind is clear and fresh. Chattergee thinks he can see a light. . . ." There was a general scrambling, scratching noise, and Heather understood that Chattergee had bounded off to investigate.

"Isn't he going to get lost?" Veronica asked.

"Should I light a match?" Doggett suggested.

"I don't want that thing to find us," Heather hissed.

"Besides, he'll sniff us out," Doggett agreed.

"A squirrel's sense of smell is better than his eyesight," Heather pointed out. "Nature Channel."

After that, the silence seemed endless as the company waited for Chattergee to return. Heather was feeling a little less light-headed now that she could feel that she was in a wide chamber with a high ceiling. Still, the darkness made her nervous, and every beat of her heart seemed to rattle her bones as she waited to find out if there was an exit after all.

What if we're stuck down here? she wondered. Stuck forever with that horrible, creeping assassin bug . . .

A scratch, a crunch, and Chattergee—or what Heather could see of him—appeared. "It's not far!" the squirrel chattered. "Not far, not far! Follow me!"

The company hurried after him, listening for the sound of his scratching paws. Now Heather could smell new scents on the air. Was that pine? She imagined herself under the twilit sky, looking up at the trees. Even the endless twilight seemed preferable to this lurking dark. . . .

And then she could see it—pale purple light. They were almost there, almost out of the caves. The twilight shone soft across the rocks to either side, casting violet shadows over boulders that shimmered with quartz.

"Right here!" Chattergee said. "Right here!"

And then one of the shadows moved.

Rising up, the boulder that wasn't a boulder revealed its long, striped legs. It crawled forward, dragging its hind leg. *Things that large shouldn't move so quickly,* Heather thought dizzily as the assassin bug lashed out, pinning Chattergee—who writhed and bucked—to the ground.

"Aiee!" the squirrel screamed as the assassin lowered its beak. The dark dagger reached toward Chattergee, and drool dripped from the insect's proboscis in anticipation of the feed.

Heather's heart froze in horror. "Veronica!" she shouted.

But Veronica had already pulled her crossbow. She let out a shout as she shot a silver bolt into the bug's segmented body. Acid gushed from the wound, and Veronica had to turn away to protect her eyes. An immense leg loomed over her. Turning her head, she saw the bug's beak lowered into Chattergee's lifeless body.

Doggett hurled a rock at the insect, but it was no use. The bug flicked him away with a single blow of his barbed leg, opening a gash over Doggett's left eyebrow.

"Stop it!" Heather screamed, and she was just about to fling herself at the bug when a howl rang through the cavern, echoing off the rock walls. It was bestial and somehow familiar, and

Heather didn't have time to register why she recognized the noise before the vile, hulking form of the Moat Beast became visible in the twilight that glowed softly in the cavern.

Doggett yelped as the Moat Beast lunged for the bug's leg and twisted, snapping it like a matchstick. Acid poured out, but the Moat Beast wrapped his mouth around the leg, slurping and licking.

Hissing, the assassin bug dropped Chattergee, who fell limply to the floor as the beast leaped. The giant insect lashed out with razor-lined legs, slashing violently at the beast's claws. The Moat Beast howled in pain and clutched his face as the insect spewed venom across his eyes.

But the only effect the venom had on the beast was to further enrage him. With a roar, he leaped onto the back of the bug and bit into its neck.

"Run!" Heather screamed as the battle raged. "Run!"

Doggett reached for Chattergee, cradling him in his arms as he ran after Veronica.

Behind them, the insect screeched again and spewed venom, but now the Moat Beast had grabbed its antennae. With a fierce yank, he snapped them off and tossed them aside. Scrambling up the bug's back, the beast snapped at the insect's narrow neck and, in a single bite, severed its head completely from its body.

The bug collapsed against the floor of the cave, legs twitching in a hideous dance.

But the company didn't look back, didn't pause, didn't think as they clambered through the opening and into the twilit air above.

ELEVEN

"Is he alive?" Heather asked as Doggett peered down at Chattergee.

The Kiblar stroked the squirrel's fur. "I feel a heartbeat," Doggett said. "But who knows how much blood he has lost." He ran gentle fingers over the squirrel's body, frowning in concentration. "I can't find the wound. . . ."

"Stop it . . . " Chattergee murmured softly. "Tickles . . ."

"Tickles?" Veronica couldn't help the grin that started to spread across her face.

Chattergee sat up, woozy. "Is this heaven?" he asked.

"That squirrel hasn't lost any blood," Heather realized. "He just fainted!"

"Chattergee takes umbrage at your tone, Princess," the squirrel announced. "Would anyone in the same position have done otherwise?"

Behind them, there was a low moaning noise; then a shadow passed over the dark mouth of the cave. In a moment, the Moat Beast appeared, pulling himself weakly out of the cave. With a hollow "murph" noise, he collapsed on the pale grass.

"Run! Run! Run for your lives!" Chattergee shouted.

"Wait," Doggett said gently.

"Doggett," Heather called as the Kiblar walked toward the weary beast. "Doggett, don't!"

The elf looked over his shoulder at her and smiled. "It's all right," he said before he turned back and knelt beside the creature.

The Moat Beast looked up at Doggett with wide orange eyes, and the elf reached into his pocket and came up with a crumpled packet.

"What is he doing?" Veronica asked.

Chattergee's tail flicked back and forth as he covered his eyes. "I can't watch!"

The monster stared at the packet a moment, then opened his enormous mouth wide.

Carefully, Doggett placed the packet in the beast's mouth. The creature waited for Doggett to withdraw his hand before munching carefully. After a moment, he let out a satisfied burp.

Doggett smiled, then reached out and touched the monster gently on the head. At first, the beast flinched and moved away. But after a moment, it laid its head down and let Doggett pet it.

"Good boy," Doggett said.

The Moat Beast gave Doggett's hand a slimy lick.

Doggett looked back at his friends. Chattergee was peeking through his fingers, horror stamped across his face.

"I think we've made a friend," Doggett announced.

⚘

"This is it?" Heather asked as she and the rest of the company plodded through the streets of the village of Karn. The rest of their trip from the Caves of Terror had been uneventful . . . although a bit smelly, thanks to the Moat Beast. Doggett had persuaded the beast to take a dip in a river, but even that had only diminished his stench a little. And it had rendered the river water completely undrinkable for miles downstream. Still, although the beast was kind of disgusting, Heather had to admit that she found him comforting in his own way. Now that he wasn't attacking them, she could see how a giant, smelly monster might be useful.

It was Chattergee who had found the path leading away from the caves, and the company hadn't walked for more than twenty minutes before coming to the outskirts of Karn—the place where they would, hopefully, pull the Helmet of Unsmellability from the dragon's lair.

A helmet like that could come in handy, after all, Heather thought, eyeing the Moat Beast.

Karn itself was a bustling little village, lined with stalls topped with red canopies. Shoppers milled along the main street, looking at the stall keepers' wares. Heather looked around. "It's a tourist trap!"

"I wouldn't call it a tourist trap—" Veronica started, but her sentence was quickly drowned out.

"Get your key chains!" called an enormous man wearing an eye patch. "Get your Dragon of Karn key chains!"

"Official dragon wallets, belts, and shoes," shouted a woman in a stained apron. "This is the only place to get them, folks."

"I've only got a few dragon stocking caps left!" cried a portly older man, waving a long hat. "Topped with an official replica of the Warning Bell of Karn," he said, giving the cap a jingle.

Heather lifted her eyebrows at Veronica and walked up to the huge man with the eye patch. "Excuse me," Heather said, "can you tell me where to find the dragon?"

"Official Dragon Tourist Office—end of the street," the man snapped, tugging at his black beard. "Key chain?" He dangled one in front of her. It was tipped with a beautifully wrought, fierce-looking red dragon.

"Um, no, thanks," Heather said. "But it's very nice." She walked over to where the others were standing, all except for Chattergee, who was chatting up a woman in a low-cut shirt who was selling dragon beer. "Up the street," Heather said, leading the way.

"Why don't you take that foul-smelling thing out of here?" screeched the woman in the stained apron as the Moat Beast passed by.

The Moat Beast reached for the woman, who let out a shriek.

"No! Bad!" Doggett shouted.

The beast looked guiltily at Doggett and dropped his head. Doggett tossed him half a cookie, and the beast caught it in his mouth. "Good boy," Doggett told the beast.

"Here it is," Heather said, staring up at the sign that read, OFFICIAL DRAGON TOURIST OFFICE. Actually, the "office" was nothing more than another red stall with a skinny man asleep behind the counter. "Excuse me," Heather said.

A little snore escaped the man's nose.

"Excuse me," Heather repeated.

The little man's mouth twitched, and he smacked his lips.

"Hey," Veronica said, shoving him on the shoulder. "Wake up."

"Hm? What?" The little man started, then blinked at the company through eyes that appeared enormous behind his thick glasses. Catching sight of the Moat Beast, he frowned.

"What is it?" he snapped.

"We want to see the dragon," Heather explained.

The little man let out a hissing laugh. "Sssss-ssss-sss!"

"What's so funny?" Doggett asked.

"Sssss-ssss-sss!" The little man rocked back and forth in his chair. "Sssss-ssss-sss!"

"Hey, creepy little dude, quit hissing at us," Veronica said. "We want to see the dragon—now let's go!"

"Sssss-ssss-sss! Nobody sees the dragon!" the little man said, wiping a tear from his eye as he continued to giggle in his snaky way. "Oh, hoo-hoo! Sssss-ssss-sss!"

"What?" Heather glanced at Veronica, who had clearly had enough.

She pulled her battle-ax from her belt and held it against the little man's neck. "Take us to the dragon," she said.

The little man's huge eyes rolled wildly as he stared at the blade. "You don't know what you're saying!" he cried. "Nobody sees the dragon. It's much too dangerous! But I can offer you a tour of the exterior of his cave. It leaves in ten minutes."

"Good enough," Veronica said.

So the company grabbed a few overpriced official Dragon of Karn corn dogs while they waited around, killing time before the next tour. Actually, Veronica thought as she munched one, it wasn't at all bad. Kind of spicy. Doggett bought a packet of dragon snaps for the Moat Beast.

Finally, the little man hauled himself out of his chair. "Right," he said, holding out his hand. "That's ten frilligs, payment in advance."

"Ten?" Doggett demanded. "How do you get ten? The sign says two frilligs each."

"And there are five of you," replied the skinny little man.

"You can't count the beast!" Doggett insisted. "He doesn't even speak English!"

"Ten. Frilligs." The little man held out a stubborn palm. His enormous eyes flashed.

"Just give it to him," Heather said with a sigh.

Doggett handed over the money, grumbling.

The little man shoved the frilligs into his pockets, donned a flat-topped straw hat, and started toward a steep slope. "This way!" he called. "Up the hill! To your left, you'll see the official Dragon of Karn Watchtower, built in the year 764. The Warning Bell of Karn is rung if the dragon is spotted more than twenty paces from his cave." The little man pointed to the tower, where a short sentry paced back and forth before a large bell.

"When was the last time you had to ring it?" Heather asked.

The little man glared at her. "It's never been rung," he snapped, stopping in his tracks. "Let me tell you something, missy: if that dragon ever left his cave, we'd all be dead! We have to feed him a sheep every day to keep him happy."

"Then why have a bell?" Veronica asked.

"Why have a—?" The man shook his head as if to say that he wouldn't even dignify that question with a response. "And here we have the path to the Cave of Karn. Over the course of two centuries, more than a hundred men have passed this way in an attempt to slay the dragon."

"But why are they trying to slay him if he never leaves his cave?" Heather asked.

The little man gaped at her. "He's killed a hundred men!"

"But they were trying to kill him," Heather countered. "It was self-defense."

"Self-de—?" Turning on his heel, the man *harrumph*ed and led the way up the rest of the hill in silence.

"I think you've made him mad," Doggett whispered to Heather as they trooped up the hill.

"People around here are very touchy," she replied.

Once they reached the top of the hill, the little man pointed down and said, "Take a look and see what your 'self-defense' has wrought."

Heather, Veronica, Chattergee, and Doggett peered over the edge of the ridge. The ground was scorched black in front of the natural cave that lay at the rocky bottom. Bones and twisted, misshapen metal—the remnants of knights and their armor—lay strewn around the perimeter. A plume of smoke wafted out of the cave, curling toward the sky.

"Almost feeding time," the little man announced. "We'd better get back."

"Oh, I want to see him get fed," Heather exclaimed.

"No, no, no!" The little man turned pale in horror. "Nobody watches the feeding—it's far too dangerous! You can come back later and have your portrait painted in front of the cave. That's it."

"Well, I guess we'll just turn back—" Chattergee started.

"We're going to watch it," Veronica announced. She turned to face the others. "I think we need to see what we're up against."

The little man's jaw dropped in horror. "It's not up to you! By order of the mayor, no person aside from the official Dragon Keeper shall be present at the feedings. It's for your own safety!"

"We'll take the risk," Veronica told him.

"Hey," Heather said, pointing to a large boulder nearby. "Let's hide behind this and take a look at feeding time."

"Good idea." Veronica and the others followed Heather, crouching low behind the rock. The beast crouched too, even though he was about three times the size of the rock and it barely hid his legs.

The little man's eyes bulged as the company settled in. "You can't stay here!" he cried. "I'm getting the Dragon Guard. They'll clap you in chains before you can say—"

"Hold up there, pip-squeak," Veronica said. Leaping after him, she grabbed him by the collar.

"Help!" the man cried.

"Doggett," Heather said. "Can't you do something?"

"Beastie?" Doggett looked over at the Moat Beast, who stood up. He gave himself a good stretch, then walked over to the little man and sat on him.

"Oh, my!" cried the little man. "Oh, my! The smell! I feel faint! I think I'm going to—" He passed out from the stench.

"Good boy," Doggett said, giving the beast a pat.

The beast belched.

"Sorry you're unconscious," Doggett said to the little man. "I really liked the tour. Very educational."

Veronica peered down at the entrance to the dragon's cave. "I wonder how long we'll have to wait for him to show up."

Answer: not long. After a few minutes, a young boy in rough brown pants tied with a piece of rope and a stained shirt appeared at the top of the path. He had a gray bag slung at his side. He scrambled partway down the ridge, then stopped and reached into the bag. Taking out a chunk of meat, he heaved it toward the front of the cave, then clambered up the ridge and ran down the path as fast as he could, disappearing into the trees.

Heather frowned at the chunk of meat. It was about the size of a tennis ball. "Doesn't that seem like kind of a small portion for a big dragon?" she asked.

Just at the moment the words had left her mouth, the dragon himself waddled out of the cave. He was covered with brilliant scales that gleamed alternately red and gold in the soft twilight, and he looked very much like a picture of a dragon in an old storybook—with a long snout and small, scaly wings. Veronica recognized him immediately from Fabiella Banks's description. Curls of smoke rose from his nostrils as he stretched his long, snakelike body, revealing golden talons. He looked exactly the way she had said he would. There was only one difference.

"He's . . . smaller than I expected," Doggett admitted.

"Smaller?" Veronica repeated. "He's the size of a Chihuahua."

Chattergee nodded. "A fierce and noble fighting dog," he proclaimed.

Heather leaned forward for a better look. "He's adorable!"

"Adorable?" Chattergee demanded. "That thing's a killer!"

Heather rolled her eyes. "Chattergee, don't tell me you're falling for that propaganda."

Doggett shook his head. "The legends of the dragon are known far and wide—"

"Oh, spare me," Heather interrupted him. "That doesn't make them true. Look, this whole town is founded on the Dragon of Karn tourist trade. They probably set up these fake bones and stuff to make it look more dramatic. That's why they don't want anyone to watch the feeding—because then the world will know he's perfectly harmless." She glared at the little man, who was just coming to.

"Where am I?" he asked faintly.

"You're here—in front of the sweet little dragon." Heather snapped her fingers in his face. "I think you'd better rewrite your tour."

"Good lord, he's out of the cave?" the man cried.

"Yeah, and your secret's out too," Heather told him. "Let him go, beastie."

The Moat Beast shifted just enough for the little man to squirm away. "Get away from the dragon while you still can!" he cried, scurrying away. "He'll kill you all!"

"Wow, he really can't let it go," Heather said.

"I don't know," Veronica said dubiously. "Maybe the dragon really is dangerous." She remembered the scene in *Queen of Twilight* in which Princess Arabelle fought the dragon. In the book, it took all of her skill, plus that of Ibharn and the three giants, to defeat the beast.

So, okay, the dragon was smaller than Veronica had expected. That didn't mean he was harmless. . . .

The Dragon of Karn nibbled the meat and stretched out in the pale light.

"Oh, he is so cute!" Heather said. "Look at the way he's cleaning his paw!"

"You mean his razor-sharp talon?" Doggett corrected.

The dragon rolled over onto his back and wiggled happily. He looked about as dangerous as a cone of cotton candy.

"Don't let the fact that he's small fool you," Chattergee

pointed out. "Many a man has met his match at the tip of Chattergee's sword."

The Moat Beast yawned.

"So what's our plan?" Veronica asked, wondering how they would get the Helmet of Unsmellability. "How are we getting inside the cave?"

"Plan?" Heather repeated as the dragon stretched and waddled back into the cave. "Why don't we just walk in?"

"Are you mad?" Chattergee demanded, his tail fluffing indignantly.

Veronica tugged at her ponytail. She had to admit, the dragon didn't look dangerous. And Fabiella Banks did have a gift for exaggeration . . . like with the spider. Except that there really had been a giant bug in the caves, and it really had attacked them. "I don't know," Veronica hedged, but Heather was already on her feet.

"Princess!" Doggett hissed after her. "Princess!"

Heather ignored him, marching straight down the steep incline.

"She doesn't even realize how brave she is," Doggett whispered as he stared after her in awe.

"Some might call it brave," Veronica said as Heather disappeared inside the cave.

A short while later, she reappeared, hurrying up the slope. "I got it!" she said triumphantly as she reached the boulder.

"The Helmet of Unsmellability?" Veronica asked.

"No," Heather replied in a duh-what-are-you-thinking? voice. She patted a bulge in her pocket. "The dragon."

༺༻

"Who's a good boy?" Heather asked, tickling the dragon's

golden stomach. "Who's a good wittle dwagon? Hmm?"

"Prrt?" Karn's golden talons flopped in the air as he wiggled happily under Heather's attention.

"Would you stop touching it?" Veronica demanded. "We don't even know if it's dangerous or not."

"Ooh, who's a wittle killer?" Heather asked Karn. She scratched him under the chin. "Who's a vicious, vicious wittle baby?"

The dragon clucked happily. Turning over, he crawled into Heather's lap and looked up at her with huge golden eyes.

"He's purring!" Heather cried joyously.

"Is that . . . good?" Chattergee asked dubiously.

"It means he loves me," Heather announced, running her fingers along the golden red scales that lined his back. They were surprisingly soft—more like feathers than scales, really.

Karn hopped off Heather's lap and trotted over to the Moat Beast, who reached out for the little dragon. Karn scooted away playfully, then tentatively approached again. But the Moat Beast had already lost interest. He started sniffing at Doggett's pack. When Karn discovered that he couldn't rouse the beast's notice, he gave up and started chasing his tail.

"He's like the puppy I always wanted." Heather sighed. She tossed Karn a leftover piece of corn dog.

"Are you sure he should be eating that?" Veronica asked.

"It's meat, isn't it?" Heather shot back. "Besides, he loves it—look."

Sure enough, the tiny dragon was munching at the corn dog eagerly. Once he had gobbled it up, he let out a tiny burp, sending up a small puff of smoke.

Giggling, Heather reached out to give him another pat.

Karn sniffed her fingers, then butted his head against Heather's bicep. He wrapped his snakelike body around her upper arm.

"By the Great Squirrel, he's attacking you," Chattergee said, half rising from the ground.

"Would you relax?" Heather shot back, holding up her arm. Karn was looped around it, like a red-gold ornament. He seemed to be there more or less permanently, because his eyes were closed and he was purring again, as though he had fallen asleep. "Can you believe it?" Heather squealed. "He's the perfect combination of pet and accessory!"

"And deadly killing machine," Chattergee added.

Heather gazed adoringly at Karn. "I just wish I had one in every color."

Heavy footsteps sounded behind them. Someone was trudging up the steep slope. A moment later, Doggett's head appeared, then the rest of him. He was breathing hard, lugging an enormous oblong object that looked something like a gray watermelon.

"Well, I got it," Doggett said as he tossed the watermelon to the ground, where it landed with a heavy thud.

Chattergee hopped over to inspect the thing. "That's the Helmet of Unsmellability?" he asked.

"How do you see out of it?" Heather asked.

Doggett frowned at her. "Are you wearing the dragon?"

"Okay, let's not get into some kind of fashion discussion, because I might have a few comments on your squid-head helmet," Heather shot back.

Doggett sighed. "Well," he said, turning back to the helmet, "I guess this heavy visor can come up. But I think, generally speaking, you want to leave it down—for maximum smellessness."

"It looks kind of heavy," Veronica said doubtfully.

"Whatever," Heather put in. "I'm not wearing that thing on my head."

"I expect you'll be glad to have it before the end," Doggett said with a shrug. "Besides, Strathorn said we needed it, so . . . "

Everyone was quiet for a moment at the mention of Strathorn.

"Well," Veronica said finally, "I guess we should get going. We've wasted enough time here."

"I'm ready." Heather stood up, and the dragon fidgeted in his sleep.

"All right," Veronica said. "We'll all wait while you put the dragon back."

Heather stared at her as though she had just sprouted a snout. "I'm not putting him back."

"You have to put him back," Doggett said. "This town is based on that dragon."

"I'm not leaving him here to be gaped at by strangers and to have lies told about how dangerous he is," Heather insisted. "One of these days, those crazy people are going to start believing their own propaganda, and they'll come out here and kill him!" Karn snuggled tighter against her arm.

"Be reasonable . . . " Veronica started.

"No!" Heather cried. "No—Karn is the one good thing that's happened to me since I got here, and I'm keeping him."

Veronica shook her head. "But you can't—"

"Why not?" Heather demanded. "Doggett gets to have a pet!"

"The Moat Beast is not a pet," Doggett insisted.

Hearing his name, the Moat Beast looked up from the bag he had been sniffing and gave Doggett a wet, sloppy lick on the cheek.

"You know," Chattergee chimed in, "the princess has a point."

"Oh, be quiet or we'll leave you behind," Veronica grumbled. "Fine," she snapped, turning to Heather. "But this is a big mistake. Mark my words."

"Don't listen to them, Karnie," Heather told the sleepy little dragon as she rubbed him beneath the chin with a finger. "They're just meanies."

# TWELVE

It's a strange thing, going to sleep when it's still twilight, Heather thought as she rolled over in a futile attempt to get comfortable on the rocky earth. It seemed that no matter which way she twisted, a stone would dig into some region of her body. Before she turned, it had been her upper thigh, but now a spiny stone roughly the shape of an ax was digging into her navel. But besides the torture rocks, Galma never got dark enough for a proper sleep. The strange purple glow bothered Heather, reminding her of the many times when—back in her other life—she'd tried to fall asleep with the television on. But the blue lights kept her awake, which was why she often found herself watching infomercials into the early morning . . . she couldn't bear to turn off the tube and listen to the absolute quiet of her house, nor could she fall asleep.

Beside her, Karn snored lightly, his chubby little hamster belly rising and falling with each breath. Delicate tendrils of sweet smoke curled from his nostrils. Heather smiled and stroked his feathers with a tender finger. It was nice to have a pet that always smelled like incense at Christmastime. A dragon was actually a practical thing to have. Especially when traveling with a slightly smelly Moat Beast.

Rolling onto her back, Heather looked up at the faint stars above and breathed in a deep lungful of the sweet air. The nights were turning colder already, and she couldn't imagine how dismal a land of eternal twilight would seem in the winter.

Now something was pressing against the back of her head—an odd lump. *Why doesn't anyone else seem bothered by the uncomfortable ground and the weird violet haze?* Heather wondered, glancing over to where Chattergee lay curled by the dying fire, his fluffy tail serving as a blanket. Doggett was propped up against a tree, supposedly on watch, but his head lolled against his chest, and it was clear from the slight snorts he gave at regular intervals that sleep had overwhelmed him. Veronica was lying nearby without moving at all. Sometimes Veronica's complete stillness in sleep freaked Heather out a little, and she would have to poke her to make sure that she was still alive. Which she always was, by the way.

Heather reached behind her head and adjusted the light pack she had been using as a pillow. Reaching inside, she fiddled with the contents in a vain attempt to rearrange them into a less skull-crushing position.

Finally, her fingers brushed across the offending shape—a smooth round ball. It was cold, though, colder than ice, and it almost hurt Heather's hand. For a moment, the bag glowed blue, every inch of its dull tan fiber lit up from the inside.

She yanked her arm out of the pack, her heart jackhammering in her ears.

What was that? she wondered, but even as the thought whizzed through her brain, she knew the answer—it was the Orb of Neftalion. Glowing.

Heather pinched herself to make sure that she wasn't dreaming, then slapped herself to make extra sure. Okay, she was awake. Awake and in pain. And now the Orb seemed to want to tell her something.

Don't touch it, she commanded herself, but Heather's fingers—as you well know—were disobedient creatures, and before she knew what she was doing, Heather had reached into the bag and pulled it out.

At her touch, the smooth round ball glowed blue and glittered like a glacier. It felt like a glacier too. "Ow!" Heather cursed under her breath as she dropped the ball.

The blue light immediately went out.

At her feet, the Orb shone softly in the purple light.

Grinding her teeth, Heather reached down and wrapped her hand around the Orb. The blue glow rose again, but Heather wasn't sure that she could hang on. The pain, the pain, it was searing her palm—cold so frigid it was hot, her flesh was burning, and she wanted to drop it, but then . . .

The light flickered and grew, sending rays like probing fingers, like embracing arms that reached through Galma for leagues. It grew and grew until Heather held a miniature sun in her hand, a violent explosion of light. But it was light now, all light, no heat—the ice had cooled, had taken on the warmth of her palm. And it throbbed. It pulsed with a heartbeat that matched her own, almost as though the Orb had become part of Heather.

It was brilliant, blinding, but Heather wasn't blinded. Her eyes widened as she gazed into the light. She saw every racing atom as it hurried to rearrange itself within the confines of the brilliant Orb.

The atoms swirled and danced until they took on a shape. Hazy and dull at first, but then sharp and clear as Chattergee's diamond sword.

Heather gasped as she saw herself.

She was dressed as she was now but standing in a strange place. It looked like a library or some other room lined with shelves and shelves of books.

Was she alone? She couldn't see.

Her lips were moving, but the Orb revealed no words. And then Heather saw herself holding out the Orb. Giving it away.

A mottled claw at the end of a long loose sleeve reached for the Orb. The sleeve was the purplish color of twilight, and on one clawed finger was a ring with a large yellow jewel. . . .

The Orb went dark.

Heather blinked the pulsing stars from her eyes and waited a moment for her vision to clear. Her mind swam. *What was that? What did I just see?* A million thoughts collided at once as Heather attempted to sort out the vision.

Because it looked like . . .

Well, it looked like . . .

Bile rose in her throat and her chest squeezed against her cold heart. It looked like she was giving away the Orb to the Queen of Twilight.

But I wouldn't do that, Heather thought. *I wouldn't!*

Guiltily, she peered around the camp. The others were still sleeping peacefully. She looked down at the Orb in her hand. *Maybe I didn't see what I thought I saw,* she told herself. *Maybe this didn't really happen.*

But if it didn't happen, why am I sitting here, awake, holding the Orb of Neftalion? Why is my face still stinging from the slap I gave myself earlier?

Swallowing hard, Heather shoved the Orb back into her pack, burying it deep. *Don't think about it,* she commanded herself. *That isn't going to happen. You aren't even the One, so how could you see the future?*

Feeling only slightly comforted by this, Heather rolled over again. She didn't move as she lay there, blinking sleeplessly up at the twilight.

⁊ɔɕɤ

"This is it," Doggett announced, staring at his feet. The tiniest of trickles ran just past his toes, coursing lightly over smooth oval rocks.

"What is what?" Heather asked as Karn scrambled down her arm and leaped lightly to the ground. He sniffed the water warily, then started to lap it up, apparently deciding it was safe.

Doggett looked at her with his serious gray eyes. "This is the border of the Eastward Hold."

"Talan Majeur," Veronica said, remembering the words that began chapter sixteen in *Queen of Twilight.* "'The Great Heart.' The Kingdom of Men."

"Once we reach the top of Tabla Monsoor, we'll be able to look down at Palast Anoor, the Blue Castle," Doggett went on. "They say it's almost blinding in the full sun."

"Then I guess we should be glad it's always twilight," Heather replied.

Chattergee pulled his sword. "Across the Fjord of Banata!" he cried, splashing through the trickle. Karn leaped playfully after him, and the Moat Beast followed, lumbering.

Heather shrugged. "Whatever," she said, stepping into the ankle-deep water.

Doggett went next, and Veronica brought up the rear, her heart thudding in her chest. This was it. The scene in which the final stand took place. Once Princess Arabelle and Ibharn reached Palast Anoor and met King Rellett, they would lead the army to victory against the Twilight Queen. And now—well . . . something would happen, although just what was anyone's guess.

Heather was silent, her lips pressed tightly together, as her toes squashed inside her damp shoes on the far side of the shore. She was still feeling a little unsettled from her vision the night before. But the sky overhead was clear twilight, and the air was cool and crisp. Fall had always been Heather's favorite season. With every step she took in the sweet, clear air, she seemed to leave her vision farther and farther behind.

After the fjord, the landscape shifted, and the company found itself plodding up a slight slope that seemed to go on forever. In fact, the slope was so subtle that Heather didn't even notice it for a long time, not until she found her chest tight and her legs aching. "Is everything uphill in this country?" she muttered.

"Just in this direction," Veronica said, catching Heather's words. "Once we reach the top, we'll have reached the tabla—the table. It's completely flat, and you can look down into the valley, where the Blue Palace was built."

"Why is it blue?" Heather asked.

"It's lined with thousands of painted tiles," Veronica explained, remembering Fabiella's vivid description. "The tiles tell the history of the race of men, and each is painted on a blue background. It's built in tiers, and from a distance, the palace looks like the shifting sea. It took a thousand artisans a hundred years to make it."

"Is it my imagination," Doggett said after a while, "or are we leveling off?"

"I think you're right," Veronica said.

The Moat Beast let out a howl.

"Up ahead!" Chattergee called from his place on the beast's shoulder. "I see the top of the ridge!"

In the same way that a school of fish twists and changes direction as though every member is of the same mind, now our company found themselves running, running together toward the top of the ridge. A fleeting thought passed through Heather's mind—this was the first time since she had arrived in Galma that she was running toward something instead of away from it. The endless journey was almost over. She laughed out loud, thinking of it, and her body felt light, barely skimming over the grass.

It was the Moat Beast who reached the top first. He stopped short and stood perfectly still, gazing down at the valley below. Chattergee remained stock-still on his shoulder.

"Oh . . . " Veronica said as she reached the top of the ridge. She stood looking down at the Kingdom of Men, which stretched as far as the eye could see.

Heather was the last to catch up. As she stood looking down at the vast expanse, her already-short breath seemed to disappear. "It can't be. . . ."

"We're too late," Doggett announced.

For miles below them, nothing was visible but black, scorched earth. A column of oily smoke drifted up from the center of the destruction . . . the bluish tint of the few remaining walls in the eastern wing told Heather that this was all that remained of Palast Anoor. Suddenly, the wind shifted, and Heather caught the thick smell of something burning. Not the sweet, clean smell of a wood fire, but the heavy, acrid smoke of dead bodies, and stone buildings, and devastation. The ground was littered with corpses—men in armor and Ookies in their strange leather garb, goblins and trolls scattered everywhere, like garbage blown by the wind. Among the bodies were glass statues that winked coyly, catching the dim twilight.

Above the hold hung a black cloud, and a light rain misted over the burning devastation.

"She's been here," Veronica said, half to herself. "The queen. She does have the Hag's wand after all."

"And her sister, the Drizzly Witch," Doggett added, eyeing the clouds that hung like misery over the scorched scene.

Heather couldn't breathe. Her throat was closed. Her body felt heavy, and she swayed on her feet. Suddenly, the meaning of her vision seemed clear: she herself had handed Galma over to the Twilight Queen. The vision had already come true. "I did this," she whispered.

Veronica stared at her. "What?"

Heather couldn't see—her eyes were blinded by tears. "If I hadn't been captured by the Galag Nur . . . we wouldn't have been too late—"

Veronica shook her head. "If I hadn't suggested that we go around the Lake of Woe—"

"If we hadn't gone by the northern route," Heather insisted. "If I hadn't opened that golden box—"

"If a lot of things," Doggett said simply. "But here we are."

They stood in silence for a moment, each contemplating the desolation below.

"What are we going to do?" Veronica asked the sky.

Heather closed her eyes. She wanted to lie down, to sleep. Karn slunk over and nuzzled her ankle, but she didn't reach down to pet him. She didn't have the energy. She felt like Chattergee. *Let's give up,* she thought. *Let's go home.* . . .

Only she couldn't go home. Not ever.

Doggett was looking at Veronica, his head cocked. "What are we going to do?" he repeated. His gaze shifted to Heather's face, then back to Veronica's. "Why, we're going to go on, miss," he said. "What else can we do?"

Heather's anger flared, and she felt a violent urge to kick Doggett or to scream. But neither of those things was any use, and she knew it. There was no point in anger—Doggett was right. They had to go on.

Slowly, slowly, she felt her breathing return to normal. As much as she wanted to pretend that this wasn't happening . . . well, it was happening. She picked up Karn and he wrapped himself around her arm. Her eyes sought out Veronica's.

Swallowing hard, Veronica nodded in understanding. "Okay," she said at last. "Let's get going."

The Moat Beast let out a howl as Doggett took the first step down the ridge.

"Hey, wait a minute," Veronica said. "Where's Chattergee?"

Everyone looked around—but the squirrel was nowhere to be found. "He's disappeared," Heather said. "That coward."

"Oh, no," Doggett insisted. "Squirrels are known for their bravery, Princess. He's probably disappeared to go find us some help."

Heather sighed. In a way, it was sweet that Doggett always believed the best in people. But in another way, it was kind of annoying. "Okay, Doggett," she told the Kiblar. "Whatever you say."

Veronica snorted. *Maybe Chattergee is the smart one*, she thought miserably. But her feet didn't change direction as she and the others plodded forward, down into the valley of destruction, Talan Majeur.

Up close, Heather could see that the damage done to King Rellett's castle was even worse than she had thought from afar. Entire walls and sections of the palace lay in smoking ruins. Pieces of glittering blue tile were scattered like trampled confetti over the blackened earth. The sight of the fallen stronghold filled Heather with a different sort of sadness than the individual corpses she had seen lying on the battlefield. Doggett had told them that the Palast Anoor had always been an impregnable fortress for King Rellett's ancestors, famous for surviving countless battles with its beauty intact. And now huge chunks had been torn from its body, and it lay flattened like a piece of roadkill that wouldn't even see a proper funeral. It looked like what it was—the destruction of a nation.

The east wing, however, was still standing, and Doggett made straight for the tall iron doors that were bolted against intruders. Two battle-weary sentries stood at either side.

"Tell the king that the One has come!" Doggett shouted to the sentries.

"Shh—Doggett!" Heather punched him on the shoulder lightly as one of the sentries scrambled inside. "Jeez!"

"What?" Doggett asked as Heather blushed furiously.

The other sentry knelt before Heather, bowing his head. "Princess Arabelle," he said gravely, "long have the men of the Eastward Hold awaited this day."

Veronica gave Heather a kick.

"Um, pleased to meet you," Heather mumbled, and before she knew it, she was following Doggett through the open doors and into the Great Hall.

"You wait here," Doggett commanded the Moat Beast, who grunted in understanding. He crouched on his haunches beside the wary sentry.

The sentry sniffed warily. "Are you sure he's all right?" he asked Doggett.

"Oh, he's fine," Doggett said. "Just take him for a walk if he gets restless."

Every warrior of the Eastward Hold who could still walk or stand had gathered inside. Women and men, all with the typical dark hair and cocoa skin of the people of the region, lined either side of the Great Hall. Most were lying or sitting, sharpening weapons or straightening shields. Two hundred pairs of dark eyes flashed up at Heather as she stepped into the hall. Instantly, she felt dwarfed by the towering cathedral ceilings. She wished she had time to stop and stare at the colorful murals that lined the walls, but her attention immediately went to the tall chair—the throne—at the end of the hall. A man sat there, large and barrel-chested, with a dark beard that came down to his heart. His dark face was almost perfectly round and made Heather think of a bearded hazelnut. This, of course, was King Rellett, and standing beside him was the sentry who had opened the door. He was whispering in the king's ear, and when Rellett saw Heather, his dark eyes sparked and his round face broke into a weary but hopeful smile.

"Princess," King Rellett said, and the moment he spoke the word, the hall began to ring with the rattle and clink of soldiers clattering to their feet. Nobody spoke as Heather, Veronica, and Doggett made their way toward the throne. The warriors' eyes followed every step.

Heather looked up at the room full of expectant eyes, all focused on her face. She felt weak under the weight of their glance. She thought of the battlefield, covered in corpses. She felt like the hall was filled with their presence. Heather locked eyes with one warrior—a girl about her age. Her dark eyes were full of relief, as though she expected Heather to put things right, to make all of those deaths okay somehow.

But Heather couldn't do that. Nobody could do that.

It isn't fair, Heather thought. In her entire life, nobody had ever expected anything of her. Nobody cared if she brought home good grades or cleaned her room or showed up on time for a movie. Nobody cared. But now—now people expected everything of her all at once. And it just . . . wasn't . . . fair.

King Rellett stood up. He was a tall man, massive as an oak. "The One has come," he said. His voice was a hushed whisper, but the silence of the hall was so absolute that nobody missed the words. "The prophecy has been fulfilled."

The hall rippled with murmurs and then fell silent. The warriors were waiting—holding their breath, it seemed—for the One to speak.

Heather opened her mouth, then stopped. *What should I say? Something inspiring? Something helpful? Something—?* And then, as her brain whirred, a voice from the depths of her mind whispered, *Tell them the truth.*

King Rellett smiled encouragingly, his kind brown eyes crinkling at the edges.

I have to, Heather realized. *I have to tell him. And it has to be now.* She couldn't let these men go on fighting because they believed in some crazy prophecy that wasn't even about her.

Heather's knees felt wobbly, like Slinkys, as she stood before him. She took a deep breath, collecting herself. There were so many things she wanted to say. So many explanations. But how to begin? And her voice—she was so overwhelmed, she could hardly speak. Finally, she found that she could say only one word. That word was, "No."

The great hall echoed with the soldiers' whispers.

The king's smile evaporated. "Ah," he said, folding his hands over his immense belly. "I see." Understanding dawned over his face, and Heather felt awash with relief. She could feel Veronica's eyes on her, boring into her skull, but Heather didn't care. There it was. The truth was out. And the king understood.

King Rellett's beard twitched as his face rearranged itself into a thoughtful frown. "It is just as I thought," he went on. "You speak wisely, Princess. Of course, the prophecy has yet to be fulfilled."

Murmurs of agreement ran through the assembled ranks as the king curled his hand into a fist and held it to his heart. His voice took on a deeper tenor. "My army is weak," King Rellett boomed. "But now the One will lead us into triumphant battle, and the words of Landron the Sage shall ring across the land!"

The warriors let out a chorus of cheers.

Heather felt the color drain from her face. He hadn't understood her at all! "No—no, wait." Heather shook her head, finding her shaky voice. "I can't lead the army—"

"Oh, certainly not. Not alone," the king said firmly, wrapping his thick fingers around the hilt of his sword. "I shall ride with you at the head of the column! Onward—into battle!" Drawing his blade, he swiped through the air, slicing it with a deadly hiss.

The hall rang with shouts of "Hear, hear!" and cries of "To the witch!"

Heather stared about her in horror. That wasn't what she'd meant to say. *Okay, stay calm,* she ordered herself. *Start from the beginning.*

"No, you don't understand," Heather said, touching the king on the shoulder.

King Rellett arched an eyebrow. Heather wasn't sure how, but she managed to go on. "You see, Princess Arabelle has been shattered."

The great king took Heather's hand in his massive paw. "Of course she has, my dear," he said easily. Then he turned back to his troops. "The princess has been shattered," he called, "and shall be born anew as the Queen of Galma!" He held Heather's hand high over their heads in a symbol of victory.

"Hooray!" shouted the soldiers.

Wearing a huge grin, Doggett leaned toward Heather. "You're doing great!" he whispered. She could hardly hear him over the noise of the soldiers. "They love it! Keep it up!"

Heather groaned and looked helplessly at Veronica, who had gone pale. She knew that Heather was right. They had to tell the truth—now. "You're not getting this," Veronica said, stepping forward. "What we're trying to say is—we come from a different world, okay?"

"A world where right shall rule and evil be vanquished!" The king waved his sword in the air, and the hall rang with whoops and shouts.

"No, no!" Yanking her hand out of the king's grip, Heather took a step toward the throne. "Look—I'm not the princess!"

"So are none of us ourselves!" the king cried. "We have no titles! We have no divisions! We are all one! We are," he shouted, brandishing his shield bearing the golden unicorn that was the standard of the Eastward Hold, "warriors of Galma!"

Veronica looked at Heather and shrugged helplessly.

Heather sighed. There was no point in saying anything else—she'd probably only whip them up into a further frenzy. *I'll just have to figure out some other way to get out of this,* Heather decided. *The only question is—how?*

Heather sat cross-legged on her bed, staring at the Orb laid out before her on the blue-and-white coverlet. The room was in the part of the palace that had survived the attack and was surprisingly opulent . . . although the foul stench of death that hung in the air had permeated even this elegant little room.

Karn happily explored the washbasin, nuzzling the pitcher with his snout.

But Heather didn't care. She didn't even care about the nice, hot bath she had just stepped out of or the fresh clean clothes in the Majeurean style that she had just put on. What Heather needed was an answer.

Still, she was afraid to touch the Orb.

What if she had the same vision—or one that was worse?

What if she watched the warriors as they fell to the queen? What if she had to watch her friends die in battle, beheaded by Ookies?

But what if the Orb showed her a new vision—a better vision? What if it showed her how to help these people? What if it showed a way out?

What if it showed her nothing at all? Would that be better? Worse?

"My head hurts," Heather muttered as Karn flopped into the washbasin.

Sighing, she hauled herself off the mattress and picked up Karn. He purred softly, his warm chest vibrating, as she carried him to the bed.

"I don't know what to do," Heather admitted, gazing at the Orb. "I just don't know." She stared at it, and her eyes defocused as her mind wandered.

A tiny firefly dove and fluttered inside the Orb, then died.

Heather squinted. "Did you see that?" she asked Karn.

The dragon yawned, then started licking himself beneath his right wing.

Heather looked at the Orb again. She hadn't touched it . . . but she could have sworn that it . . .

Shaking her head, Heather stared at the Orb again. Nothing happened.

How did I do it? she wondered. *What was I doing? Well . . . I wasn't doing anything. Okay.*

Standing tall, Heather let her mind go blank as she looked at the Orb.

A spark pulsed, then soared toward the top of the Orb. It was joined by another, then three more. In a moment, a crowd of sparks whirled and danced, cutting through the dim twilight, filling the room with brilliance.

Karn stopped licking himself and looked into the Orb, mesmerized.

The minuscule fireflies leaped and frolicked, and Heather felt her heart fluttering.

The sparks shimmered, then grew less restless, more still. The dance came together and formed a picture. An image. A company was on the march. Veronica rode on a dappled gray horse. Beside her was King Rellett. Behind them was a column of horsemen, followed by foot soldiers. The Majeureans.

But Heather was not with the company. . . .

"What are you doing?" Veronica cried.

The Orb went dark, but Heather's eyes still pulsed with light. Her head swam and she heard the door being slammed shut and Veronica's voice whispering, "Ay, Dios mio, que hace aquí?"

Heather blinked hard, clearing the explosions from her eyes.

"What did you do?" Veronica asked. Her voice sounded strangled.

"Nothing," Heather insisted, shaking her head. "That is, nothing . . . on purpose."

Her vision was clearing enough so that she could see Karn nudging the Orb inquisitively on her bed.

"Did you . . . did you see something?" Veronica asked.

Heather felt herself go pale. "No," she lied.

Veronica planted her hands at her hips. "You're a decent thief but a crappy liar."

Heather sat down on the bed. "I saw . . . I saw you and King Rellett riding into battle. I think you were going to fight the Twilight Queen."

"Really?" Veronica seemed pleased.

"But I didn't see me," Heather went on.

Veronica took a moment to absorb this information. "Well, maybe you were doing something else," she suggested.

"I had another vision," Heather admitted. "Last night."

Veronica narrowed her eyes, like maybe she didn't believe Heather. "Why didn't you mention it?"

"Because . . . " Heather had to swallow hard to clear her throat. "Because I saw myself giving away the Orb. To her."

Veronica looked stricken. "But . . . you wouldn't. . . . "

"Wouldn't I?" Heather asked. She sighed. "I don't know. In a way, I already have."

Veronica didn't say anything, and in the next moment, Heather had hopped off the bed.

"Now what are you doing?" Veronica asked as she watched Heather gather her things, which the servants at Palast Anoor had kindly unpacked for her, and shove them back into her bag.

"What does it look like I'm doing?" Heather demanded, tossing her extra pair of elfin capris onto the bed. "I'm pulling a Chattergee and squirreling out of here. And you should do the same."

Karn buried himself in the pile of pillows at the head of the bed.

Veronica folded her arms across her chest. "Where are you going to go?"

"Who cares?" Heather snapped. "All I know is I'm not leading some army to die at the hands of the Queen of Twilight, okay? Maybe I can't get out of this stupid fantasy world, but I can get out of here. If these people want to die, that's fine, but I'm not going to be responsible for it. And I'm not handing over that Orb to the witch. I'll leave it here. Let the king deal with it. That's what we said we were going to do, and that's what I'm doing." Heather pulled Karn away from the pillow he was chewing and wrapped him around her arm, where he snuggled tight.

"They're going to die anyway," Veronica pointed out. "I mean, if the queen wins . . . "

"She's already won!" Heather's blue eyes seemed lit with fire as she wheeled to face Veronica. "Look around you! This place is wrecked! Don't you get it? She won the minute we showed up and screwed up what was supposed to happen."

Veronica sat heavily on the bed and covered her face with her hands. Heather was right. They had ruined everything, and now they were supposed to lead King Rellett's army on a suicide mission. Slowly, Veronica raked her fingers through her long hair. "What about Doggett?" she asked.

Heather looked at the floor. "I don't know," she admitted.

"Are we just going to leave without saying good-bye?" Veronica asked. Her voice wasn't challenging, though. She really didn't know what to do.

"I—" Heather's voice caught, and she had to swallow hard to clear the lump in her throat. "I can't tell him—"

Veronica sighed. "Me either."

The girls stared at each other for a long time. Heather's eyes were pleading, and her face looked fragile somehow, as though it might shatter at any moment.

"Look, I don't know what to do," Heather admitted in a quiet voice. "All I know is that I'm not Princess Arabelle. I'm just a girl who knows a lot more about makeup than magic. And I can't pretend to be something I'm not anymore. I can't let all these people die because they believe in me."

"Okay," Veronica said at last. "Just let me get a few things, and I'll come with you."

Heather turned to the door and pulled it open.

Doggett stumbled in, ear first.

"Doggett!" Heather cried.

"Sorry, sorry!" he apologized. "I was just passing by to check on Beastie, and—"

"And you happened to shove your ear against the door?" Veronica demanded.

Doggett planted his hands on his hips. "I heard my name, if you must know," he said, blushing.

Heather huffed. "So you decided to listen to our conversation?"

Doggett narrowed his eyes. "And quite a conversation it was, too," he said in a low voice.

Heather felt the heat rise to her face, and she had to look away from Doggett's eyes. "Doggett . . . " she whispered. Her mind raced as she wondered how much he had overheard. But a single glance at Doggett's face told her that he had heard plenty. He knew everything.

"You." Doggett pointed a thick finger right in Heather's face. "You are not the person I thought you were!"

"I wanted to tell you," Heather pleaded. "But I—"

Doggett shook his head in disgust. "Leaving without saying good-bye." He slapped his palm against his chest. "How did you think that was going to make me feel?"

Heather opened her mouth to speak, then stopped. "Wait—"

"And giving up!" Doggett turned his piercing gaze to

Veronica. "I never would have thought that you . . . " His voice trailed off. Then he shook his head and recovered. "Look, all great leaders have doubts sometimes," he said. "But you have to move past it. Get on with it. There's a job to do."

"Doggett," Veronica said, "don't you get it? This person"—she pointed to Heather—"she isn't Princess Arabelle."

"My name is Heather Simms," Heather added. "I'm not a princess. I'm just . . . nobody."

"Oh, you're nobody." Doggett folded his arms across his chest. "You're the same nobody who survived the Shadow Forest. The same nobody who defeated the Fragile Hag. The same nobody who holds the legendary Dragon Karn on her arm as though he was a bracelet, hey? That nobody?"

Heather looked at her feet. She couldn't even face Doggett. It seemed impossible to believe that he still had faith in her even now. "I'm not the One," Heather said simply.

"Yes, you are!" Doggett cried. "I don't care what your name is or where you came from! These people"—he spread his arms wide, as if to embrace everyone, not only Talan Majeur, but all of Galma—"you're their only hope!"

"But I'm a fake," Heather whispered.

"No, you aren't," Doggett shot back. "Don't ever say that."

Heather looked up at him then, and she felt like his gray eyes were stabbing into her. He had looked at her like that before—like he could only see what was good in her. It hurt her when he looked at her like that. "It's sweet that you believe in me, Doggett," Heather said. "But you're wrong."

"Did you or did you not look into the Orb of Neftalion and have a vision?" Doggett demanded.

"A bad vision," Heather corrected. "A vision of giving

away the Orb. A vision of Veronica leading a battle."

"But a vision nonetheless," Doggett said. "Only the One can do that."

Heather heard the blood rushing in her ears. For a moment, no one spoke.

"He does have a point," Veronica admitted.

"But how can I be the One if I shattered the One?" Heather asked.

"How can you claim you're not the One when you clearly are?" Doggett cried.

"What's the point, Doggett?" Veronica asked. "What's the point of leading these people to their deaths?"

"Who can say?" Doggett asked. "But all I know is that the only certain death is if we do nothing. Because even if we live under her rule, our souls will die. But if we march on the Twilight Queen . . . well, even if we do die, it will be a noble thing and worth doing!"

"God, I wish I was like you," Heather said. "But I'm no hero."

"Princess, I'm no hero either. I'm just a Kiblar elf. But I know one thing. I know that these people need you." Doggett's gray eyes were pleading. "And you can't tell me . . . you can't tell me that everything that's happened—even Strathorn's death—was for nothing." Doggett took a ragged breath and added in a whisper, "Please don't tell me that."

Reaching out with gentle fingers, he took Heather's hand in his. She felt the warmth of his blood beneath the flesh. She looked into his gray eyes. He wore the same look—the look of utter faith. But it didn't hurt as much anymore.

Heather looked at Veronica, her eyes questioning. Veronica

stood motionless for a long time. Finally, her head gave the tiniest tilt, the smallest nod. There it was. Heather's answer.

"Okay," Heather said finally. "Okay, Doggett. We'll do it."

"All right, listen up, everybody," Veronica called, clapping as she strode into the Great Hall, Heather and Doggett behind her. "We've got to talk plan."

King Rellett looked up from the long table, where he was seated with his captains, poring over a map of Galma.

"Okay, King, here's the deal." Heather grabbed an apple from the fruit bowl in front of the king and placed it on the table. "Let's say this apple is a small band of your best fighters."

"And the fruit bowl is the Twilight Queen's castle," Veronica explained.

"What's the banana?" King Rellett asked as Doggett took one.

Doggett flashed the king a guilty look. "Um . . . a snack?"

"Okay, these two grapes," Heather explained, "are me and Doggett. While you and your fighters go to the front of the castle . . . " She positioned the apple before the fruit bowl. Somehow, her experience with the Orb and Doggett's faith had left her with a sense of unshakable confidence. "Doggett and I will work our way around back. . . ." Heather moved the grapes behind the bowl. "And sneak into the castle."

"Madness!" said one of the captains.

"Look, the whole thing is madness," Heather said calmly. "Let's just talk about what has to be done, okay? Anyway, so while you're creating a disturbance, Doggett and I sneak into the castle with the Orb of Neftalion and steal the queen's other two orbs. Then the future of Galma lies in our hands, not hers."

"You can't take the Orb of Neftalion into the queen's castle," the first captain said, pulling his beard. "It's too risky."

"Look, as long as we hold the Orb, we have some power," Heather pointed out. "And the moment we hold all three, it's game over. Besides, it's not like we can leave it behind."

"But what you're saying is impossible," another captain—the short one—put in.

"You got a better plan?" Veronica demanded. The short captain clamped his lips together. Veronica shot him a withering glance. "I didn't think so."

"Look, I know we've only got a slim chance of success," Heather admitted. "But I still think it's our best shot."

King Rellett stared at the fruit on the table. "If the One says it shall be thus," he said, "thus it shall be."

Just then, there was a disturbance at the far side of the hall, and a small voice shouted, "No squirrel shall be denied entry to a stronghold of men! This is an outrage!"

"Chattergee?" Doggett said, half to himself, and a moment later, the squirrel clambered atop a curtain. The men below squawked and gave chase as the squirrel jumped to a carved pillar, then jumped again, landing at Heather's feet.

"It's okay," Heather told the warriors who were closing in on him. "He's with us. I guess," she added, cocking an eyebrow.

"Princess Arabelle," Chattergee said, bowing low. "I am sorry to have left so unceremoniously after we crossed the Fjord of Banata. And I must especially apologize to the very beautiful, lovely, and highly curvaceous Lady Veronica."

Veronica rolled her eyes.

"It's okay," Heather said. "But you might not be so happy

to have come back, Chattergee. We're about to take on the Twilight Queen."

"Why else would Chattergee have returned?" huffed the squirrel. "When I saw the desolation at Talan Majeur, I immediately left to find an army to help us fight."

Veronica snorted. "Yeah, right," she muttered.

"You did?" Doggett cried. "By the nose, Chattergee, I knew you'd come through!"

"Company, march!" Chattergee shouted, and at that moment, there was a great sound of feet on stones and with all of the suddenness of a summer rain, Chattergee's army appeared at the door.

"Chipmunks?" King Rellett said.

"Not just chipmunks," Chattergee cried, missing the sneer in the king's voice. "Badgers, groundhogs, beavers, squirrels . . ." There was a fluttering overhead as birds began to pour into the Great Hall. "Not to mention sparrows, finches, larks, jays, cardinals, chickadees . . . "

"Oh, my—" Veronica gasped as small people, no more than three feet high, with green skin . . . no, not skin; they were made of leaves, with branches for arms and legs . . . no, on second thought, they were people . . . people with rough brown skin like bark and hair like moss . . .

"And shrubbery!" Chattergee said triumphantly.

"Where are the trees?" King Rellett asked.

"They won't fight, the cowards." Chattergee spat on the floor. "But who needs them?" He brandished his tiny sword. "We'll cut the queen's army off at the knees!"

King Rellett looked up at Heather. "Princess . . . " he said in a low voice. "Surely you won't allow these tiny creatures to fight?"

Heather shrugged. "It seems to me we need all the help we can get," she said.

"This is perfect!" Veronica cried.

Heather gave her a dubious look. "Are you kidding?"

A broad grin spread across Veronica's face. "I'm dead serious," she said. "Think *Redwall* meets *Macbeth*."

Heather rolled her eyes. "I've never heard of those guys."

"Not guys," Veronica said, her brown eyes twinkling. "Books."

"Okay," Heather prompted. "So?"

"So?" Veronica wiggled her eyebrows. "I think it's time to set the woodland creatures and Birnam Wood on the attack."

THIRTEEN

Heather tucked her dagger into her belt, then pulled on a greenish-brown cloak. She put her pack on the bed and shoved the Orb of Neftalion inside. Karn looked up at her from the head of the bed, where he was snuggled between two pillows. "Prrt?" the dragon cooed. Giving a long stretch, he stood up and waddled over to the pack, sniffing it inquisitively.

"This thing is heavy," Veronica complained as she slipped a shirt of chain mail over her head. "How am I supposed to move?"

"Just think of it as resistance training," Heather prompted.

"Oh, of course," Veronica shot back, her voice thick with sarcasm as she pulled a cloak over the mail shirt. "I'll just focus on how many pounds I'm sweating off while trying not to get killed."

Heather smirked. "That's right—if you live, you'll have fabulously firm glutes. Karn, stop that," she said pulling the little dragon from her pack, which he had been nibbling. Flashing her a sheepish look, Karn disappeared between two pillows. "Oh, great, now he's going to sulk."

"Aren't you at all concerned that this plan won't work?"

Veronica asked. "You seem freakishly calm to me."

Heather twisted her lips into a rueful smile. "I think I might just be a little burned out on worry," she admitted. "Like, I have too much to think about. There isn't any room in my brain for anything else."

"Yeah," Veronica admitted, sitting down on the bed. "You know what I keep thinking about? How—if, somehow, this crazy plan actually works—we might just get to go home. I keep picturing my mom's face . . . how she'll look when I show up again." Veronica faced the window, and the pinkish twilight glowed on her olive skin. "She must be so freaked out right now, not knowing where I am. . . ."

"Yeah," Heather agreed quietly. An image of her parents flashed in her mind. *I wonder how long it took them to realize I was gone,* she thought. *I wonder if they've even realized it yet.*

There was a knock at the door, and Doggett poked his head in. "Ready?" he asked. Behind him the Moat Beast gurgled and belched.

"I guess," Veronica admitted, hauling herself off the bed.

"Okay, Karnie," Heather said, pulling the pillows away from the headboard. "You stay here and be a good dragon, okay?"

But Karn had disappeared.

"Karnie?" Heather asked, peeking under the bed. "Damn—where did he go?"

"Princess," Doggett said gently. "The army awaits."

"Yeah, yeah . . . " Heather yanked back the covers. No Karn. "Where is he?"

"He'll be fine," Veronica said. "Don't worry. Just be sure to lock the door behind us so he can't get out."

The Moat Beast gurgled in agreement.

Heather sighed. "Okay, fine."

Doggett slung a huge pack over his shoulder and turned to leave.

"What have you got in there?" Heather asked, shouldering her own small bag.

"The Helmet of Unsmellability, of course," Doggett said.

Heather snorted. "You can just leave that behind," she said as she followed Doggett into the hall. "I am so not wearing that stupid helmet."

"As you wish, Princess," Doggett said. "But I will bring it along nevertheless."

Veronica shut the door carefully behind them.

They met King Rellett at the end of the hall. "The army is assembled," he announced. Shoving open the enormous iron doors, the girls looked out over their army of woodland creatures, men, and small shrubbery. A feeble wind blew, rustling the leaves of the Shrub People, and from a distance, the whole thing did look like nothing more than a wide . . . if rather short . . . forest.

At the sight of the princess, the army let out a cheer. The sound vibrations rolled over Heather, settling into her chest, making her giddy. She turned to Veronica. "Are you ready for this?"

Veronica's mouth twisted into a wry smile, and Heather knew that she had felt the effect of the vibrations too. Her dark eyes sparkled. "Let's hit it," she said.

⁊ɔɔ

As the army neared the outskirts of the Twilight Queen's lands, the skies began to grow ever dimmer. The usual twilight was blanketed with a heavy cover of dark gray clouds, and a chill fog hung over the landscape. Heather felt like she had wandered from Galma into a land of eternal November, when even light itself seems to have surrendered to the gray gloom of foul weather.

"This is the work of the Drizzly Witch," Doggett whispered. "She's here with her sister, mark my words."

At the sound of the words *Drizzly Witch*, Heather felt the chill in the air seep deeper into her bones. Suddenly, her brilliant plan didn't seem so brilliant anymore. *What am I doing here?* she wondered as she followed Doggett along the rocky path that led to the rear of the Twilight Queen's stronghold. *I am so unqualified for this task, it's ridiculous.*

She and Doggett had left Veronica, King Rellett, and Chattergee at the edge of the Phantom Wood. Chattergee had looked much fluffier than usual, and Heather assumed his fur reflected his fright. The Phantom Wood was a dark and mysterious place, and King Rellett had explained that men avoided it. Even now, many of the men in the army seemed visibly uncomfortable and cast furtive glances from one to the other, as if to assure themselves that they were not alone.

"Princess," Chattergee had confided, "this squirrel is actually looking forward to attacking the Twilight Queen—if it means getting out of this place."

"I hear you," had been Heather's reply. Somehow, that spooky forest actually made her feel glad that she and Doggett were going another way . . . over the rocks to the queen's castle.

Before they'd parted, Veronica had touched Heather lightly on the shoulder. "Hey," she said. She opened her mouth, like she wanted to say more, but in the end, all she said was, "Don't get killed."

Heather placed her hand over Veronica's fingers. "Right back at you."

"Good luck, Beastie," Doggett told the Moat Beast. "Take care of Veronica, okay?"

The Moat Beast let out a plaintive yelp, but he stayed put behind Veronica as Doggett and Heather started away.

The fake princess was replaying this scene in her mind as she and Doggett peered cautiously from behind a boulder. The exterior of the castle was made of some strange rock—gray and perfectly smooth, almost as though the walls had been carved from a single giant stone. An archway flanked by Ookie guards led inside. There were only two guards, but still—

Clang!

"Jeez, would you please put down that stupid helmet?" Heather hissed as Doggett yanked his pack away from the giant rock. "I already told you, I'm not wearing it."

"You want me to leave it here for Her to find?" Doggett looked horrified.

"What's this?" asked a sibilant voice behind them. "Bickering? Tsk-tsk. You'll never get anywhere with such a negative attitude."

Fear snaked up Heather's spine, disabling her limbs. It took an enormous effort for her to turn her head. . . .

"It's the Drizzly Witch," Doggett said in a low voice.

A short, fat woman with a round face smiled at them. The witch wore a robe that shimmered with different shades of gray, and she resembled a cross between a plump rain cloud and the fairy godmother in Disney's *Cinderella*, Heather thought.

"Well, well, my dears, we meet at last," said the witch. Her face darkened, like the sky before a storm, and suddenly, Heather felt her skin grow damp as the moisture in the air settled over her. "You have met my sister, the Duchess of Breakable Objects, it seems. And now we have a score to settle."

"How did you find us?" Heather asked.

The witch smiled. "Oh, I get around." She cast a vague glance up at the clouds, and suddenly, Heather understood— the Drizzly Witch traveled on the clouds.

Fear clung to Heather's spine, and she had to bite her lip to keep from screaming. Beside her, Doggett shifted uneasily. "If you're going to kill us, then do it quick," he said.

Heather kicked him. "Shut up, Doggett."

The Drizzly Witch stroked her nubby chin. "Yes, the princess is right," she said. "There's no need to resort to violence . . . unless it's absolutely necessary." She narrowed her eyes. "Perhaps we can strike a deal. You do have something I want. . . . " A slow, ugly smile crept up her face. "The Orb of Neftalion."

"Never," Doggett said. "We'll never let you take it for your sister."

"Now, why would I want to give it to her?" the Drizzly Witch asked. "She has two Orbs already. And she's really quite impossible about it. No . . . I think I might like to keep one for myself. So, you see, you'd actually be doing a good deed by handing it over to me."

"Never," Doggett repeated.

"Hmm," the witch said thoughtfully. "Yes, well, it isn't really your decision, is it, Kiblar?" She turned her stormy gaze to Heather. "Come, Princess, hand over the Orb."

Heather felt her fingers twitch as the witch's cloudy eyes flicked to her hand.

"Don't listen to her," Doggett said. "Don't look at her."

"Yes, that's it," the witch hissed. "Hand over the Orb, and avoid a fate like that of your friend, Strathorn."

"No!" At the mention of Strathorn, Doggett lunged toward the witch. With a flick of her wrist, she flung him aside. Doggett landed on his arm with a sickening crack. He cried out in pain and grabbed his elbow.

"Do not toy with me!" the witch cried, and as she did, she seemed to grow a foot, two feet, five feet, ten. . . .

Heather backed against the boulder.

"Hand it over." The witch's voice boomed as she reached her now-giant hand toward Heather.

Suddenly, Heather felt something sharp digging into her shoulder, and a moment later, a giant gust of flame shot forth over her shoulder. It was a column of fire, as wide as a school bus. The witch let out a shriek, then a hiss, and a cloud of warm moisture washed over Heather's skin, opening her pores as though she was getting a facial. In a moment, the witch had disappeared in a cloud of steam.

Doggett seemed momentarily distracted from the pain in his shoulder by the sight. "By the Nose," he whispered.

"Karn?" Heather said, plucking the small dragon from where he stood on her shoulder. He had stowed away in her pack, that sneaky dragon.

Karn butted his head against her neck. He sniffed, and a slight puff of smoke rose from his nostrils.

"I told you he was dangerous," Doggett said.

"Don't be silly," Heather insisted, scratching Karn under the chin. "That was just a little burp."

ᴄⷢᴄ

From the edge of the woods, King Rellett gazed out at the queen's battlements. The fog was thickening, but it was still possible to survey her forces. Along the edge of the top battlements was a row of goblin archers, black arrows held ready in deadly looking bows. The base of the castle was defended by Ookie infantry, clad in their traditional dull green-gray metal. Their foul yellow eyes peered furiously through the long rectangular slits in their visors.

A screech tore through the sky, and one of the Galag Nur wheeled into view.

The king gazed up at the terrifying sight, his expression unmoved. *He looks like he's watching a movie,* Veronica thought as she surveyed his profile—his soft nose, his puffy cheeks. A sudden image of her father popped into her mind—her father as he watched television, the eerie light flickering across his face. He never laughed. Never seemed afraid. Never responded to the images on the screen in any way. He just watched, as the king was watching now.

King Rellett's face betrayed nothing as he raised his fist, then lowered it. The horsemen—his warriors—made no move, but around them, leaves and branches began to twitch, as though they were being blown by a tricksy wind. The ground shook gently; then a wave of earth washed forward.

There go the moles, Veronica thought as she watched the advance guard move out. In the next moment, the shrubbery stepped forward.

"Squirrels right forward," Chattergee commanded from his place at Veronica's horse's neck.

The squirrels fell into line, moving with the shrubbery. The chipmunks were close behind. Chattergee turned to the king. "Do not let your warriors move until Chattergee's signal," he commanded.

Finally, the king's expression changed—his lips twitched into a wry smile. "I wouldn't dream of it, Commander Squirrel."

"Fair lady," Chattergee said to Veronica with a bow, "it is an honor to step onto the field of battle with you. It is quite possible that we go now to our deaths, but these deaths will be as honorable as they are full of pain, suffering, and misery." The squirrel's tail twitched nervously, and he cast a quick glance at the queen's fortifications.

Veronica lifted her eyebrows at the squirrel. "Uh," she said. "Thanks, I guess."

With that, Chattergee bounded off after his army, disappearing into the thick mist.

Veronica watched as, with every beat of her heart, the shrubbery and woodland creatures crept toward the castle. The Ookies still hadn't noticed that the woods were drawing near. In the next moment, the wave of earth reached the queen's outer walls.

Seconds passed and then—a shout.

"A breach!" shouted a deep, ugly voice. "A breach!"

Whizz! Whizz!

Arrows sliced through the air, bouncing off nearby rocks. A cheer went up and the woodland creatures surged forward. Veronica was overwhelmed by wild flapping. She ducked as a cloud of birds streamed over her head, plummeting toward the battlements.

"Men! To the gates!" King Rellett's voice boomed. The horses plowed forward, and Veronica found herself galloping headlong toward the castle. After that, things began to happen quickly.

Above, the Galag Nur wheeled and screamed, ready to attack. But the finches and chickadees were too small to grab. They slipped through the talons of the giant crows and made right for their eyes, pecking madly.

"Argh!"

A line of goblin archers staggered and fell under a tremendous glob of stinking goo. Veronica looked over her shoulder, where the Moat Beast was heaving piles of sludge at the battlements. The goblins retaliated with arrows, but the Moat Beast flicked them away in annoyance and lobbed another pile of goop at the archers.

Meanwhile, the Ookies—who have a natural fear of mice and rats—were driven to positive fits by the squirrels and chipmunks, who were biting their ankles.

"They have rabies!" shouted one of the Ookies.

"Stomp them!" shouted another, but the small animals were too nimble. Soon, the Ookies were stomping like mad and stabbing each other in the feet with their swords in a desperate attempt to kill the small creatures.

The moles, too, were doing their job, destabilizing the earth beneath the retaining wall. An entire section had collapsed already, thanks to their work, and the king's warriors made their way to the chasm, ready to race through it.

"It's working!" Veronica shouted in disbelief. "We're win—"

Boom.

The ground shook. Veronica's horse stopped short and refused to take another step forward. Beside her, the king's horse had pulled up also.

"What was that?" Veronica asked.

Boom.

Boom.

"I'm not sure I want to know," the king confessed.

BOOM. BOOM! BOOM!

The goblins cleared the battlements, and the Ookies scrambled away—many of them limping—in fear.

Bricks and stones rained down as the monster appeared. It was enormous. Tall as the queen's tallest tower. It stood like a giant, but with a misshapen face, pale fish-belly skin, and black lips. It looked like the very vision of death.

"Gorak," King Rellett whispered.

The front line of moles, poor blind things, had no idea that a horrible monster was hovering over them.

"Go back!" Chattergee shouted. "Go back!"

"What did he say?" asked one of the moles.

"I think he said, 'Attack,'" replied the other, and in the next moment, the line of moles surged ahead.

With a single sweep of his hand, the monster grabbed the moles and stuffed them into his mouth.

Chattergee's armies let out a collective scream as the Gorak lurched forward, sweeping destruction before it.

✶⊙✶

"Don't touch it," Doggett said as Heather reached for his arm.

Her fingers hovered above the twisted blue flesh. She was no doctor, but she knew a broken bone when she saw one.

Doggett looked up at her, his eyes cloudy with pain. "I'm fine."

"You're not."

"Princess," the Kiblar said in a low, steady voice, "I'm fine." He struggled to stand, and Heather helped him, hauling him to his feet with his good arm. "Thanks," Doggett said through gritted teeth. "At least I'm right-handed, and she only got my left arm."

Heather peered down at the Ookie guards. Not far from their large webbed feet, along the edge of the smooth castle wall, was a hatch. This, King Rellett's spies had told her, was the entranceway to the drains beneath the castle. It was narrow, they said, and dark, and Heather wasn't looking forward to sliding her way in there, even if there was any way to get past the Ookies. . . .

Doggett leaned forward for a better look.

Clang!

Heather and Doggett froze as one of the Ookies—the tall one—started. "You hear that?" he asked the short one.

Heather's hand slipped into Doggett's and he squeezed.

"Eh—we're right above the dungeon," the other Ookie replied. "Probably just one of the queen's torture devices."

The other Ookie peered around suspiciously but eventually settled back down.

Releasing the breath she hadn't realized she was holding, Heather shook her hand free of Doggett's. "Oh my God, leave the dumb-ass helmet," Heather hissed. "It's going to get us killed!"

Doggett looked hurt. "It'll save us before the end, I'm telling you," he insisted, hitching it higher onto his shoulder. He winced.

Heather shook her head. That elf could be shockingly stubborn.

She went back to peering at the guards. Also according to King Rellett's spies, the chamber that held the Orbs was not far from this entrance. But how were they going to get into the drain with the guards standing there? And how could they be sure that the spies' information was reliable?

Just then, a horn blew. There was shouting and a sickening splat, as though a vat of pudding had just landed against a slate wall. Heather knew what those sounds meant—the battle had begun.

One of the guards—the tall one—gripped his battle-ax and looked around.

Heather followed Doggett as the Kiblar picked his way down the knoll. When he reached the boulder closest to the entrance, he stopped and whispered, "How will we sneak into the drain?"

Heather shook her head. It was impossible. That much was obvious. The drain was right there, out in the open. "Maybe we can create some kind of distraction," she suggested.

"Like what?" Doggett asked.

Picking up a baseball-sized rock, Heather tossed it toward the guards.

Have I mentioned that she is bad at sports? Well, Heather had intended to throw the rock to the side of the guards, near their feet, to distract them. But as the rock sailed through the air, it was clear from the very first moment that its trajectory was off. It flew out of its arc and smacked right into the face of the taller Ookie, who let out a shout and stumbled backward.

Seeing his chance, Doggett let out a cry and lunged toward the guards, sword drawn.

The guard with the battle-ax darted forward, but Doggett was quick—he ran his sword through the belly of the injured guard.

But the tall guard swung his ax.

"Doggett!" Heather screamed. The Kiblar dodged the blow, and sparks flew from the stone where the ax landed a foot from his head.

Stumbling, Doggett fell to the ground. The Ookie raised his ax, and Heather felt her heart race in panic. She dug her hand into her pack, searching for something, anything. Her fingers wrapped around a cold, hard object.

"Ouch!"

As the cold burned her palm, Heather's first instinct was to let go of the Orb, but she fought it. Keeping her hand wrapped around the bag, she stumbled forward. As though sensing the danger, Karn tightened his hold on her arm.

The Ookie turned, hearing the noise behind him.

Doggett's eyes were round. "Princess, what are you—"

"Don't look at me!" Heather shouted as she pulled the Orb of Neftalion from the pack. Brilliant light cut through the twilight, blinding the Ookie. "Now, Doggett!"

With a fierce jab, Doggett thrust his sword through the Ookie's back. The ghoulish creature barely had time to register his surprise before he fell to the ground, dead.

The Orb blinked out, and Heather tucked it back into her pack.

Doggett stared at her in awe. "That was amazing," he said.

Heather smiled. "You weren't so bad either," she told him.

Swallowing hard, Doggett hauled himself to his feet, then brushed himself off. "So . . . " he said awkwardly after a few moments. "Should we . . . should we sneak down the drain?"

Heather flashed a dubious look in the direction of the narrow, dingy grate. "I don't know about you," she said, "but now that the guards are dead, I'm going in through the door." Turning on her heel, she headed through the castle entrance.

Doggett hesitated a moment, then followed. Inside, the castle was cool, almost as though the smooth gray stone was radiating cold. Aside from the shouts and noise coming from outside, the place was eerily quiet. Torches flickered along the wall, giving off a pale greenish light. "So unflattering," Heather pointed out. "You couldn't pay me to try on bathing suits in this light."

"What?" Doggett asked.

Heather rolled her eyes. "Nothing."

They came to the end of a long hall. After a moment's hesitation, they turned right. The hall led up a flight of stairs, then down a flight, then zigzagged like a drunken man until it finally branched off in two directions again.

"Which way?" Doggett asked miserably.

Heather looked around. "Aren't we back where we started?"

Doggett bit his lip. "I think you're right."

Heather shrugged. "Left, then."

She and Doggett hurried down the hall. Neither of them said what they were both thinking—that the sooner they found the Orbs, the sooner the fighting would end . . . which meant that fewer would die.

This hall led up a spiral staircase, then down a long, long corridor. It cut quickly to the left, then led down a wide staircase, and finally spat them out exactly where they started.

"It's a maze," Heather said.

"We should have known," Doggett moaned.

"What now?" Absently, she reached into the bag for the Orb, tracing her fingers along its smooth surface. She had been doing that often lately—making sure it was there. But this time, something about it was different. "It's warm."

"Really?" Doggett's eyebrows flew up.

"Wait a minute," Heather said, wrapping her fingers around the Orb. She took two steps to the right, and the heat faded. Four steps to the left, and the warmth was back. "I think it knows where the other Orbs are," Heather said.

"We might as well try it," Doggett told her.

"Prrt?" Karn's tail swished.

She hurried down the hallway. But after thirty paces, the Orb grew cool. She backed up, and it grew warm again. "But there's no door here!" Heather cried in frustration.

"Maybe we should rest a moment," Doggett said. He put down the pack with the Helmet of Unsmellability. At that moment, the bag tipped over—and fell through the wall.

Heather and Doggett gaped at each other. "It's just an illusion!" she cried, stepping through after the helmet. Doggett followed. Sure enough, there was a long expanse of gray hall beyond the wall. Doggett picked up his pack and followed as Heather gripped the Orb. This time, she closed her eyes. Soon, she was racing through the castle, stepping through paintings, into mirrors, even walking over what looked like a gap over a screaming abyss.

Finally, they reached a set of enormous, intricately carved wooden doors. Heather's heart began beating quickly, like bird wings fluttering against a cage. The room was emanating fear.

She picked up her foot to cross the threshold. It paused in midair.

"I can't do it," she said. "I can't go inside."

Doggett's left arm hung limply at his side, so he reached for her with his right. He looked deeply into her eyes. "Do you want to wear the Helmet of Unsmellability?" he asked.

Heather glared at him . . . and put her foot down. In the next moment, she found herself in the room.

Doggett was right beside her. "Whoa."

Karn purred approvingly.

It was as though when Heather crossed through the doorway, she had passed through an invisible wall of fear. From the outside, the room had appeared gray and cold. It had looked bare, with nothing but tall, Gothic arches sliding toward the ceiling. But once they were inside, the room looked very different. The light was still dim, true, but a warm, buttery glow was coming from a large fireplace. The walls were lined with books, and it made Heather think of movies she had seen in which rich British people sat around in their country libraries. Intricately woven carpets of deep maroon and slate blue lined the floors. There was a comfortable leather couch and two luxurious chairs. Behind the couch was a heavy wooden table, and on the table stood three tall silver (or platinum, perhaps? Heather wasn't sure) stands that looked almost like candlesticks. Two held small glass spheres. They were cloudy with a purple haze and didn't even reflect the bright orange flames from the fireplace. The third stand was empty.

"The Orbs," Doggett whispered.

Looking around, Heather realized that the room was filled

LISA PAPADEMETRIOU

with magical accoutrements. On a low table lay a silver bowl filled with dark liquid that Heather hoped wasn't blood. A dark cauldron hunched heavily on a high table in the corner. Purplish flames danced inside the rim of the bowl, sending up an occasional green spark.

"That's it?" she asked. "All I have to do is take the Orbs, and we're out of here?"

Karn yawned.

Doggett looked doubtful. "I don't think . . . "

But Heather had already taken a step toward the Orbs. She reached out, but the moment her hand crossed the edge of the table, an alarm so loud she felt like her brain was exploding filled the room. Something shifted, and dark arms reached up from the floor itself, grabbing Heather by the ankles. She felt the cold, clammy chill of their inhuman touch.

"Doggett!" Heather screamed. "The doors!"

Immediately, Doggett dashed for the exit, but the heavy wooden doors clanged shut before he could reach them.

I can still get them, Heather thought, turning back toward the Orbs. She reached for the one nearest to her. . . . Too far. She strained. . . .

A hand reached out and slapped her fingers.

"Ouch!" Heather cried.

A tall figure stepped out of the shadows. It wore a long, black cloak and was as thin as the Drizzly Witch had been round. The only part of the Twilight Queen's face that was visible was her cruel, crimson mouth.

"You aren't too bright," the red mouth sneered, "are you?"

Heather didn't get a chance to answer that, because

Doggett let out a fearsome shout and lunged toward the queen, sword raised.

The queen hardly moved. She simply flicked her hand through the air as though she was warning away a bothersome gnat, and Doggett flew across the room. He slammed against the wall and fell to the ground in a heap.

"Doggett!" Heather screamed. She tried to run to him, but the clammy fingers held her fast. She fell half to her knees.

Doggett didn't move.

"That was fun," said the Twilight Queen. "Almost as fun as killing you will be."

Heather narrowed her eyes. "Oh, yeah?" she said. "Well, guess what? I've got a secret weapon. It's time to get toasty!" She held up her wrist, where Karn was nuzzling happily. "Get her, Karn!"

Karn blinked at Heather. "Prrt?"

"Don't look at me!" Heather shouted, pointing at the queen. "Get her!"

Karn stared at Heather's finger.

With a derisive snort, the Queen of Twilight unleashed a ball of fire at the dragon.

A scream choked in Heather's throat as the fireball hit Karn. But it simply bounced off the dragon's head. Karn looked at the ball of fire as it rolled across the room, and he darted after it. He batted it around happily for a moment, then started to chew on it.

Heather sighed. "Hopeless."

"I hope that wasn't your secret weapon," the Queen of Twilight said. "Because I think he's occupied. And now, Princess, I'll take what is mine."

FOURTEEN

"Bloooorrrgg!" cried the Gorak as it stomped furiously into the fray.

"It just stepped on eight Ookies," King Rellett announced. "That's good."

In fact, the Gorak had just fallen backward on its haunches and was now occupied in picking squashed Ookies from between its toes. But the respite didn't last long. In one moment, the Gorak stuffed its foot in its hideous mouth and licked the Ookie guts with its enormous, horrible brown tongue, and in the next, the monster was back on its feet.

"Ech," Veronica said as the Gorak belched and stood up. "Disgusting."

As if on cue, a huge glob of Moat Beast slime glided through the air overhead, landing with a wet smack against the Gorak's skull. The Gorak roared, then wiped off the slime and flung it back at Chattergee's army, wiping out a battalion of chipmunks.

The small woodland creatures scrambled about ineffectually as Chattergee chattered instructions. "To the left! The left! No, no—to Chattergee's left!"

"Who's Chattergee?" one of the woodchucks asked another.

The other woodchuck didn't even reply—he was too busy running away.

Some of the shrubbery had engaged the Ookies in branch-to-hand combat, and from Veronica's seat atop her horse, it looked as though the ground was a swirling, seething sea of green. Occasionally, a dagger or sword caught the light, winking playfully.

"Growr!" Bending down, the Gorak reached into the sea of Ookies and shrubbery and shoved a handful of green into its mouth. The shrubs screamed as their branches broke with a crackle under the Gorak's cruel teeth.

Despite the fact that the monster had just eaten part of their own forces along with the shrubbery, the Ookies seemed emboldened by the Gorak. With a fierce shout of triumph, their line surged ahead as goblin arrows whizzed toward the line of men on horseback. Three of them fell as King Rellett pressed onward.

With a mighty crunch and scrape, the Gorak tore an enormous chunk from the queen's stone battlements and heaved it at the line of men. Two captains and their horses barely had time to scream before they were crushed beneath the smooth gray stone.

That thing will kill us all, Veronica realized as she watched the Gorak swipe wildly at the brave group of squirrels that were attempting to bite it between the toes. Veronica kicked up her horse as, with a single step, the squirrels were no more.

Ziip! Ziip!

"Veronica!" King Rellett shouted. "No!"

Fierce dark arrows flew past as Veronica thrust herself into battle. Luckily, her horse was one of King Rellett's finest and wore battle armor of its own. It was used to the noise and confusion of battle and seemed instinctively to know that Veronica wanted to go to the scene of greatest danger.

But just before she reached the monster, a spear pierced her horse's armor. The horse sank to its knees.

"Oo-ha!" the Ookie cried.

In one fluid motion, Veronica fired with her crossbow and leaped from her horse. The Ookie lay dead at her feet.

"Blooragh!" the Gorak roared, aiming another rock—this time at King Rellett.

Veronica dashed over to its foot—her head barely came to the top of its shin—and drove a crossbow bolt into the soft, thin flesh behind its knee. Howling in pain, the Gorak dropped his boulder—this time on the top of a troop of goblin archers.

Green blood splattered Veronica as she yanked the bolt from the Gorak's knee and plunged it into the monster's toe. The Gorak screeched in fury and reached for her.

"Oof!"

Her lungs constricted as the Gorak's fingers closed around her ribs. Hot, rank breath that smelled like a mixture of dead dog on a summer day and year-old cottage cheese washed over Veronica, making her feel sick, as the Gorak brought her before its eyes, peering at the tiny thing that had caused it so much pain. *Its teeth are as long as my brother's left arm,* Veronica thought as it lifted her to its lips. *And I can't believe that's the last thought I'll ever have. . . .*

But at that moment, a horn blew. It was a fresh, clear note

that made Veronica think of bells, and of silver light on clear blue water, and of mossy trees in deep woods. It was a sound she knew—not from her memory, but from her imagination. A thousand pages in a thousand stories told her that a sound like this could only mean one thing. . . .

Elves.

The Gorak paused, mouth still open, and stared off into the distance. Veronica twisted in its hot, sweaty palm until she could see what he saw—along the ridge was a line of elfin riders. And behind them . . . giants. At the head of the column was a figure in a red robe. He rode a black horse and carried a long staff.

Who are they? Veronica thought. *Which side? Which side are they on?*

It was as though the field of battle had fallen silent. Weapons clashed and warriors fought, but Veronica felt like the scene itself was holding its breath, waiting. Waiting to see what would happen next.

A slight breeze blew across her face, lifting her damp brown bangs away from her forehead. And in the next moment, the breeze caught the pale green banner along the column of elves. The silver tree unfurled at the head of the army.

Ibharn.

The red figure raised his staff, and as one body, the warriors descended into the fray.

A horrible scream rose from the Ookies, and then there was the sound of clashing metal as the elves attacked. Arrows whizzed by—all futilely—as the giants heaved boulders at the battlements. In the next moment, Veronica felt herself falling, falling, as the Gorak dropped her and turned, to run into the castle . . . and then everything went black.

ᴖᴖᴖ

There was hardly time to register the twitch of the queen's scarlet smirk before she lunged at Heather. With a yelp, Heather tried to dart away, but the clammy hands still held her feet firmly against the wooden floor. The sudden motion of her body sent Heather pitching forward, and her arms flailed wildly as she struggled to right herself. It was no use—she fell right into the queen's arms.

"Get off me, you klutz!" shouted the Queen of Twilight. She shoved Heather aside.

But Heather had twisted her fingers into the queen's shadowy robe, and as she fell again (backward, this time), she yanked the cape clean off the queen's body.

Thud!

"Ow!" Heather cried. She fell to the floor, the gray cape billowing around her softly.

The Queen of Twilight let out an ugly shriek and tossed a mottled gray arm across her eyes. "It burns!" she shouted, staggering away from the lamp on the table.

Perhaps surprised by the queen's weakness, the clammy hands on the floor fumbled at Heather's feet, and she kicked at them. The fingers faltered for only a moment, but that was enough. Heather scrambled away.

The queen staggered against the table as Heather made for Doggett. She touched his neck—a pulse! She nearly shouted for joy. He was alive! *Now all we have to do is get out of here,* Heather thought, looking up at the doors. No good. They were locked.

"You hideous witch!" the queen screamed.

Right, Heather thought as she stared at the scrawny figure before her. *That's like disco calling sixties retro "tired."* The queen might have been pretty once, but she definitely looked like her evil deeds had caught up with her. *Like that picture of Dorian Green,* Heather thought, proud to have come up with a literary reference for once in her life. *Only the queen is the picture.* She was tall and slim, that much Heather would give her, but her skin was mottled gray and green. Her hair was sparse and had a greenish tinge, like fuzz on a boiled egg. And she was wearing a long greenish gown that really did nothing for her. *Hello, who's your designer, House of Burlap?* Heather thought. It was a mystery what color the queen's eyes were—since they were squeezed shut tight against the dim light in the room—but her nose was way too long, with wide nostrils. *She's right to play up her mouth with the red lipstick,* Heather decided. *Really, it's her best feature. . . .*

"I'll kill you!" the queen screamed.

Except when she's flipping that attitude out of it, Heather amended mentally, darting behind a nearby curtain.

The queen staggered away from the table, pointing her nose in the air. Her nostrils flared as she sniffed. "You can't hide from me," the queen announced. Sniffing again, she took a step toward Heather. "Your scent has changed, but I can still smell your fear, Princess," the queen said. "It's the same smell that gave away your parents as they tried to hide from me . . . the night I killed them." A smile curled at the queen's lips, and she sniffed again. "This will be so easy."

Heather bit her lip. *Crap!* she thought. *I can't believe Doggett was right about that stupid Helmet of Unsmellability!* But she couldn't reach it now. The queen was standing between her and Doggett. *Why do I always think of things too late?*

The queen stepped closer.

If only there was some way to throw her off, Heather thought desperately. *Like if I could throw my smell the way some people throw their voices . . .*

Wait a minute!

Heather plunged her hand into her pocket and pulled out a perfume atomizer. She leaned as far out of the curtain as she dared. . . .

Squirt!

The queen sniffed again. She hesitated, then headed toward the smell of the perfume as Heather dodged away, beside a bookcase.

Reaching out a black-nailed claw, the queen ripped through the empty space that had just been filled with perfume. "Argh!" the Queen of Twilight shouted in frustration, then sniffed again. "You can't hide forever," she announced. "I'll find you!" She took a step toward Heather's bookcase.

Heather squirted again and again the queen padded off in another direction as Heather scrambled to hide beneath a table. Sniffing like a hound dog on cocaine, the queen lashed out, knocking several objects—a crystal vase with a black rose, a silver plate, a golden box the size of a deck of cards—from the table. The vase shattered and the silver plate rolled away, but the golden box landed right in front of Heather, flipping open. Heather was too busy watching the queen to notice the box . . . until it spoke up.

"Hello, Princess from Hell," the box said spitefully. "Remember me?"

Her eyes wide with horror, Heather reached out to shut the box, but it was too late.

"She's down here!" shrieked the box. "Get her!"

Blue eyes peered down at her from the folds of a deep scarlet robe. The figure had a long white beard, but his face was smooth, without a wrinkle. There was something about the owner of the face that seemed familiar to Veronica, as though she had known him when he was older . . . but that wasn't possible. She was confused. . . .

"My head hurts," Veronica said.

The edges of the blue eyes crinkled slightly. "You're lucky you aren't dead," the old-young man said.

Veronica gasped. It was the voice that did it—the voice was unchanged, even though the face was altered. "Strathorn," she whispered.

The old-young man nodded slightly.

Veronica struggled onto her elbows. "I knew it!" she screeched, then surrendered to a fit of coughing. She took a deep breath and managed to choke out, "I knew it was a psych-out!"

Strathorn's eyebrows crept upward in confusion. "What?"

"I knew that bloodsnake couldn't kill you!" Veronica insisted.

Strathorn nodded serenely. "It tried . . . but it couldn't kill me," he agreed.

The happiness coursing through Veronica's body was enough to make her feel like she could take on the Gorak single-handed. She knew that she had to get inside the castle to help Heather, but she couldn't go—not yet. "So— what happened?"

Strathorn sighed. "Well, when the bloodsnake swallowed me, I dropped my blade. It was dark and fearsome inside the snake, but eventually I realized that my sword must be lodged in his belly. It took several hours, but I managed to feel my way through the muck of his innards. Let me tell you, that snake had eaten some foul things. . . ."

Veronica cleared her throat. "Um, yeah—okay . . . "

"But eventually, my fingers wrapped around the handle of my blade. I spent several moments collecting my strength, but I was weak after several hours of being partially digested. . . ."

"You know, I'm not sure I really want to hear—"

"But once I had gathered myself, I thrust the blade through the snake's belly. Blood gushed everywhere, like a fountain of red! I was bathed in the lifeblood of the Snake of Nithral! It entered my body, streaming into my ears, dripping beneath my eyelids, pressing past my lips. . . ."

Veronica thought she might barf.

"And for a moment, I feared that many more snakes would be born of the blood. But I reached for my staff, and—though my magic was barely an ember—I summoned everything I had. I unchained the great snake's magic and took it upon myself. And now—I am Strathorn the Red! The life of the Blood Snake of Nithral flows in my veins!" He stared down at her, triumphant.

Veronica didn't know what to say. "Um . . . ew?"

Strathorn blinked. "Anyway, then I remembered what you had said—about the giants being important. So I headed south to try to gain their help. But when I reached them, I found Ibharn already there with a troop of elves."

"Yeah—what happened there?"

"Well, it seems that once Ibharn refused the quest and let a 'servant' go in his place—he became persona non grata at the palace. The Kiblars began refusing to do his errands, and Linnea stopped talking to him. So he tried to catch up with us. But, as you remember, we were supposed to go to the Drizzly Witch's palace. When he arrived, he found it deserted, so he pressed on to the giants."

"And that's where you found him."

"Indeed."

Veronica smiled. "So it all turned out all right in the end," she said.

Strathorn cocked a white eyebrow. "Well—it's not quite the end . . . is it?"

A loud roar shook the castle.

"Good point," Veronica said, scrambling to her feet.

Before she knew what she was doing, she found herself running toward the queen's castle. But Strathorn was faster.

"Quickly!" he shouted over his shoulder. "We have to find the central chamber—before it's too late!"

꘎꘎꘎

"Shut up, you stupid box!" Heather shouted, lunging at the golden objet d'art. With a furious growl, the queen reached under the table. Her nails dug into Heather's calf. "Ow!"

"Ha, ha! It's no worse than you deserve," the box taunted. It was just a finger length beyond Heather's reach. She tried to dig her fingernails into the floor as the Queen of Twilight hauled her backward, out from under the heavy wooden table. Heather kicked furiously, but it was no use. The queen was freakishly strong.

"Bye-bye!" said the box.

The queen grunted with effort as one final heave freed Heather from the slight protection that the table had offered.

"Get off me, bitch!" Heather screamed.

"I'll enjoy killing you," snarled the queen. "Perhaps I'll make you into a lovely sculpture so that I can look at it and always remember this tender moment." Reaching into her pocket, the queen pulled out a long, slender wand.

The Fragile Hag's wand.

The witch stroked Heather's chin tenderly with the wand, and her crimson lips curled upward as she squinted blindly at her captive. "I do wish I could see the look of fear in your eyes," the queen hissed.

Suddenly, a fierce war cry sounded from the corner of the room.

"What the—?" The queen turned just in time to see a short figure with a giant head lunging at her with a sword raised in his right hand. She dodged away awkwardly, but not quite in time—Doggett's sword landed on the Fragile Hag's wand, slicing it in half.

"Doggett!" Heather cried.

"Princess?" It was him, all right—and he was wearing the Helmet of Unsmellability. Visor down, for maximum smellessness. Of course, he couldn't see a thing.

Which puts me in the minority, Heather thought as she watched the queen stumble backward.

"You ruined my wand!" the witch screeched. She lurched forward but managed to trip over Karn, who was still chasing his ball of fire. The queen went sprawling and the fireball landed on the couch, sending it up in flames. Karn leaped onto the fire and rolled about in delight.

"To the left!" Heather shouted as Doggett lurched away, swinging his sword wildly. "More left!"

"Aha!" Doggett cried as he swung his sword into the velvet curtains. "I've got you!" The heavy drapes swung back, wrapping him in their folds. "She's got me! Princess—save yourself!" The curtains fluttered and bounced as Doggett struggled to free himself.

Heather sighed.

"Hotter, hotter!" shouted the golden box as the Queen of Twilight crawled along the floor toward Heather. Sensing movement from the drapes to her right, she veered off. "No! No!" the box cried. "Now you're colder!"

Damn you, box! Heather thought. Skirting the queen, she pulled the box from beneath the table.

"She's right here!" the box screeched. "She's got m—"

Heather flipped closed the lid and tossed the box into the cauldron of fire.

"Aiiiiiiiiiiiiiiiiiiiiiiiiiiiiieeeeeeeeeeeeeeeeeeeeeeeeeeeeeeeeeee!"

The purple flames danced, sending up a shower of green sparks, as the fire gobbled up the golden box.

"Box?" the queen cried. "Box!"

There was a thud at the wooden doors.

Crap, Heather thought, *Ookie guards!*

"Aha!" Suddenly freeing himself from the drapes, Doggett lunged in the direction of the queen's voice. He missed her by a yard and a half, driving his sword deep into the table. Nearby, Karn had begun nibbling on one of the beautiful carpets, the edge of which was in flames.

"Who's this?" the queen asked, sniffing near Doggett. "I don't smell anything. . . ."

The thudding against the doors was growing more intense as Doggett struggled with his sword.

"Stand back!" said a voice from behind the doors.

Thinking fast, Heather dug out her perfume. She squeezed the atomizer, spraying the queen right on the nose.

"Argh!" the queen screeched in frustrated rage.

The doors exploded inward in a shower of splinters and wood chips, and the smoke-thickened air grew even more viscous as two figures darted into the room. The first wore a red robe. He passed his staff over the burning couch and carpet, and the flames blew out. Karn looked up in surprise and sniffed at the smoking edge of the carpet. The little dragon flashed an accusing look at the figure, who slowly pulled back his red hood.

"Strathorn?" Heather said just as Doggett managed to yank his sword free of the wooden table. "You look great—did you have some work done?"

"Doggett!" Veronica shouted as she stepped farther into the room.

"Die, witch!" Doggett shouted.

"No, wait!" Heather cried, but it was too late—Doggett had lurched directly at Veronica, who stepped aside as the Kiblar went careening into the wall.

Unfortunately, Veronica stepped just a fraction of an inch too close to the queen, who lashed out and caught her by the leg. With a fierce yank, she pulled Veronica to the floor beside her and held a razor-sharp fingernail against her neck.

"Stand back, wizard!" the queen shouted. "Or I'll kill this one."

"Let her go!" Heather cried.

The queen laughed harshly. "And who's going to make me? You?"

Heather looked into Veronica's eyes, seeing her fear as the fingernail sank farther into the flesh of her neck. A bead of blood appeared against the skin.

We can't give up now, Heather thought. *Not when we're so close to getting home.* . . . Reaching into her pocket, Heather pulled out the only card she had left to play. "Let her go or I drop the Orb into the cauldron," Heather announced, holding the smooth round globe over the dancing flames.

"Heather, what are you doing?" Veronica screeched.

"Heather?" Strathorn asked. "Who's Heather?"

"You wouldn't dare . . . " the queen said. But she didn't sound sure.

"Oh, I'd dare," Heather announced. "See—I don't give a flying flip about this thing." She tossed the Orb into the air, catching it just before it hit the flames. "So believe me, I'd dare."

There was a clang and a clatter as Doggett pulled the helmet from his head and let it drop to the floor. "Princess—" he began.

"Don't call me that," Heather snapped. "I'm not your princess, and you know it."

"I think I've missed something important," Strathorn said, half to himself.

"I knew it!" the queen screeched. "I knew your scent had changed! You aren't Arabelle at all, are you?"

"Would someone explain to me what's going on?" Strathorn demanded.

Heather didn't even bother to reply. "Listen to me closely,

witch," she said, dropping her voice an octave. "You're going to let go of her, and I'm going to hand over the Orb."

"Don't do this," Veronica begged.

Heather ignored her. "Then you're going to send me and my friend back to where we came from."

The queen sneered. "Done."

Heather narrowed her eyes. "How do I know you'll keep your word?"

The queen rolled her eyes. "I swear by the Orbs," she said in a bored voice.

Heather looked dubiously at Strathorn.

"That'll do it," the wizard said with an absent nod.

"No," Veronica said. Her voice rose to a scream as the queen pulled her finger away from her neck. "No!"

Doggett didn't say anything, but his expression spoke volumes.

"Don't look at me like that," Heather snapped at him. "Don't you get it? We've already lost here, okay? And I've got to . . . I've got to get home. . . ."

Veronica stumbled as the queen shoved her toward Heather. But Veronica wouldn't even look in Heather's direction as she placed the Orb in the queen's mottled greenish-gray claw. Suddenly, Heather recognized it—this moment. It was her vision. So it had come true after all.

The queen held the Orb close to her eyes. Snow fell softly within the crystal, swirling around a dark tower. "The Orb of Neftalion," she whispered. "I have all three Orbs! Darkness shall reign!"

As she stared at the Orb in the queen's hand, Veronica's eyes widened in realization. Catching her eye, Heather nodded.

Quickly, she reached into her pocket as Veronica drove her dagger into the witch's shoulder. The queen let out a cry of surprise and pain just as Heather pulled the real Orb of Neftalion from her pocket. The room exploded in light.

"Doggett!" Veronica shouted as the queen clawed at her face. Strathorn brought his staff down on the queen's back.

"Oof!"

The Kiblar realized what was happening and lunged toward the table for the other two Orbs, but his ankles were caught by the guardian floorboards. No good.

"Karn!" Heather shouted. "Fetch!"

The little dragon looked at Heather's hand, and she pretended to throw in the direction of the Orbs. Seeing the two balls, Karn bounded over to them. He stopped at one, then hesitated. He looked at the other one in confusion.

"Come on, Karn!" Heather shouted. "Come on!"

Suddenly, the little dragon seemed to make a decision. He grabbed one in his mouth. Then he grabbed the other.

"Way to go, Karn!" Heather shouted, just as one of the Orbs dropped from Karn's mouth. Heather groaned as Karn tripped after the lost Orb.

The queen zapped a fireball at Strathorn, and he deflected it. *Boom. Boom! Boom!*

"Okay, just bring me one of them, Karn," Heather urged desperately, but the little dragon wasn't paying attention. He bounced after the Orb, then snapped it up in his jaws. This time, the other Orb fell out.

"Either one," Heather said. "Either one!"

Karn nuzzled at the Orb, pushing it forward . . . unfortunately, in the opposite direction from where Heather was standing. She was about to scream in frustration when a hand reached down and grabbed the Orb. Straightening up, Doggett tossed it to Heather.

She caught it single-handed.

In a moment, Karn bounded toward her, and suddenly Heather found herself holding all three Orbs. The purple haze that had filled the other two Orbs lifted. Then, deep in their cores, the Orbs began to glitter, then glow. . . . Like a flame licking the edge of a newspaper, the two silver spheres caught the light of the Orb of Neftalion, and the brilliance that had lit the room only moments before doubled, then tripled. The light was so bright that Heather felt like she was being sucked into the center of the sun, and yet she found that she could look at the Orbs. And in them, she saw the entire future of Galma, the joy that would last two hundred years now that all three Orbs were in her hands.

The light spilled through the room, pouring down the hall, threatening to lift the castle off its very foundations.

A brain-splitting screech shuddered through the room, threatening to tear the tapestries from the walls. It was as though the castle itself was screaming. It took Heather a moment to realize that the noise was coming from the witch, who appeared to be . . . shrinking.

At the same time, Strathorn seemed to be growing. It wasn't that these two magic entities were exactly changing size, but more that the space that surrounded them was shifting. Heather was struck with the realization that the queen's power was fleeing her . . . while Strathorn's was flooding back.

After a moment, the brilliance of the Orbs seemed to diminish. At first, Heather wasn't sure it was really happening, and then she was certain. The Orbs were dimming. They grew paler and paler until they sat in her hands, glowing only slightly.

"Wow," Veronica said.

"You've killed me!" the queen cried. "You've killed me, you little turd!"

"Oh, be quiet," Strathorn commanded. "You aren't dead. You're going to stand trial, just as you should, and you'll probably spend a lot of time enjoying the hospitality of your own dungeons."

The ex-queen let out a miserable wail.

Boom! Boom! Boom! "Growr!" In that instant, a hideous yellow Gorak eye appeared at the door.

Veronica cowered, waiting for the worst, but the beast bashed his hand through the door frame and reached for the wretched queen.

Strathorn the Red bolted forward, raising his staff. Light flashed from the polished wood, streaming toward the Gorak.

The beast only had time to let out a confused, "Urt?" before it burst into a shower of pink and white rose petals. They fell softly to the floor, creating a carpet from the hallway to the room.

Strathorn grinned. "I've still got it," he said, half to himself.

"No! Nooooo!" the queen screamed as the flower petals scattered across her ruined Oriental carpet. "My beautiful Gorak!"

Turning, Strathorn sent out another blast with his staff, and the Twilight Queen found herself standing in a cage of liquid fire. "Oh, be quiet," Strathorn snapped.

Karn bounded over to the fire cage and looked up at the queen expectantly.

"Shoo," the queen told him. "Go away."

Karn bounced up and down and let out a "Prrt?"

"I'm not making any more fireballs for you, so forget it," the queen told him. "Get away from me, or I'll kill you!"

"Karnie, get away from there," Heather said, looking worried.

"Never fear," Strathorn told her. "That little dragon is more than capable of defending himself, if need be."

Heather looked dubious as Karn rolled around playfully on his back, desperate to get the queen's attention.

Veronica put a hand on Heather's shoulder. "Hey—you can pick your friends, and you can pick your dragons . . . but you can't pick your dragon's friends."

Heather rolled her eyes. She opened her mouth to say something but then seemed to change her mind. "I guess you never really know who'll make a good friend," she said after a moment. Her voice was almost shy as she looked up at Veronica, a question in her eyes.

Veronica was taken by surprise at the feeling that rushed over her. *Friends—is that what we are?* she thought, but instantly she knew it was true. A smile broke out across her features and seemed to spread through her body. Before she had time to stop herself, tell herself that it was a bad idea, scream, *Stupid!* in her mind, Veronica wrapped Heather in a warm hug. "I guess you never can tell," she whispered into her friend's hair.

ⵟⵕⵝ

"Beastie!" Doggett cried as he and the others burst from the castle. Strathorn had healed his arm, so he didn't cry out in pain when the Moat Beast bowled him over, giving his face a sloppy lick. In a moment, Karn had joined in, and Doggett was giggling and laughing as two beasts tickled and tumbled with him.

"Hoo-hoo!" Doggett cried. "No! Stop! That tickles!"

Just then, there was a quick *clop-clop-clop,* and a gray pony trotted up to Doggett and nickered.

Doggett looked up. "Franklin?"

The pony stamped and nodded.

"Franklin!" Doggett cried, leaping up. He wrapped his arms around the pony's neck and covered his long nose in kisses.

"He followed Ibharn the entire way," Strathorn explained. "It seemed he missed his friend."

"Strathorn!" King Rellett rode up with a weary-looking squirrel on his shoulder. It was Chattergee who was doing the shouting. "Strathorn, where have you been?" the squirrel demanded as he leaped from the king's shoulder to the ground in front of the wizard. "I've been looking all over for you!"

"Chattergee!" Veronica said. "You just used a first-person pronoun!"

Chattergee ignored her, instead gesturing to the field, where many small animals lay beside broken branches and fallen leaves. "Strathorn, there are many wounded. . . ."

"We have a surgeon," King Rellett put in, "but he is only one man and has no magic. . . ."

"You have to help them!" Chattergee cried. "They're small, but they fought so bravely and all because I asked them—"

"Calm yourself, squirrel," Strathorn said. "Of course I'll help them." His ice blue eyes twinkled and a smile twitched at the corner of his mouth. "I'm looking forward to this."

The king rode off to find his healer and Chattergee scrambled toward the battlefield. Strathorn followed, then stopped suddenly and turned back to Veronica and Heather. "Did I understand this correctly," he said suddenly, his intense blue eyes boring into Heather's. "That is to say, that you are . . . not . . . the Princess Arabelle?"

Heather felt the color drain from her face.

"Well, the princess," Veronica said quickly, "met with an unfortunate accident."

"It was totally an accident," Heather agreed.

"And then we—sort of—well, you thought Heather was Arabelle. . . . "

Strathorn held up his hand and Veronica's voice trailed off. "I see," he said, nodding.

"Strathorn!" Chattergee called.

The wizard waved to signal that he was coming. When he turned back to the girls, his face was serious. "I think it might be best if we don't mention this to anyone. Hmm?"

"Well . . . " Veronica said, "I guess it doesn't really matter now. . . ."

"Oh, but it does," Strathorn corrected. "The One must stay. The people need their new queen."

"But—wait." Heather held up a hand. "I'm not the One. Didn't you get that? I'm not—"

"My dear . . . whoever you are," Strathorn replied, "you seem to have a very strange idea of what being the One means."

"Bu—but . . . isn't the One . . . Arabelle?" Veronica asked.

The wizard's sharp eyes hooked onto hers. "The One," Strathorn said calmly, "is the one who delivers Galma from the hands of the Queen of Twilight. The One is the one who does. Not a name from a legend."

Heather shook her head. "But the prophecy—"

"Prophecies often come true in the strangest-possible ways, my dear," Strathorn pointed out. "Sometimes a hero must make her own destiny." And with that, he turned and strode away, his red cape trailing behind him.

Veronica rolled her eyes and gave Heather a knowing glance. "Boy, does he have a brutal shock coming," she said.

Heather smiled uncertainly, but she didn't have time to reply, because at that very moment, Ibharn strode up with four very, very good-looking guys behind him. "Queen Arabelle," the elf prince said, bowing low, "may I present to you the princes of the Eastern Isles, Narok, son of Darok . . . "

Hot Salsa bowed low.

"Imogen, son of Frellig the Mighty . . . "

This was Dark Chocolate. He kissed Heather's hand, which made her giggle.

"Fan, son of the great queen Islingmara . . . " Ibharn indicated Mega-prep, who nodded seriously. "And Donnogh, of the Clan of Dulingleath." Paddy O'Hotcakes gave a courtly bow as Imogen stepped forward.

"Queen Arabelle, you knew us as the Galag Nur," he said as he knelt before her. "Our souls were imprisoned by the Queen of Twilight. With her death, our period of enchantment has ended, and we wish to pledge our allegiance to the new queen."

The other princes—even Ibharn—knelt before her.

Heather lifted her eyebrows at Veronica. "When I agreed to be a princess," she murmured just loud enough for her friend to hear as she grinned at the five hotties at her feet, "this was more what I had in mind."

᙭

Of course, the work wasn't over. It took a day and a half to tend to the wounded. Strathorn used his magic in the most dire of cases, and everyone—Heather and Veronica included—worked feverishly to organize and care for the more lightly injured. The Moat Beast dug an enormous pit and helped pile the bodies of the fallen in a great funeral pyre at the far edge of the battlefield so that the smoke wouldn't disturb the living. Luckily, once the queen's enchantment had ended, even the enemy Ookies had lost their foul temperaments. They were grateful not to have to work for such a nasty queen and went about helping Queen Arabelle—as everyone was calling Heather now—quite cheerfully.

During this time, Heather was strangely silent. It was a mystery to Veronica, who wanted nothing more than to talk about going home. She hated worrying her family for even an extra day, but she knew that Strathorn was busy healing the wounded, so she didn't bother him.

Finally, the last dying shrub was made right, and the last splint was placed on an injured woodchuck, and Veronica pulled Strathorn aside.

"Strathorn," she said to the wizard, "we need to talk to you."

The wizard looked at her keenly. The glance was heavy, and Veronica had difficulty forcing herself to go on. "You see . . ." Veronica cleared her throat. "Heather—Queen Arabelle—and I . . . we're from another world. We're not really sure how we got here, but . . . " Her voice drifted off.

"But . . . " Strathorn prompted.

"We have a wish," Veronica said. "We were thinking that—now that you have your powers again—you could send us back to our world."

Strathorn nodded thoughtfully. His eyes moved from Veronica to Heather and back again. They hesitated there for a moment. Then he seemed to make up his mind. "I could."

"Well—will you?" Veronica asked.

Sighing, Strathorn planted his staff more firmly in the ground. "I will."

"When?" Veronica's voice was breathless.

Strathorn thought for a moment, stroking his beard, and Veronica was afraid that he would tell her that it would take months, maybe years for him to learn how to do it. But in the end, what he said was, "I will send you now, if you like."

"We like! Oh, we like!" Veronica cried, throwing her arms around Heather. "We're going home!" She started to dance around wildly, and it took her a moment to realize that Heather wasn't dancing with her. In fact, Heather wasn't even looking at her. She was staring at the ground. "What's wrong?"

Swallowing hard, Heather looked up at her friend. When she spoke, her voice was almost a whisper. "I'm not . . . "

Realization broke over Veronica like a wave over stone. "Oh my God," she said slowly. "You're not coming."

As she faced her friend, Heather blinked, and the tears that had collected at the rims of her eyes spilled down her cheeks. She looked around at the battlefield, now littered with recuperating soldiers and woodland creatures, and at the castle, being rebuilt stone by stone. She couldn't really see them through her tears, but Veronica saw them for her.

This is the thing about friends—often, they understand us without words.

But Heather tried to explain anyway. "They need me. . . ."

Veronica's mind reeled. She couldn't believe what Heather was telling her. "Your parents," she protested.

"Veronica . . . " Pressing her lips together, she shook her head. Taking a deep breath, she tried again. "I don't have a family like yours . . . " she said. She thought of her home—the huge, quiet rooms. The empty space, empty hours. The absence that was the presence she lived with. "You're lucky, Veronica," she said finally.

Veronica didn't know what to say. She took her friend's hand and squeezed. "But—what about me?" she asked.

Heather laughed through her tears. "You should stay too," she said, sniffling.

Veronica thought about it for a moment. Part of her was tempted. Galma was the kind of place she had been dreaming of her entire life. And now there would be two hundred years of joy and light . . .

But what about Mama? she thought. *What about Luz? Even stupid Esteban. They'll miss me. . . .*

No.

No, I'll miss them, Veronica realized. *I do miss them.* "I can't stay," Veronica said at last. "I need to go back to my family."

Heather ran a finger beneath her bottom lashes, wiping away the tears. "I knew you would say that."

Veronica looked Heather squarely in the eye. "Now, tell me the truth—do those four hot Galag Nur have anything to do with this?"

Heather laughed softly and shook her head. "Well, you know I never mind being surrounded by hotness," she admitted. Without even realizing it, she looked over at the castle wall. Doggett was there, shouting instructions to the Moat Beast, who was lifting some of the heavier stones. Her eyes lingered on Doggett's face, and she smiled softly. "But . . . in the end, it's what's inside that counts," she said, half to herself.

Almost seeming to feel her glance, Doggett turned around. When he caught sight of Heather, he waved. Heather waved back.

Signaling to the Moat Beast, Doggett started walking toward Heather. The beast lumbered behind.

I have to say good-bye, Veronica realized. Suddenly, she felt like Dorothy in *The Wizard of Oz*, and Frodo at the end of *The Return of the King*, and Wendy at the end of *Peter Pan*, and Digory at the end of *The Magician's Nephew*, and about a zillion other examples all rolled into one.

A gentle hand touched Veronica on the shoulder. "Are you ready, my dear?" Strathorn asked. At his ankle stood Chattergee. The squirrel had lost half an ear in battle, and he looked much older, although his posture was straight.

"I hear you're leaving," Chattergee said slowly. "I wish you wouldn't. It's rare to meet such a lady, who is both lovely and a good fighter."

Kneeling, Veronica looked Chattergee in the eye. "I'll never forget you, Chattergee."

And then the squirrel surprised her by bursting into tears.

Veronica touched him on the head. "It's okay. It's all right."

"It's not all right!" Chattergee insisted. "This is terrible! Terrible! Oh, how will I survive?"

"What a drama queen," Heather muttered.

"What's wrong?" Doggett asked, joining the group. "Chattergee, are you all right?"

"No, I'm not all right," the squirrel snapped. "The lady Veronica is leaving us!"

Doggett sighed. "Back to the dwarves?" he asked.

Veronica gave him a rueful smile. "It's a little farther than that," she admitted.

Doggett thought about this for a moment. "Will you visit?"

"I don't think I'll be able to," Veronica told him.

Strathorn cleared his throat.

"Well, maybe," Veronica amended.

Doggett's face crinkled into a worried frown. "You aren't . . . you aren't taking the queen with you, are you?" he asked, looking over at Heather.

Heather slipped her hand into his. "I'm not leaving," she said gently, and relief washed over Doggett's face.

"Oh," he said, blushing a little. "Well, I'll miss you, Veronica."

"I'll miss you too, Doggett," Veronica told him. She looked up at the Moat Beast, who was wearing Karn like a ring. The beast's orange eyes looked misty, and suddenly, emotion threatened to overwhelm Veronica. "I'll miss all of you," she said, her voice choking.

"Then why are you leaving?" Chattergee wailed, dissolving into sobs.

"Because I have to," Veronica told him, and it was true. She turned to Strathorn and cleared her throat. "I just want you to know because I don't think I ever told you," she said, "that I'm sorry."

Strathorn's icicle eyes softened. He knew what she meant—that she was sorry about the Lake of Woe, about the bloodsnake. "My dear," he said gently, "there is nothing to forgive. You do not need to fear your mistakes so much."

Leaning close, she whispered in the wizard's ear. "You were exactly like I knew you would be."

"Same to you," Strathorn whispered back.

Veronica looked up at him in surprise and was delighted to see his blue eyes dancing. But she didn't have time to ask him what he meant, because Heather wrapped her in a warm hug. "I'll miss you," she whispered.

Veronica nodded. "Me too."

"Excuse me, Queen Arabelle," said a voice at Heather's shoulder. "I seek a boon."

Turning, she came face-to-face with the skinny little man who had given her the tour of Karn's cave. Behind him were the burly key chain man with the eye patch and the sweaty wallet lady and a few other tchotchke sellers from the village.

"What's a boon?" Heather asked, and Veronica hid a smile.

"We've come here all the way from Karn, see?" the skinny little man whined. "And we need our dragon back."

"Our economy depends on it!" said the sweaty woman.

Heather looked over to where Karn was curled happily around the Moat Beast's finger.

Heather sighed and looked at Veronica.

"Hey, queens deal with economies," Veronica said, shrugging. "It's your headache now."

"Okay, look," Heather said, turning back to the skinny man. "I think Karn is happy where he is. . . . " She wrapped an arm around his shoulders and they fell into step together. "But I have an idea that might bring a lot of money into Karn. Have you ever heard of a destination spa? Well, there is a great cave near your village, and . . . "

As Veronica watched Heather walk off with the Karnish villagers, she smiled to herself. *Maybe Heather really was born to be a princess after all,* she thought.

Sighing, she looked over at Strathorn.

"I'll make sure you land somewhere comfortable in your world," the wizard said kindly.

Veronica nodded. "I think I'm ready now."

"How can you be ready?" Chattergee wailed. "How?"

"Well . . . maybe I'm not ready," Veronica admitted. "But it's still time to go home."

ॐ

"Knock, knock."

Veronica rolled over in the soft bed. When she opened her eyes, she had a momentary flash of—*where am I?* After weeks of sleeping on the ground, the sweet, familiar-smelling sheets were strange. The things around her were well known, but she couldn't quite place them . . . like that beat-up dresser with a book propping up one leg . . . that old brass lamp . . . that dark head poking into her door. . . .

"Luz!" Veronica shrieked, realizing in a flash just where she was. "Ohmigod, Luz!" She leaped off her bed and wrapped her sister in a huge hug.

"Ow! Would you get off me?" Luz griped. "Jeez."

Veronica gaped at her sister. "Didn't you miss me?"

Luz gave her a heavy-lidded look. "Considering that you were the last person I saw before I went to bed and now you're the first person I'm seeing this morning, um—no."

"What?" *Ohmigod,* Veronica realized. *So no time had passed in this universe after all! Of course—rule number one of fantasy: whenever you get sucked into another world, the adventure takes no time at all in your own. I did all that worrying for nothing!*

Thank goodness.

"So, can I borrow your brush or what?" Luz asked.

"Borrow anything you like!" Veronica said, giving her sister another affectionate squeeze.

Luz looked slightly weirded out as she made her way to Veronica's dresser. Just then, Esteban staggered through his bedroom door, bleary-eyed.

"Esteban!" Veronica shouted. "I love you!"

"Ow," Esteban complained. "Don't bug me."

"Good morning!" Carmen sang as she walked down the hall, fastening a hoop earring. There she was—looking exactly as she had ages ago, before Veronica's adventure. Her hair was still a little damp from the shower, and she wasn't wearing any makeup. But to Veronica, her mother had never looked more beautiful.

"Mom!" Veronica nearly knocked her over as she bounded toward her, giving her an enormous hug.

"Buenos días, early bird!" Carmen said, stroking her daughter's hair. "You're in a good mood."

"I'm just so happy to see you," Veronica whispered.

"And I'm happy to see you, amorcita," Carmen said, squeezing back. "Now—you'd better get ready for school, or you'll be late." She winked at her daughter and finished putting in her earring.

"School?" Veronica repeated.

"Hey—did you finish that paper?" Luz asked, strolling out of Veronica's room dressed in Veronica's favorite sweater.

Veronica shook her head. "What paper?"

"Hel-lo?" Luz rolled her eyes. "*Queen of Twilight*? You were totally freaking out last night that it wouldn't be done."

Now Veronica's head really was reeling. She stepped into her room and looked around. There it was—on her desk. A paper.

"*Queen of Twilight*: A Traditional Epic Reimagined," the title read. Veronica flipped through it. A seven-page paper. Double-spaced. Printed out and ready to go.

"I guess I did it," she said slowly.

"Oh, that's good," Luz said lightly. "That way I can copy it next year."

But Veronica didn't hear her. She sank into her desk chair. *It was a dream,* she realized. *The whole thing. Strathorn. Heather. Doggett. Karn.* She had to grab the edge of her desk as her mind swam. It was all just . . .

With the motion of her hand, something rolled from the edge of her desk and plopped heavily onto the thick carpet. It had been there all along, lying right next to the paper. Veronica blinked down at it.

"Nice snow globe," Luz said, her voice dripping with sarcasm.

Veronica picked the globe up and turned it, looking at

it from all angles. Inside, snow fell softly around a dark tower.

Standing up, she crossed the room and tucked the snow globe into her top drawer, along with her socks and underwear and other private things.

Luz lifted her eyebrows as Veronica gently closed her drawer. "Where'd you get it?"

Veronica smiled as flashes from her adventure ran through her mind. "Oh," she said vaguely. "A friend gave it to me."

Are you ready for another kind of fantasy? The kind that includes Matrix-style martial arts, a demon that exists as liquid darkness, a mysterious magical tattoo, and a roller-coaster adventure that goes from London to Hell itself?

Well? Are you?

Turn the page for an advance peek at

by Sam Enthoven
Coming in October 2006

SKILLS

Charlie answered the door in his sunglasses. Once Jack was safely inside, however, he took them off—and Jack had his first shock.

"I know," said Charlie, looking away before Jack could even think of what to say. Charlie's eyes were red and puffy, with thick dark-blue smudges underneath them. He looked awful.

"Mum was up crying most of the night again," he said. "She's asleep now, so we'll have to be quiet."

"Oh, mate," said Jack stupidly.

"Anyway," said Charlie, and a glint appeared in his eyes, "listen, before we go, I want to show you something. What do you know about tattoos?"

"Er . . ." said Jack—but Charlie had already got his T-shirt up round his neck.

"What do you think," he asked, "of this?"

He turned his back, and Jack had a second shock.

"Eh?" said Charlie, when Jack didn't answer at first, then again: "Eh?" He stretched out his arms.

"Blimey," said Jack finally.

From shoulder to shoulder and right down Charlie's back, almost as far as the waistband of his jeans, was a huge black tattoo.

Jack stared.

It was an odd sort of pattern. The tattoo's broad, curving shapes reminded Jack of certain tribal designs, Celtic or Native American ones, but it wasn't quite like anything he'd ever seen before. The shapes seemed to radiate out from Charlie's spine, scything across his back like a crest of broad feathers or a set of great curved sword blades. The shapes were black against Charlie's pale skin—completely, utterly black—and each and every one of them ended in a perfect, razor-sharp point. Charlie clenched his arms, and the black shapes seemed to bunch and shift of their own accord as his muscles moved underneath them.

Even apart from the fact that it had just appeared on Charlie's back, the tattoo made Jack uneasy. Still, he thought, with a twinge of envy: it was certainly impressive. In fact, no denying it, it was most definitely. . . .

"Cool," he breathed.

"Huh. Yeah," said Charlie, turning, casually. "Got the surprise of my life when I caught sight of it in the mirror this morning."

"Does it hurt?"

"Naaah," said Charlie. "Not really."

"And that's the . . . thing? From yesterday?"

"Well, I don't think Mum drew it on me in the night."

"Wow," said Jack. He meant it.

"Come on," said Charlie, pulling his T-shirt down and getting into a short-sleeved shirt. He left it unbuttoned and untucked, hanging over the waistband of his black jeans, showing his black T-shirt underneath. He stuck his shades back on and turned to Jack.

"Let's go," he said.